The cover was a [...] [...]
no masonable ena [...] [...]
who wanted Abigail to marry an older
man not the one,

The Second Surprise

I couldn't put this book

Lady Mary Spence had been surprised once that
night, when hands had whirled her around and a
man's lips had evoked a startling response from her
own. Fortunately, Lord Kenmare had come to her
rescue.

down cause of the battle of waterloo

"Foolish, idiotic woman, going into the gardens
without an escort," Kenmare murmured.

just for the Blood & gut you got
to rate it at 8

"How did you know?" Mary whispered.

The corner of Kenmare's mouth quirked upward.
"I, too, had designs on your virtue. But he was
before me. I was enraged to be so upstaged."

"And so you hit him," said Lady Mary. She gave
him a faint smile. "I thank you for your chivalry,
my lord."

But her smile faded as Kenmare laughed, and his
hands tightened on her shoulders . . .

GAYLE BUCK free-lanced for regional publications,
worked for a radio station, and as a secretary. Until
recently she was involved in public relations for a major
university. Besides her Regencies, she is currently working on projects in fantasy and romantic suspense.

SIGNET REGENCY ROMANCE
COMING IN AUGUST 1991

Irene Saunders
Talk Of The Town

Margaret Westhaven
Country Dance

Barbara Allister
A Love Match

Laura Matthews
The Seventh Suitor

The
Waltzing Widow

Gayle Buck

A SIGNET BOOK

SIGNET
Published by the Penguin Group
Penguin Books USA Inc., 375 Hudson Street,
New York, New York, 10014, U.S.A.
Penguin Books Ltd, 27 Wrights Lane, London W8 5TZ, England
Penguin Books Australia Ltd, Ringwood, Victoria, Australia
Penguin Books Canada Ltd, 2801 John Street,
Markham, Ontario, Canada L3R 1B4
Penguin Books (N.Z.) Ltd, 182-190 Wairau Road,
Auckland 10, New Zealand

Penguin Books Ltd, Registered Offices:
Harmondsworth, Middlesex, England

First published by Signet, an imprint of New American Library,
a division of Penguin Books USA Inc.

First Printing, July, 1991

10 9 8 7 6 5 4 3 2 1

BOOKS ARE AVAILABLE AT QUANTITY DISCOUNTS WHEN USED TO PROMOTE
PRODUCTS OR SERVICES. FOR INFORMATION PLEASE WRITE TO PREMIUM
MARKETING DIVISION, PENGUIN BOOKS USA INC., 375 HUDSON STREET,
NEW YORK, NEW YORK 10014.

1

OUTSIDE the frosted windowpanes the day was gray, lending steel-blue color to the low clouds and snow-covered grounds. Set against the January cold, a cheerful fire snapped on the hearth of the sitting room. It was a tasteful room, with nothing of the flamboyant to mar its quiet elegance, and it admirably reflected the personality of its mistress.

Lady Mary Spence was sitting at her cherrywood writing desk, reading a letter. She was attired in a long-sleeved merino day dress of a becoming shade of mauve, a shawl was draped about her shoulders, and a beribboned lace cap crowned her gleaming chestnut curls. Pinned to her breast was a cameo brooch bearing inside it the likeness of her beloved husband. She was to all appearances the respectable widow in half-mourning, unless the casual observer chanced to glance at her face and discovered a countenance that should never belong to one of mourning status.

Lady Mary's face was unlined, excepting the tiny laugh lines at the corners of her eyes. Her large gray eyes were set wide, giving her a pleasant openness of expression that was inviting. But at the moment her usual air of serenity was marred by the tiny frown between her feathery brows. She reread the particular lines of the letter that had perturbed her.

The sitting-room door burst open and a young lady of dazzling beauty rushed in. ''Mama, here you are! I have looked positively everywhere for you. I have just returned from visiting Betsy, and you shall never guess what she says,'' the young lady exclaimed, pulling off her velvet bonnet and shedding her cloak, muff, and gloves in quick succession.

As always, Lady Mary was gladdened at sight of her daughter's lively, cheerful face, and the slight frown of the moment before disappeared. She laid down the letter she had been reading and said with a smile, "I await with bated breath, Abigail. What does Betsy say?"

Abigail was too excited to acknowledge her mother's gentle teasing. "Why, Betsy has gotten herself engaged, and to a parson, no less!" she exclaimed. She watched eagerly for the effect of her announcement, and when she saw the flash of surprise that crossed her mother's face, she chortled. "I knew that the news must astonish you, Mama. I am certain that I never expected such a thing to happen. Betsy to be married, and to a stick of a parson! I should not want such a match for myself, I can tell you!"

"I am surprised, certainly. I had thought the engagement was to be formally announced in the spring," Lady Mary said.

Abigail regarded her mother with astonishment. "Mama, you knew all along. And you never breathed a word of it to me! How abominable of you to keep such a secret."

"It was not my secret to freely bestow, Abigail. Mrs. Evesleigh confided in me a few months past that she and Mr. Evesleigh had agreed to the Reverend Coates making his addresses to Betsy, who I understand has shown a decided partiality for the gentleman for some months. I can only be glad for Betsy. She is a delightful girl and deserves every happiness," Lady Mary said.

Abigail recovered from her astonishment. "But a parson, Mama! Why, Betsy has never been to London, and the only society she is used to is that of our own county," she said, obviously marveling at the inexplicability of her friend's actions.

The slight frown returned to Lady Mary's face. For several weeks she had been disturbed by the emerging tack of her daughter's conversation, but never more than at that moment. Unlike her good friend Betsy Evesleigh, Abigail had been up to London on numerous occasions to visit with her grandparents. Abigail had been shown much about society and had been exposed to polite circles enough to have given her a bit of polish. Unfortunately, thought Lady Mary, Abigail had also acquired the knowledge that there was more to the world than the quieter society that she had been formerly used to and that Lady Mary Spence herself preferred.

Lady Mary regarded her daughter. She had known what a

heady experience those last visits to London had been for Abigail, but she had hoped that important considerations would not be lost to sight in the excitement and glamour. She herself had renounced that grandeur and social ambition when at the age of sixteen she had fallen in love with a gentleman some fifteen years her elder who was of merely respectable birth. Her parents did not object to the difference in their ages, but rather to the gentleman's lack of social status. Viscount and Viscountess Catlin looked higher for their only daughter than a mere baronet. No amount of persuasion had been enough to sway Lady Mary's parents in the gentleman's favor, and the lovers had reluctantly resorted to a runaway marriage.

Lady Mary's parents had wholly disowned her during the period of her brief but happy marriage. After Sir Roger's untimely death, they had become willing again to countenance her existence. After all, Sir Roger Spence had had the good taste to die early and leave his spouse a wealthy widow. However, her parents had cause to regret Sir Roger's astute business sense and investments because Lady Mary was thus enabled to steadfastly refuse all their invitations and their suggestions for her remarriage.

But Lady Mary had not imposed her voluntary exile from interaction with her parents to her children. She had allowed William and Abigail to accept various invitations for extended visits in London so that they would come to know their grandparents and grow up familiar with the ways of polite society. Now, as Lady Mary listened to her daughter's prattle, she wished that she had not been so acquiescent.

"I shall make a splendid match to a gentleman as rich as Croesus, who shall grant me a positively enormous allowance and make me mistress of a large establishment. I shall be touted as the most popular hostess in town and everyone will vie for invitations to my lavish parties," Abigail said, sinking down on the settee with a grand air. She pretended to ply a fan and accept accolades with a gracious nod. She abandoned her play for a moment. "Do you know, Mama, when I asked Betsy whether she meant to put off her wedding so that she could be presented at court, she snapped her fingers at me in the most offhand fashion! Why, I would die rather than miss my court presentation, and so I told her. She and the parson are to be wedded in February, of all dreary months. Can you believe it? Not even a fine June wedding, but a hurried affair in the middle of winter.''

"I imagine that Betsy is so enamored that such considerations as a court presentation pale beside planning for her wedding,'' Lady Mary said quietly.

"So she says, but I cannot credit it. I know that I could not relinquish it so easily,'' Abigail said.

Lady Mary sighed, but she did not press the issue. "I am surprised the wedding has been moved up so early in the year. Are you certain it is to be in a month's time, Abigail?''

"Oh, yes, I am positive that is what Betsy said. Her parson has accepted a living in the next parish and he is to begin immediately,'' Abigail said.

"How delightful! I imagine that must be a relief to Mrs. Evesleigh, who was naturally dreading Betsy's leaving. They will be able to visit often, I expect,'' Lady Mary said.

Abigail was not listening, instead pursuing thoughts of her own. "Mama, I am expected to be Betsy's maid of honor, of course. But if the wedding should interfere with our removal to London, I would rather not do so. I do not wish to miss even one day of the Season. Grandmama has promised me such a high time, you see,'' Abigail said.

Lady Mary was stunned. She wondered when her sweet, sensible daughter had changed so completely. Certainly Abigail had acted differently after the last visit to her grandparents, but Lady Mary had been able to shrug off her daughter's flashes of selfishness as temporary and harmless. Perhaps the news she had read earlier in the letter was come at a fortunate time after all, she thought. She said slowly, "I fear that I must rethink your come-out this Season, Abigail.''

"Mama! How can you say so? Why, you promised that when I turned seventeen I was to come out!'' Abigail exclaimed, abandoning her languid attitude and bolting upright on the settee. Horrified dismay enlivened her blue eyes. "Grandmama has told me of all the parties she has planned for me and the gentlemen I am to meet, and Grandpapa has promised me a carriage of my own with a tiny tiger dressed in livery of my own design and . . . Mama, you cannot turn back on your word now, you simply cannot!''

Lady Mary picked up the letter that was lying on her desktop. ''I am sorry, Abigail, but—''

Abigail leapt to her feet. Bright anger sparkled in her corn-flower-blue eyes and indignation charmingly pinkened her cheeks. ''It is because I said that I did not wish to be Betsy's maid of honor, isn't it? Well, I don't. I want to go to London. I don't care about Betsy's idiotic wedding or her stick of a parson or—''

''Abigail, sit down!''

Abigail had seldom in her life heard her mother use that particular tone of voice, and she instinctively quailed. She slowly sank down on the settee, her fearful eyes held by her mother's awful gaze. She said haltingly, ''I . . . I am sorry, Mama. I should not have ripped up at you so. It is just that I have pinned all my hopes on a Season, and it is so unfair that—''

Lady Mary flung up her hand. ''That will be enough, Abigail. I am quite aware of your hopes. You have aired them frequently and far too publicly for my taste,'' she said. Her haughty expression softened with regret. ''But that is not what has disappointed me so in you, Abigail. You have been fast friends with Betsy Evesleigh since the cradle; but now, on the eve of Betsy's most important decision, you are willing to abandon all that you have meant to her for the sake of a few paltry parties. I am deeply ashamed of you, Abigail, and also I am saddened. I had not quite realized what a selfish and self-centered creature you had become. I had believed that you had grown up enough to be allowed to establish yourself in polite society, but now I must confess to grave doubts.''

''Mama, no,'' breathed Abigail. She folded her hands in her lap and sat up in the most demure posture of which she was capable. ''Mama, I promise you that I am grown-up, truly I am. I did not mean to slight Betsy even by words, and I will be delighted to act as her maid of honor. Of course I shall be. Mama, pray do not look at me like that. Truly, truly, I never meant to distress you.'' She leapt up and ran over to fling herself against her mother's knees and burst into tears.

Lady Mary sighed. She laid her hand gently on her daughter's bowed head and caressed her soft hair. "Oh, my dear girl. What trials we must all go through," she murmured. She let Abigail cry for a little while before raising the girl's face and offering her own fine handkerchief. "Come, Abigail, blow your nose and take hold of yourself. There is something that I wish to discuss with you."

Abigail took the handkerchief and did as she was bidden. She dried her eyes and blew her nose delicately. "What . . . what is it, Mama?" she asked.

Lady Mary again picked up the letter that she had dropped a few moments before. "I have received this letter from my dear friend Emily Downing."

Abigail nodded, not very interested. "Oh, your London friend."

Lady Mary sighed in exasperation. "Abigail, she writes that London is unusually thin of company for this time of year and daily becomes more deserted. The abdication of Bonaparte last April set off a marked exodus of the *ton* to Europe that has not abated. London has been deserted while the peace negotiations are pounded out in Vienna; and in the Low Countries, where the Army of Occupation has been stationed and the festivities have begun upon the installment of William of Orange as the King of the Netherlands, Brussels has become one of the gayest capitals in all of Europe." She had briefly referred to the sheets of paper, and now she looked up to catch her daughter's puzzled gaze. "Abigail, do you quite understand what I am attempting to convey to you?"

Abigail frowned, knowing that there was something important in all her mother's talk of politics. It came to her in a sudden flash of understanding, and her eyes widened. "Oh! You mean that the *ton* have all left London. But that means . . . why, there won't even *be* a proper Season in town this year."

"I am afraid so, my dear," Lady Mary said. "Your grandmama's plans for a dizzying round of parties will hardly live up to your expectations, I fear. And according to Emily, who may be depended upon for her good sense and information, the situation is not likely to change for some months, at least until the Congress of Vienna is concluded and our statesmen and our army return home."

"But what am I to do? I will be on the shelf before I am much older," Abigail wailed. Lady Mary went into a peal of laughter. Her daughter regarded her with a mixture of astonishment and resentment. "Mama, it is not at all amusing," Abigail said with injured dignity.

Choking back her laughter, Lady Mary shook her head. "No, I can see that it is not," she said with an attempt at sobriety, quite ruined by the gurgle that escaped her. "I am sorry, poppet. I am a perfect beast for laughing at you, but you are such a baby, and hardly in any danger of becoming an old maid, believe me."

"But you were married at sixteen, Mama, a year younger than I am now, while I haven't yet been presented or come out or met a single eligible gentleman," Abigail said.

Lady Mary was reduced to silence. As she looked at her daughter, she recalled herself at the same age, deeply and irrevocably in love with her kind, good husband, and already a mother. She had lived life with such passion as long as Sir Roger had lived.

Her grief at his death had tempered her and had served to mature the undisciplined person. Overnight she had changed from a protected, well-loved, and cosseted wife to a young widow and mother of two, very much aware of her responsibilities and determined to carry out her duty as best she could.

Despite the openly expressed doubts of family and friends who considered her too young to raise a young son and baby daughter, or to handle her own financial affairs, she had succeeded. She had succeeded without assistance, gently but firmly turning aside the several attempts made by her parents to draw her back into their orbit. Only once did she accept her parents' aid, and that was to allow her father to buy a commission in the army for her son, William. It was a difficult decision that had cost her many sleepless nights, but in the end she had capitulated to her son's entreaties to be allowed to make a career of the army.

Now, gazing upon Abigail, who was so very like her younger self, and thinking of her son, William, whom she had not seen in several months, Lady Mary came to an abrupt decision. "Very well, Abigail. You shall have your Season. We shall go to Brussels for the spring and summer, and though you won't be presented at court until next year, you may at least make your formal entrance into society," she said quietly.

"Brussels, Mama!" Abigail squeaked, completely bowled out. Recovering in an instant, she threw her arms about her parent. "*Thank* you, Mama! You are so good to me. You can have no notion how happy you have made me."

Lady Mary emerged from the fervent embrace somewhat breathless and with her lace cap knocked askew. "Have I not, indeed!" she retorted, laughing as she straightened her beribboned cap. "Now, do go away, Abigail. I should like to pen a congratulatory note to Mrs. Evesleigh regarding Betsy's upcoming nuptials."

"Of course, Mama," Abigail said. She crossed gracefully to the door. With her hand on the knob, she was struck by a sudden thought. "Mama! Wasn't William's last letter from Brussels?"

Lady Mary smiled at her daughter. There was a twinkle in her gray eyes. "Why, I do believe that it was, Abigail. A fine coincidence, certainly."

Abigail giggled. "You are the most complete hand, Mama." She sighed. "I shall enjoy seeing William again, I confess. I have sorely missed him these last months."

"As have I," Lady Mary said.

Abigail sent a saucy glance at her mother. "Besides, what is the use of having an older brother if he is not available to introduce one to his rakish friends?"

"Abigail," Lady Mary said in a warning tone; but she smiled even as she spoke, aware that she was being teased. Abigail laughed again. She skipped out the door, humming happily. Lady Mary shook her head in affectionate exasperation before turning her attention to her correspondence.

2

THE LETTER to her friend Emily Downing went swiftly and crossed several pages. She sanded the sheets and folded them into an envelope that she addressed in her firm clear hand, sealing the missive with hot wax. Lady Mary sighed as she pulled a fresh sheet of vellum to her. The letter to her parents, Viscount and Viscountess Catlin, would be more difficult to compose. She sat chewing the nib of her quill pen, forming and discarding a dozen openings. Finally, when she had decided on the best approach, she discovered to her irritation that she had completely frayed the tip of her pen, and she had to sharpen it with a small penknife before she could begin writing.

Dipping the newly sharpened point of her quill into the inkwell, Lady Mary took a breath and started upon the letter. It was always difficult to communicate with her parents, for the sole reason that whatever she wished to convey was invariably rejected as errant nonsense.

Viscount Catlin still clung to his obstinate position that the independent and respectable widow was the same lavishly spoiled and petted daughter that had grown up in his house. As for the viscountess, she cherished the fond notion that her out-rageously wayward daughter must one day yet take her rightful place at the forefront of society. But by her very character, Lady Mary violated every conception that her parents held of the ideal dutiful and dependent daughter.

Lady Mary caught herself sighing again. She knew that the news that she and Abigail would not be going up to London for the Season after all would excite strenuous protests from her parents. She thought with a flash of humor that she would not require the return post to know of her letter's reception; she would be bound to be able to hear the repercussions on the very air.

She finished the difficult letter, sanded it, and readied it for posting. Rising from the desk with the two letters in her hand, Lady Mary went out of the sitting room. The footman immediately inquired her wishes and she gave him the envelopes with instructions to post them. Then she asked, "Is Miss Abigail in the drawing room, John?"

"Yes, my lady. Tea is being brought round this moment," the footman said.

"Thank you, John," Lady Mary said. She walked to the drawing-room door, which was partially open. Hearing the murmur of voices, she paused with her fingers on the panel, disconcerted. She had not known that her daughter was entertaining a guest.

A young gentleman in desperate tones said, "I swear to you, Abigail, I shall do it. I shall join the army if you will not."

Abigail's high clear voice sounded irritated. "Pray do not be so absurd, Colin! I cannot possibly marry you. "Do, *do* get up! Tea will be brought in at any moment and it will be all so embarrassing."

Lady Mary closed her eyes for a second of resignation. Then she pushed open the door, saying brightly as she did so, "Abigail, I have just recalled—" She had the briefest impression of a red-faced young gentleman scrambling up from his knees and her daughter snatching back her hands from the inopportune suitor's slackened grasp. She pretended not to notice either of their flushed faces. "Oh, it is you, Colin. I am happy to see you, as always. How does your dear mama?" She advanced toward him smiling, her hand held out to him.

The young gentleman, who was dressed in riding clothes, awkwardly took her hand and sketched a bow. "Mama is much better, thank you, Lady Mary."

"I am happy to hear it. Influenza is such a particularly fatiguing ailment. But I expect we shall soon see Mrs. Rollings to be her usual self again," Lady Mary said. She seated herself beside her unusually quiet daughter. She chose to ignore Abigail's swift wondering glance. "We were just about to take tea. I hope that you will join us, Colin." As she spoke, the butler entered with the tea tray and set it down on the occasional table before her. She thanked him quietly.

"No . . . no, that is to say, Mama must have been expecting me back long since. I but stopped to . . . to pay my respects to yourself and Miss Spence, my lady," Colin stammered. He appeared extremely uncomfortable and cleared his throat.

Lady Mary calmly nodded her understanding, betraying nothing of the amusement she felt. "Of course. We must not keep you, then. Pray give my regards to your mother. I shall make a point of calling on her in the next few days," she said, once more holding out her hand to him.

He took it, mumbling his excuses before turning to Abigail. Faced with her gleaming eyes and lovely countenance, Colin swallowed hard. His voice was hoarse as he took a lengthier leave of her. With one last anguished glance cast in Abigail's direction, Colin exited the drawing room.

When the door closed behind him, Abigail let out her breath on an exasperated sigh. "*Thank* you, Mama. Before you came in, I did not know what I was to do. You have no notion what a cake Colin was making of himself."

"Of course I do," Lady Mary said. She gestured for her daughter to pour the tea. "That boy has been head over heels in love with you for months. I am not at all astonished that he was at last able to screw up his courage enough to make an offer for you."

"You heard! Oh, how glad I am that you did not say anything. It was such an embarrassing moment in any event, and I most certainly would have laughed if Colin had turned one shade redder," Abigail said, handing her mother a saucered cup. "Mama, I have known Colin Rollings simply forever. I do not understand why he should suddenly take it into his head that I would make him a good wife."

"My dear daughter, have you looked in the mirror today?" Lady Mary asked with a gathering twinkle in her gray eyes.

"Of course I have," Abigail said. She blushed when her mother laughed at her. "Oh, you know what I meant, Mama. But Colin—he has seen me every day of our lives, except when he was away at school and this last time that I spent visiting with Grandpapa and Grandmama in London. Colin has always known what I look like, but he never paid the least attention to me until now."

"You forget that you have changed considerably in the last few months, Abigail," Lady Mary said.

Abigail instinctively glanced down at herself, and a slow satisfied smile curved her lips. "I have gotten my figure, haven't I, Mama? And it is quite a nice one, too."

"Really, Abigail, your vanity seems to have kept pace with your increase in dress size. Yes, my dear, your figure is very nice and you have a lovely face as well. And that pretty package is what has Colin completely bowled out." She saw that her daughter was immensely pleased with herself and she shook her head. "What was that Colin was saying about the army just before I entered?"

Abigail brushed aside her query. "Oh, that. Colin swore that if I refused to marry him, then he would run away to the army and I would never see him again. Such stuff! It was all nonsense, of course."

"So I should hope. I do not like to think what Mrs. Rollings' feelings would be if Colin were actually to do such a harebrained thing. She positively dotes on that boy," Lady Mary said, somewhat disturbed. She took a biscuit from the tray, reflecting upon the matter. "Perhaps I shall drop a hint in her ear when I call on her. She will know best how to discourage any such ridiculous ambitions, I am certain. The army is no place for one so young as Colin."

Abigail regarded her mother in surprise. "Mama, I did not know you felt that way about the military. Why ever did you give permission for William to go if you dislike the idea so?"

"Your brother is altogether different from Colin. He has always been army-mad, and when your grandfather offered to purchase a commission for him, and William begged me to agree to it, I could not very well refuse him his dream," Lady Mary said. She sighed softly. "I did worry over William, of course. But the long war is done with at last, and he is not likely to see battle again now, so I am content."

"I do not think that William will be. Content, I mean. He wrote a vastly exciting letter about the battles that some of his acquaintances participated in, and he was quite envious of all their daring deeds. He rather thought his own experience paltry by comparison. Do you remember, Mama?" Abigail asked.

Lady Mary gave a slight shudder. "Too well, I thank you. He described it all so cheerfully and took such pride in breezing through with but a 'scratch' across his brow. A scratch! When he came home on leave I almost fainted at sight of that scar. He might have lost his sight."

"I secretly thought that William's scar made him appear terribly romantic," Abigail said.

"Abigail! I hope that you did not tell him so," Lady Mary said, appalled.

"Of course not, Mama. I did not wish him to get a swelled head over it, and besides, we did not know then that the war was finished. I knew that he would think nothing of being wounded again if he believed that it would make him appear even more interesting," Abigail said.

"I am so glad that you said nothing, my dear. William has always been more heedless than he should be," Lady Mary said. "I am just happy that Bonaparte abdicated before William had a chance to set foot on another battlefield."

Abigail nodded. "That is just what I thought. I was remembering how he tried to take that high fence on a dare and the horse refused at the very last minute. William flew over its head and broke his shoulder against the post. As soon as he was healed, he set himself for the fence again."

"And fortunately on the second round the horse landed safely and William was unscathed," Lady Mary said. "I was never more angry with him than when I learned of that stunt. But he explained in that way of his that he could not allow himself to have failed in any endeavor. How *very* glad I am that the terrible war is over."

"Even if it wasn't, Mama, you needn't have been anxious on William's account. He leads a charmed life, so Grandpapa says," Abigail said.

"Your grandfather does not rule fate, my dear," Lady Mary said somewhat tartly. She was recalled by mention of the viscount of her letter. "Abigail, I have written to your grandparents to inform them that we will not be going to London for the Season."

"Oh." Abigail drew out the syllable in an excess of understanding. "That shall not be well-thought-of at all."

Lady Mary smiled. "I am fully aware of that. However, I have explained the reason and that I am taking you to Brussels. Hopefully that will assuage their natural disappointment not to have you with them this spring." Her daughter looked dubious, but she did not give voice to her thoughts.

Lady Mary could not but feel that Abigail's instincts were correct. Undoubtedly Viscount and Viscountess Catlin would be extremely angered by her communication, and she fully expected a blistering reply. For that reason, for the next few days she dreaded the coming of the return post.

But a fortnight passed and there continued an odd silence from London.

3

WHEN Lady Mary called on Mrs. Evesleigh to relay her congratulations on Miss Evesleigh's upcoming nuptials and expressed her willingness to aid her friend in whatever manner she could, the lady thanked her warmly for her offer and then turned to another topic that greatly exercised her curiosity. Mrs. Evesleigh had naturally heard from her daughter the exciting news that the Spences were traveling to the Continent, and she sympathetically asked Lady Mary what the reaction from London had been toward her travel plans.

Lady Mary shook her head, frowning slightly. "It is the most puzzling thing, Maggie. I have heard not a single word. I begin to wonder whether my letter went awry."

"Depend upon it, your letter was received. This silence must be your answer," Mrs. Evesleigh said.

Lady Mary reflected a moment. "Perhaps you are correct. But it is very unlike the viscount. My father is not one in the habit of keeping his opinions to himself, as you know. It would be more like him to post down and demand an explanation of me," Lady Mary said with a wry grimace.

"Do you truly think so? Then perhaps you should prepare

for company,'' Mrs. Evesleigh said, casting her a sympathetic glance.

"I devoutly hope that it will not be necessary to do so,'' Lady Mary said with a light laugh.

"Let us hope not, indeed,'' Mrs. Evesleigh said. She had been Lady Mary's staunch friend and confidante for many years, and though she had never breathed a word of her stronger feelings to her ladyship, she had often thought privately that the viscount and viscountess must be unnatural and unfeeling indeed to have treated their own daughter as they had.

She smiled at Lady Mary, a twinkle in her clear blue eyes. "I am quite selfishly counting on your undivided attention in aiding me with Betsy's wedding, you see. It is come up so sudden, since the good reverend is accepting the living in the neighboring parish and must take up his duties sooner than we anticipated. As you know, I was making plans for a June wedding, but now everything must be readied and accomplished in only a month's time if Betsy is to have a proper send-off. As a consequence, these days I do not know whether I am on my head or my heels most of the time.''

"Of course you may rely upon me,'' Lady Mary said warmly. "I know that if our positions were reversed and it was Abigail who was suddenly wedded, I would wish to be able to call upon you.''

"And certainly you could have done so,'' Mrs. Evesleigh said comfortably. She smiled with a touch of sadness. "I shall miss you terribly when you have gone.''

Lady Mary reached out for her friend's hand and pressed her fingers. "And I you, Maggie. But it will be just for a few months. I could not disappoint Abigail after giving my solemn word that she could come out when she became seventeen. Perhaps she will contract an eligible match her first Season, though I admit to being in two minds about the possibility. In the meantime let us see what we can do to plan for your daughter's successful establishment.''

"And what of you, Lady Mary?'' Mrs. Evesleigh asked.

"Whatever do you mean?'' Lady Mary asked, even though she had a fair notion. There was a certain look in her friend's eyes that she had seen far too often of late.

"I shall have Mr. Evesleigh when Betsy is wedded. If Abigail does become engaged this Season and marries, how will you go on?"

"I shall go on as I always have," Lady Mary said. She laughed at her friend's exasperated sigh. "Maggie, if you mean to urge me yet again to reconsider my own unwedded state, pray spare your breath, for I shan't change my mind. I assure you, despite the number of eligible *partis* that you have managed to bring to my notice these several years, I have not developed an interest in a single gentleman."

"But it is such a waste. You are still young. Why, you don't appear above nine-and-twenty, and—"

Lady Mary laughed. "I am four-and-thirty, as well you know, Maggie!"

"Of course I do, but no one else need know it unless you confess to it. Do but look in the mirror, my dear. You've not a wrinkle to mar your face, nor a gray hair on your head, though how anyone may tell it when you insist upon wearing those ridiculous matron caps, I do not know," Mrs. Evesleigh said.

Surprised, Lady Mary put up her hand to touch her lacy cap. "Why, Maggie, you told me it was vastly pretty."

"So it is, and appropriate for one such as myself. But a matron's cap is hardly suitable for you, my lady. Believe me, you would do far better to leave it off," Mrs. Evesleigh said, earnestly.

"You forget, Maggie. I am a matron, and a widow to boot. I should appear ludicrous if I were to ape a younger lady's fashions."

Mrs. Evesleigh flushed with the strength of her heartfelt asperity. "What I find ludicrous is that you masquerade as a dame of sixty years!" When she saw Lady Mary's astonished and somewhat hurt expression, she sighed. "Forgive me, my dear. I know that I do not often speak to you in such a fashion, and perhaps it is forward of me to presume to do so now. But I wish only your happiness, and I do not believe that should mean that you spend the rest of your life alone. You have too much to offer some fortunate gentleman for you to do so, Lady Mary. You are kindhearted and gay and compassionate and loving, besides having preserved an enviable figure."

"In truth, I begin to see that I am quite a paragon," Lady Mary said humorously.

"Exactly so," Mrs. Evesleigh said firmly. When Lady Mary greeted this conclusion with a laughing protest, she reluctantly smiled. "Oh, very well, perhaps you are not a paragon precisely. You do have the most obstinate nature that I have ever encountered in a female, and you have the most infuriating way of distancing yourself when you do not wish to acknowledge someone's insistence. Yes, just that expression exactly. Quite arrogant of you, actually."

"Really, Maggie!" Lady Mary exclaimed, torn between laughter and affront.

Mrs. Evesleigh was not to be deterred. Ruthlessly she plunged on. "And then there is this idiotic refusal of yours to admit how very attractive you are. It is beyond anything. I would call it false humility, except that I know you too well."

"I see that I am quite sunk beyond reproach," Lady Mary said quietly.

Mrs. Evesleigh threw up her hands in frustration. "My dear Lady Mary, I am merely pointing up the fact that you are as human as the rest of us mortals and that you cannot spend your life behind that wall of glass that you so easily erect about yourself. You are not a porcelain figure, but a woman of warmth and feelings and flesh and blood. Mary, I am your friend. Pray listen to me this once with an open mind. William has already flown the nest and Abigail must soon follow. Pray consider what your life will be like once Abigail is gone."

"I have considered, Maggie. And if I had ever met another gentleman who compared favorably with my beloved Roger, then perhaps . . ." Lady Mary paused for a moment before she smiled. "But I have not. Maggie, do not look so anxious for me. I shall be content enough with my memories, I do assure you. And the time will come when I shall have grandchildren to occupy my thoughts and keep me busy. But for now, tell me what I may do for you for Betsy's wedding."

Mrs. Evesleigh shook her head, not really ready to let go of the subject of her friend's unwedded state. But she knew from old that to attempt to pursue a topic that Lady Mary had made obvious she did not wish to dwell upon was futile.

Though Lady Mary would have been aghast at the observation, Mrs. Evesleigh had always privately thought that when her friend wished it, she was every inch the daughter of an autocratic peer of the realm. Lady Mary Spence could don the cloak of haughty superiority and command without thought or effort, and Mrs. Evesleigh was reluctant to bring about the transformation. Already she had noted the little warning signs in her friend—a certain coolness of expression in the wide gray eyes, the slightest rise of the delicately winged brows. No, she must be content with what she had already said and hope that something might take root in Lady Mary's thoughts. Therefore Mrs. Evesleigh, not without a certain relish, turned her attention to that which had most nearly occupied most of her waking thoughts for several weeks.

When Lady Mary finally stood up to take her leave, it was felt by both ladies that much had been accomplished. Mrs. Evesleigh walked with her guest to the door, remarking, "Your help is all the more appreciated, Lady Mary, since I know that you shall have your hands full in making preparations for your journey to the Continent."

"I shall manage, never fear. I always have," Lady Mary said, a gleam of humor in her eyes. She climbed into her carriage and leaned out the window for a last word, but as it happened, Mrs. Evesleigh forestalled her.

"Oh, I know that you will. Manage, I mean. I but wish that you could feel free to rely on another's strength now and again," Mrs. Evesleigh said. She waved good-bye as the carriage got under way.

Lady Mary returned her friend's wave before she sat back against the seat squabs with a sigh. She could not help pondering Mrs. Evesleigh's parting shot, and that led her to their previous conversation. Perhaps Maggie had the right of it after all, she thought. It would be very lonely without Abigail to enliven her days. Perhaps she should remarry. Of course, such a marriage would not bring with it the blissful happiness that she had been blessed with in her marriage to Sir Roger Spence. But perhaps she was too nice in her requirements. A marriage based on mutual kindness and respect could prove quite comfortable once she became adjusted to it.

She thought about the possibility for several more minutes before she shook her head in almost a regretful way. A faint smile played about her full mouth. Such comfortable dependence was not for her. She had known something so precious and, she supposed, so rare with her late husband that she knew she could never be satisfied with less. It was better to remain alone than to enter into another relationship that was from the outset certain to prove a disappointment.

The weeks that followed were a blur of activity. Lady Mary helped with the preparations for the Evesleigh wedding and getting Abigail ready for it, as well as making their own travel arrangements. She had written again to her friend in London to request her help in finding a reputable agent who could locate a respectable residence to lease for the term in Brussels. Meanwhile, she and Abigail oversaw the packing of those possessions necessary for a prolonged stay abroad and made several visits to the local seamstress.

Lady Mary arranged for a caretaker for her home and paid off the staff, with the assurance that the major portion of their wages would be paid to them while she was gone. The servants were free to go on holiday or might choose to remain on the estate under the caretaker's watchful eyes or even take up temporary positions elsewhere in the neighborhood while she was gone. She did not have a large staff, consisting as it did of a housekeeper, two parlor maids, a cook, a scullery maid, a footman, a butler, a groom, and a stableboy. Her own personal maid and Abigail's dresser would accompany the ladies to the Continent, as would their paid companion.

Miss Steepleton had first come to the house as governess and had remained on as Abigail's chaperone and as companion to both ladies because Lady Mary had not had the heart to thrust the timid woman, who was now well into middle age, into the awkwardness of finding a new position.

Lady Mary eventually heard from the agent that Emily Downing had written to for her, and he respectfully notified her that he had engaged to rent a residence with household staff intact that he felt humbly certain would meet all her expectations. She sent her approval by the return post and made arrangements to meet with him before leaving England so that she could get all the particulars from him and settle his fee.

Lady Mary also received the long-overdue letter from her parents. She broke the seal and unfolded the pages rather reluctantly. But as she read, she felt a gathering astonishment. It was unusually short for a communiqué from Viscountess Catlin and it expressed approval for Lady Mary's good sense in providing the best possible Season for Abigail, with her love, etc. etc.

Lady Mary stared at the crossed sheets for some seconds before she thoughtfully folded the letter away. Later, when she had occasion to mention the letter's contents to Mrs. Evesleigh, she said, "It was the oddest letter of my life. Not one word of reproach, not one counterproposal, nor even a word of complaint over my selfishness. In short, my decision to take Abigail to Brussels was received with unprecedented approval. I was never more astonished in my life."

"I must admit to surprise at what you tell me. I do not recall that you have ever received such a gentle communication," Mrs. Evesleigh said, not looking up. She was embroidering the last delicate silk rose onto her daughter's wedding dress. Rather than depend upon the services of the seamstress, Mrs. Evesleigh, who was a notable needlewoman in her own right, had elected to add such exquisite touches to her daughter's gown as a visible expression of her love. She held up the train to look critically at the effect and she felt a glowing sense of pleasure. It had turned out just as she had hoped, she thought happily. She looked at Lady Mary, again returning her attention to her friend's preoccupation. "It occurs to me that perhaps the viscountess has mellowed."

"One can hope, can't one?" Lady Mary said with a smile. She ran her finger lightly over the embroidery that bordered the train of the white satin gown. "The roses are truly exquisite, Maggie. I do not think that I have ever seen a more beautiful gown."

"Oh, do you truly think so? I so wish everything to be perfect for Betsy and—" Mrs. Evesleigh choked up and tears came to her eyes as she stroked the silken roses. "I shall miss her so very, very dreadfully."

Lady Mary put her arm about her friend's shoulders and hugged her. "I do know, believe me. It seems only yesterday that we carried Abigail and Betsy to church for their christenings. Now they are young ladies and so terribly grown-up. Oh, dear, now you have me started as well!" Crying and laughing at once, the two friends eventually mopped their eyes and blew their noses.

"Well, we *are* a pair of watering pots. We mustn't let our daughters discover us in such a state or they will think us the silliest gooses alive," Lady Mary said.

"No, indeed," Mrs. Evesleigh agreed with a watery smile.

4

ONE WEEK LATER, Miss Betsy Evesleigh exchanged vows with the Reverend Clarence Coates in the old neighborhood church that had seen her christening seventeen years before. The bride and groom were resplendent in their bridal clothes, Betsy in her white satin gown standing beside the reverend in his smart dark blue frock coat with its gleaming gilt buttons. Mrs. Evesleigh quietly cried her eyes out, all the while clinging to Mr. Evesleigh, who appeared every inch the proud beaming sire.

Lady Mary's gaze traveled from the bridal couple to her own daughter. Abigail appeared nearly as radiant as the blushing bride, and it was hardly any wonder, she thought without rancor, when one considered the cost of Abigail's gown. Abigail had positively insisted upon the most expensive cloth that one could possibly acquire. There was not much that Lady Mary had ever denied her daughter, but yet she was satisfied that she had brought a firm-enough hand to Abigail's raising.

Lady Mary frowned slightly. It was just in the last few months that she and Abigail seemed to have more frequent differings of opinion. She thought that she could directly attribute those instances to the increasing influence that Viscount and Viscountess Catlin had on an impressionable and unworldly young girl. Abigail's grandparents had always indulged her and cosseted her, but now that she was seventeen and on the verge of womanhood, they filled her head with inflated expectations of life. Their wishes for Abigail included a distinguished social position gained through marriage, with the accompanying prestige, rich living, and unending parties and shopping that went hand in hand with it.

Lady Mary knew from her own childhood just how seductive such promises and expectations could be. She would have made the advantageous and socially prominent marriage her parents wanted for her and lived a life of glittering dissipation, bored with herself and with her neglectful husband, who would naturally have had his mistresses and his gaming and his own life quite apart from hers. She would have given her husband the obligatory heir and then perhaps have taken a lover or two of her own.

So would she have spent her life, caught in a marriage of convenience that was made on considerations of birth and wealth alone, if it had not been for meeting Sir Roger Spence.

From that fortuitous moment on, Lady Mary's whole perspective had changed. In Sir Roger she glimpsed the possibility of a different sort of marriage, one entered into with mutual love and respect. She had blithely assumed that her parents would give their blessing to her chosen suitor. It had come as a distinct shock when they did not, and even went so far as to forbid her ever to speak of or to acknowledge Sir Roger Spence's existence again. All of her tearful and disbelieving entreaties and Sir Roger's humble assurances could not alter the viscount and the viscountess's unequivocal decision.

Lady Mary had not known where to turn or what course to pursue, especially when she received a letter of farewell from Sir Roger. That evening she learned from her maid, who was sympathetic to the star-crossed lovers, that Viscount Catlin had threatened Sir Roger that he would disown his only daughter if she married to disoblige him, before he had had Sir Roger whipped from the house.

On the spot, Lady Mary had packed her portmanteau and in

the company of her maid had gone brazenly to her beloved's lodgings. There she had discovered him burning with fever from infection. He had not been in the most reflective frame of mind, and upon her proposal that they fly to Gretna Green, sent his manservant out to purchase a special license.

When the fever broke, Sir Roger had awakened to discover Lady Mary at his bedside, quite unconcerned that he was shirtless, and caring for his wounds. He had earnestly begged her to return to her parents, which she refused to do, and they had had the first quarrel of their acquaintance. In the end, Sir Roger had reluctantly come to agree with Lady Mary that if they were ever to be together the marriage would have to be born out of a scandalous flight to Gretna. So they had set forth, and upon the quiet exchange of their vows, they had spent the night as man and wife.

The following morning during breakfast, the door of their private parlor had burst open and Viscount Catlin had stalked in. He was verbally abusive to Sir Roger and ordered his daughter down to his carriage. Lady Mary had calmly told her father to swallow his threats and cease his demands that she return to London with him. "I am with child, Father," she had said proudly, not then realizing how truly she had spoken.

The viscount had drawn himself up and in an awful voice he had declared that she was no longer his daughter. Then he had stormed out, leaving Lady Mary in tears and seeking what solace her husband could offer to her for the loss of her family and all the life she had ever known.

But she had survived, and splendidly so, thought Lady Mary. Her eyes contemplated her daughter's lovely face. It had been the right choice, and more than anything in this life she wished her own daughter to have the opportunity to seek the love that should be hers. She was more glad than ever that she was taking her daughter away to Brussels, where Abigail would be far from her grandparents' insular, one-sided view of what constituted a proper marriage. Free of her grandparents' destructive influence during this important first Season, Abigail would have the opportunity to try her wings, and hopefully she would discover that there was more to life than an unending round of parties.

As Lady Mary watched the expressions flit across Abigail's face during the lovely and solemn ceremony, she could not but smile. It was definitely in her daughter's interest to remove to Brussels, but Abigail would be appalled if she knew that was what her mother thought. Better to let her think that the main purpose of the journey was that it be one of pleasure.

Betsy's wedding day ended in a flurry of good-byes as the bridal couple was seen off in their carriage. Abigail shrieked that she would write to her friend. Betsy blew Abigail a kiss before she pulled her head back inside the carriage window.

Abigail and Lady Mary stood with the other guests waving until the carriage had rolled out of sight behind the trees and hedgerows. "I shall miss Betsy," Abigail said, discovering it for the first time.

"I know you will," Lady Mary said, hugging her briefly. She did not say it, but she rather thought that they would both miss their former comfortable lives once they reached Brussels.

Two days later the Spence ladies set off on their journey, accompanied by Miss Steepleton in their own carriage and followed by a second carriage that carried their maids and the majority of their baggage.

The trip by carriage across England, with only a brief delay in London to call on Emily Downing and the agent who had procured the house in Brussels, ended at Dover, from whence they took sail across the Channel. As they traveled once more by carriage, the ancient cities of the Low Countries passed in a fascinating panorama: Ostend, fishing port and terminus of the Dover mail boat; Bruges, with its lofty thirteenth-century square bell tower that stood like a crowned giant over the flat expanse of West Flanders and the humpbacked bridges, swan-graced canals, and mellow brick dwellings; Ghent, with the soaring towers of the Cathedral of St. Bavon, the Belfry, and St. Nicholas Church.

Miss Steepleton was profoundly grateful to be allowed to travel to countries whose histories she had only read about. In anticipation of the journey she had procured for herself an extensive guidebook from which she was wont to quote entire passages.

When the travelers entered Belgium she volunteered the

information to her companions that the country derived its name from "Gallia Belica," used by the Romans to describe all of the southern region of the Low Countries, and that the political division of Holland from Belgium, decreed in 1609, had lasted until the present, when the Netherlands and Belgium were united into the Kingdom of the Netherlands under King William I in that year of 1815. "And that, of course, explains our own countrymen's eagerness to travel to Brussels. We have always loved the pomp and ceremony connected with royalty," Miss Steepleton said with satisfaction.

In Ghent, the ladies stayed in the oldest hotel in Belgium, the Cour St. Georges, which had been erected in the thirteenth century. Abigail had thought herself too old to be lectured on antiquities and history, but she was fascinated to learn that the hostel was the early headquarters of the honorable crossbowmen of St. George. She felt herself to be in love with the city of abbeys, castles, canals, quays, guilds, churches with chimes, and cobbled market squares. "Mama, is it not the most romantic place?" she sighed, staring up at the weathered stone facade of yet another ancient abbey.

Lady Mary laughed at her daughter. "Indeed, and is that not the same thing you have said about each of these fine old cities?"

Abigail shook her head. "Oh, Mama, you do not understand. *This* city speaks to my soul, truly it does."

Miss Steepleton uttered a faint but definite agreement of her young companion's passionate sentiment. "Oh, so true, Miss Abigail."

"Let us hope that Brussels does so as well," Lady Mary said, taking her daughter's elbow and urging her toward their carriage. Miss Steepleton hurried behind, casting several lingering glances back at the old abbey. To her mind, it was such a pity not to spend more time in awed admiration of such magnificence.

Though Abigail went with a laughing protest, she was actually as eager as her mother to continue their journey across Belgium, which had become an exciting exodus in itself. The flats and dikes near the coast had given way to a land of sweeping fields, beech forests, and weather-worn hills, all laced with rivers and sliced by canals. Tidy farmhouses and grand châteaus marked the distance like small jewels. Every vista, every personage and experience, was new and to be savored, serving to bring Lady Mary and Abigail closer in ways that they had never been before. Their mutual enjoyment of the traveling allowed them to relate more as friends and equals rather than as mother and daughter, and each discovered a peculiar delight in the emerging change in their relationship.

Lady Mary was glad to note that her sensible and sweet-natured daughter was still very much in evidence beneath the flashes of self-indulgence that Abigail exhibited and that had so concerned her for the past several months.

As for Abigail, she wondered when she looked at Lady Mary why she had never really noticed how young or how lighthearted her mother was. It was akin to discovering a dear friend. Abigail was also conscious of a new respect for her mother. She had always taken for granted Lady Mary's air of quality, her frank friendly manners, and her quiet and efficient organization of their home life. But until stepping foot on the Continent, Abigail had only rarely seen the steel that underlay her mother's character.

At rare points during their travels, even though the ladies were accompanied by Miss Steepleton and their small entourage of servants, they were sometimes accorded scant attention by hostelkeepers who were busily serving other and more ostentatious travelers. These individuals quickly learned their mistake, however. Lady Mary Spence could in an instant draw herself up with all the pride worthy of the daughter of an English viscount and in her well-modulated French inform the hostelkeeper of her wishes. Her icy hauteur left no room for misinterpretation, and Abigail was always amazed at the swift improvement in the service accorded them. She wondered whether she would ever be able to claim such respect simply by the way that she carried herself.

Upon arriving in Brussels, Lady Mary directed their driver to the address that she had been given by the agent who had acquired the house for them. During the drive through the city, the ladies exclaimed over the beauty of the buildings, the wide boulevards, the canals, restaurants, and shops. Their first sight of the Place Royale awed them. It was a great square that consisted of four-story seventeenth-century structures of brown stone and hundreds of windows, and decorated with elaborate gilded carvings, built around paving stones upon which rough-capped vendors offered roses, carnations, and chrysanthemums to promenading, mostly uniformed, gentlemen and their ladies.

Miss Steepleton quickly located the Place Royale in her guide-book, and she was able to tell the ladies that the buildings retained the original names of inns and noble abodes, though the structures presently housed the guildhalls. Abigail made a game of picking out the various guilds by the different adorn-ments on the buildings. The House of the Fox was the residence of the haberdashers' guild and was topped by a statue of St. Nicholas; the Horn, which was the boatmen's guild, wore a gable in the form of a ship's stern; the She-Wolf housed the archers' guild and sheltered under an eagle with outspread wings; the Sack, which belonged to the cabinetmakers' guild, had a small gilded globe riding proud above it; the Wheel-barrow, house of the grease and tallow traders, was topped by a gilded conch shell; and the bakers' hall was marked by a gilded dome accented by a Greek statue balanced on one foot.

"Which must be Mercury the Winged Messenger, do you not agree, Agatha?" asked Abigail, pressed close to the window to keep the object in question in sight as their carriage was leaving the great square.

"I do not recall my mythology as well as I should, Miss Abigail, but that does seem to fit," agreed Miss Steepleton.

"I cannot imagine what Mercury has to do with bakers," Abigail said, sitting back again against the seat squabs.

Just out of the Place Royale, in la Rue du Musée, the carriage stopped before a respectable town house. The carriage door was opened and a footman in unfamiliar livery set the iron step so that the ladies could descend. The carriage carrying their servants and baggage drove up as Lady Mary and Abigail stepped onto the sidewalk. Miss Steepleton closely followed on their heels as they went up the stairs and entered the modest residence.

The town house was well enough, being both spacious and tastefully furnished in eighteenth-century Flemish furniture, original Brussels tapestries, and Oriental carpets. Lady Mary and Abigail met the staff, which gathered in the front hall to greet them. The staff spoke French, though the butler and housekeeper welcomed the British ladies in softly accented English. Since landing on the Continent, Abigail had been at once struck by the strangeness of hearing tongues other than her own. She was never more glad than at this moment, when she realized that the household that would be serving them did not speak English, that she had attended to her French-language lessons so well.

After the ladies had settled into their rooms and bathed and changed from their traveling dresses, which had become sadly creased from that day's long drive, they enjoyed a quiet dinner of roasted chicken, tomatoes stuffed with small shrimp, and various other side dishes of vegetables, ending with a bowl of sweet grapes. They discussed their new surroundings in an overall pleased fashion, all three having been especially struck by the numerous bowls and vases of magnificent and fragrant blooms in every room.

"My room is so pretty, and more than adequate, Lady Mary. Why, after unpacking, I had an entire wardrobe left over. I am sure I do not know what to think of such luxury," Miss Steepleton said with a tittering laugh.

"Indeed, I think that we shall be very comfortable here." Lady Mary smiled across the table at her companion.

"Oh, quite, Mama! I saw ever so many shops as we drove into the city," Abigail said enthusiastically, her thoughts turning naturally to one of her favorite activities. She had always adored visiting the shops, with the eternal anticipation of discovering some wonderful trinket or other treasure.

Lady Mary laughed at her daughter. "Can you think of nothing but acquiring quantities of Belgian lace, Abigail?" she teased, knowing well Abigail's love of the delicate and expensive stuff.

"Of course I do. I am looking forward to meeting all sorts of elegant officers as well."

"There are a great many historical sights that you will be interested in visiting too, Miss Abigail," put in Miss Steepleton with a hopeful smile. She thought of her light duties as companion to be sacrosanct, and though usually pleasant enough, how much nicer it would be if Miss Abigail could be persuaded to participate in some of her own particular interests.

Abigail shrugged her slim shoulders, dismissing her former governess's suggestion. "Old buildings are the same everywhere. I surely saw enough to last me a lifetime during our journey."

"Whatever has happened to your poetic soul, Abigail? Was it perhaps left in Ghent?" Lady Mary asked, arching her brows in exaggerated surprise.

Abigail giggled, aware that she had left herself completely exposed to such teasing. "I think that it must have been, Mama. Now that we have at last arrived, I wish to spend every moment in whatever amusements may be had. I am sorry, Aggie. I am afraid that tours of Gothic cathedrals have been quite cast in the pale by expectations of all sorts of marvelous things."

Miss Steepleton appeared quite crestfallen. Lady Mary said soothingly, "Never mind, Aggie. I shall not require you to run about with my frivolous daughter to every social function. You may consider yourself on holiday and wander about as much as you like, guidebook in hand."

"I am most grateful, my lady," Miss Steepleton said, completely overwhelmed by her own extraordinary good fortune. She could not now recall why she had accepted the position with Lady Mary all those years ago, but at such sublime moments as this, she was extremely grateful that she had done so.

After the coffee was served, the ladies did not linger downstairs. The day had been a long and exciting one for them all, so they made an early evening of it and went directly up to bed.

5

AFTER BREAKFAST the next morning, Lady Mary met with the Belgian housekeeper and cook to relay her wishes on how the house should be managed to best suit her tastes and to discuss such menus as she wanted. The housekeeper and the cook were friendly enough, but distant in their manner, as though assessing their new mistress. However, after a few minutes they swiftly began to warm to Lady Mary as her firm, frank manners and her excellent French won them over. When they discovered that Lady Mary intended to entertain extensively in order to bring out her lovely daughter—"Ah, like an angel, that one!" the housekeeper had rhapsodized privately—they volubly assured Lady Mary of their complete and utter cooperation.

Once the domestic tasks were completed and she had sent a message off to her son to request his presence for dinner, Lady Mary asked that Abigail meet her in the front hall in twenty minutes so that they could begin their round of introductory morning calls. Lady Mary had been given, by her London friend Emily Downing, several letters of introduction to various personages.

When Abigail joined her mother, she was dismayed to see that Lady Mary had chosen to wear one of her largest matron caps under her bonnet. "Mama, must you wear that thing?" she asked with a grimace. "You know how very much I detest it when you do so."

Lady Mary glanced in the hall mirror. "It is quite respectable, Abigail," she said firmly, pulling on her soft kid gloves.

"But it is not at all complimentary to one of your perfect features," Abigail said as she eyed the offending article.

Lady Mary laughed, surprised and touched. "That is a very pretty compliment, Abigail, though I suspect somewhat biased in source. Now, let us be off. No, I will not remove my cap.

I am firmly entrenched in the matron circles and quite content to be so.''

''Well, I would not be so content if it were I who was supposed to give up all sense of fashion only because I had a daughter to present,'' Abigail said frankly. ''You know that is the only reason you took up those detestable caps, Mama, you know it is!'' She continued in her attempts to persuade Lady Mary to lay aside the cap until the moment that an antique coach was brought around from the stables. Breaking off in mid-word, Abigail stared at the vehicle, aghast. ''Mama, surely we are not going in *that*!''

Lady Mary firmly steered her daughter to the carriage door. ''Not another word, Abigail. No, not one! I am wearing my cap and we are making use of this wonderful old coach. At least we shall until I can arrange to procure a landau. Good heavens, there are actually holes in the seat leather!'' And so Lady Mary and Abigail set off on the first of their morning calls, which was to a Lady Cecily Wilson-Jones.

That morning Lady Cecily was in to visitors. Shortly after sending in their letters, Lady Mary and Abigail were shown into the drawing room. Lady Cecily reclined on a settee and she looked up with friendly curiosity at the entrance of her unknown callers. She saw a well-dressed woman endowed with a fine pair of frank gray eyes and attractive features and neat figure. There was something so pleasant and easy about the woman's smile that Lady Cecily took an immediate liking to her. The lady was followed by a younger female who was a striking porcelain-blond beauty.

Lady Cecily assumed that the stunning young miss was a cousin or niece, and she held out her hand to the older woman, whom she had guessed at once to be Lady Mary Spence, if from nothing more than her carriage. ''I am most happy to make your acquaintance, Lady Mary. Pray do forgive me for not rising to greet you. My physician has decreed that I must rest in a reclining position at least twice each day, and you have caught me during my morning habit.''

Lady Mary regarded her hostess with interest. Lady Cecily was a pretty brunette with laughing brown eyes, a rosy complexion, and in a most obvious condition. "I do not regard it in the least, Lady Cecily. I well remember how fatigued one may become, which happened particularly with my daughter, Abigail. She was a lively infant and her character has not changed since, to any great degree," Lady Mary said with a teasing glance toward her daughter.

Abigail blushed, slightly embarrassed. "Really, Mama!" she said with a small laugh.

Lady Cecily regarded her two visitors in the greatest astonishment. "Why, I assumed that Miss Spence was your niece, Lady Mary! I did not credit you to be much older than I am myself."

"There you are, Mama," Abigail said in some satisfaction. "Did I not tell you that it is ridiculous for someone as pretty as you to wear that monstrous matron's turban?"

It was Lady Mary's turn to feel embarrassment. She said gently and reprovingly, "I hardly think that Lady Cecily is at all interested in such a mundane topic as my headgear, Abigail."

At once Abigail threw a glance in Lady Cecily's direction. She bit her lip in vexation, aware that she had committed a *faux pas*. She had so wanted to appear up to the mark and sophisticated upon these first morning calls, and already she had made herself appear childish.

Lady Cecily noted with interest that Lady Mary's blush was vastly becoming, as was the daughter's subsequent confusion over her mother's mild reminder, and she decided that this pair of unknowns was just what she needed to put at bay the feeling of *ennui* that had seemed to hover over her so much the past few weeks. There was an intriguing frankness in their relationship that was quite out of the common way. "Pray do not scold, Lady Mary. Miss Spence is quite right. When one looks hardly older than one's own daughter, one should take advantage of such a kind stroke of fate," Lady Cecily said, smiling.

Soft color stole into Lady Mary's face yet again. She shook her head. "Thank you, my lady." Unable to think of anything else to add, she threw a laughing glance at her daughter, who could not contain the flash of triumph that crossed her face.

Lady Cecily saw that her guest was somewhat out of countenance and she gently turned the subject. They talked of

England and of the electrifying news, which Lady Mary and Abigail had heard but that morning from their butler, that Napoleon Bonaparte had escaped from Elba and was even then making his way through France. "When I first heard it, I could not quite believe it true, and naturally I wondered whether I had made an error in bringing Abigail to Brussels at this time," Lady Mary said.

"Oh, no, Mama, surely not. Why, the whole British army occupies the Low Countries, and everywhere in the streets this morning we saw so many of our brave fellows in their neat uniforms. I am positive that Bonaparte would not dare show his long nose anywhere near," Abigail said.

"I, too, have the greatest confidence in our army, Abigail. However, one must certainly pause for reflection when one hears that men are positively flocking to Bonaparte's banner," Lady Mary said.

"I think that the most shocking thing of all," Lady Cecily agreed. "The man is nothing less than a bad penny come back to haunt us all."

The drawing-room door had opened as she spoke, and a tall gentleman stepped in. "Who is that, Cecily?" he asked, going up to Lady Cecily and placing his hands on her shoulders as he bent to drop a kiss on the top of her head. He bowed slightly to the visiting ladies, who had watched his approach with curiosity.

Lady Cecily greeted him with an affectionate smile. "Why, Bonaparte, of course, Robert. He was soundly beaten, and here he is back again. It is positively indecent."

"I agree, Cecily. His manners are quite appalling," the gentleman said, nodding.

Lady Cecily twisted her head to stare up at him reproachfully. "Now you are teasing me again. What a horrid thing to do so early in the morning." The gentleman laughed as she allowed her own winning smile to break out. She indicated her visitors. "Robert, I do not believe that you have met my guests, Lady Mary Spence and her daughter, Miss Abigail Spence. My brother, Robert, Earl of Kenmare."

The ladies indicated how pleased they were to make his acquaintance. Lady Mary spoke in the easy, frank way that was characteristic of her, while Abigail responded to his polite greeting with an uncharacteristic hint of shyness. She had not been so long out of the schoolroom that titles were not still intimidating to her. However, she did send his lordship an appraising glance from under her lashes when he returned his attention to her mother, wondering with some surprise at an earl who was not bent over with age. She thought that making a splendid marriage to someone as handsome as the Earl of Kenmare would be a pleasant triumph indeed.

As for Lady Mary, she was struck at once by the earl's strong virile looks and his quiet air of authority. Lord Kenmare was attired in a tight-fitting morning coat and buckskins, which set off to advantage his broad shoulders and lean length. His features were even, his eyes a deep sea-blue, and his well-molded mouth quirked at one corner in a most fascinating fashion when he smiled. Lady Mary was surprised by the turn of her thoughts, and she concentrated instead on the affectionate and sensitive manner in which his lordship treated his sister.

Talk returned to the escape of Bonaparte and his extraordinary reception in France, but the earl seemed not to place much weight upon it. Lady Mary asked, "Do you not regard Bonaparte's return as a threat, my lord?"

Lord Kenmare reflected a moment. "I would not disregard him, Lady Mary. The man has proved himself to be an able, charismatic leader. Let us say that I have the greatest confidence in his grace the Duke of Wellington and in our own gallant army," he said.

"But the duke is not here. He is in Vienna, while every day Bonaparte marches closer," Lady Cecily said. Unconsciously her hands cradled her large belly. "I do wish we were all safe at home in England."

The earl smiled at his sister. "You need not fret over Wilson-Jones, Cecily. He is a hardy fellow and not likely to let the prospect of a battle quail him, if it comes to that at all."

"That is precisely what does make me anxious. Reginald positively dotes on what he terms a good fight. He says that it makes him feel ten times more alive," Lady Cecily said with a grimace. "I shall never understand the male mind. It is all so illogical!" The earl laughed and she threw him a look of disgust. She pointedly turned away from him. "And what of your son, Lady Mary? I believe you said that he is with the Fifth Division. Is he as battle-hungry as all the rest of these young officers?"

Lady Mary shook her head regretfully. "Quite foolishly so. At least, so I judged from his last letter. He was very disappointed to have missed all but the tail end of the Spanish campaign. This news of Bonaparte must have put him in fine fettle."

"We have not yet seen William, my lady. He comes to dine with us tonight, Mama says, and I know that he will have such stories to tell us," Abigail said with a sparkle of excitement in her large blue eyes.

Lord Kenmare was regarding Lady Mary with an expression that was faintly surprised. "Your son is surely not old enough to be already a veteran of war," he said.

"*I* do not think so, certainly," Lady Mary said, laughing. "But William would beg to differ with anyone who dared say so. He has been army-mad since he was in short coats."

"William is turned eighteen and he is quite handsome in his regimentals, my lord, besides having a most distinguished scar," Abigail said proudly.

Lord Kenmare smiled slightly, amused by her naive enthusiasm. "I am certain that he does. Perhaps I shall have the pleasure of meeting your brother one day, Miss Spence," he said.

Glancing at the clock ticking on the mantel, Lady Mary judged that their social call had been long enough, and she said, "Abigail, I believe that we have a few other visits yet to make this morning." Rising with graceful manners, she and Abigail took their leave of Lady Cecily and the Earl of Kenmare.

Upon the closing of the drawing-room door behind her visitors, Lady Cecily turned at once to her brother. "Well! What an entertaining morning I have had, Robert. I was intrigued by the letter of introduction that Lady Mary had from Emily Downing. Such a glowing recommendation from one of known discrimination in her friends. I am quite glad that I was in to callers. I found her perfectly fascinating, did not you?"

"Who, Miss Spence? She is very lovely and very young; but

fascinating? Decidedly not. I am not particularly enamored of babes-in-arms," Lord Kenmare said. He bowed to his sister, a teasing gleam in his blue eyes, and said, "Though I shall naturally make an exception in the case of my niece or nephew."

Lady Cecily threw a tasseled satin pillow at his head, which he easily caught. "Wretched creature! As though you do not know perfectly well that I am speaking of Lady Mary. I was completely bowled out when I learned that Abigail is her daughter. Why, Lady Mary could almost pass for Abigail's elder sister, so young as she appears."

"I beg to differ, Cecily. Lady Mary is too calm in manner and intelligent to be other than she is, and that is an extremely attractive young widow," the earl said, flicking the pillow back at his sister.

Lady Cecily deflected the soft missile, staring up at her brother. A kindling expression warmed her eyes. "Ah, so you did notice!"

"Cecily, stop that thought right where it is," Lord Kenmare said quietly. "You know how much I detest becoming the object of matchmaking schemes."

"But, Robert, you cannot mean to go the remainder of your life without remarrying. I said nothing to you for years after Madeline died, out of respect for your feelings and because I hoped that eventually you would cast about for someone on your own. But you have not given a single sign that you mean to do anything about it, and I can't help but think—"

"Pray do not think, Cecily!" the earl groaned. "Come, dearest sister, when shall you give up this ludicrous notion that I cannot be happy unless I remarry? You know perfectly well that I am comfortable as I am."

"Yes, I know all about your occasional companions, Robert," Lady Cecily retorted.

"Now, I wonder, who can be telling tales about me out of school?" Lord Kenmare mused. His expression was at its blandest. "You really should not listen to gossip, Cecily, especially the whispers of the ill-informed."

Lady Cecily was goaded beyond endurance. "You know perfectly well that I do not pay heed to *gossip*! At least . . . Really, Robert, surely you must realize that everyone is anxious that I am kept informed of your discreet progress. I am thought to live in dread of your begetting an heir and thus losing the title for my own firstborn. Such odious busybodies. It is quite a trial to me, I assure you. Yes, you may laugh! But if you had any feeling for me at all, you would marry tomorrow so that I may have some peace. I have often been so put out of patience with the nonsense that I have positively *hoped* that you have a bastard or two tucked away somewhere, and so I have said! *That* shut their mealy mouths, I can tell you!''

The earl laughed again. At Lady Cecily's reproachful look, he only shook his head. He rose and gently tweaked one of his sister's glossy brown curls. ''I am most sorry to disappoint you, Cecily. But to my knowledge, I have no bastards. And I do apologize for being such a cross for you to bear. I had no notion that you suffered such indignities on my behalf.''

''If you truly, truly loved me, you would remarry,'' Lady Cecily said hopefully. Her brother's gaze was startled. She tried to keep a straight face but she could not. She pealed with laughter. ''Oh, that was perfectly wicked of me, was it not! Pray do forgive me for teasing you so in such a horrid fashion, Robert.''

''Indeed, I must, for I do adore you.'' He smiled down into her eyes, then said firmly, ''But not enough to wed Lady Mary Spence or any other lady only to satisfy your notion of proper succession, which, by the by, is a most unnatural one for a mother-to-be. Any other lady would be ecstatic to have her unborn child in line for an earldom.''

''That's all very well, Robert. But you know that my dearest wish above all else is to see you settled and as happy as you were before. You see!'' Lady Cecily spread her hands with an air of injured innocence. ''I am completely unselfish.''

The earl lifted his well-marked black brows. ''Indeed!''

She smiled as she stretched out her hand to him. ''Go away, dear brother. I wish to think private and forbidden thoughts regarding your future.''

''You fill me with alarm,'' Lord Kenmare said. He bowed over her fingers, retaining her hand for a moment as though he meant to say something else. But he apparently thought better of it. He merely smiled before he left the drawing room.

6

THAT EVENING mother and daughter waited impatiently for the arrival of their invited dinner guest. When a very young gentleman attired in regimental togs was ushered into the drawing room, both ladies leapt to their feet.

"William!" Lady Mary quickly went to him, her hands outstretched. But Abigail slipped past her to envelop her brother in a smothering hug.

The young gentleman emerged from Abigail's fervent welcome to take Lady Mary's hands. He bowed with aplomb. "My lady, you look exceptionally well," he said, a wide grin belying the formality of his greeting.

Lady Mary laughed and shook her head at him. "You'll not stand on such ceremony with me, I warn you," she said. In imitation of her daughter's exuberant welcome, she threw her arms around him. She was surprised and touched when his strong arms came up to clasp her close.

The silly tears started to her eyes and she blinked them back. She released him with a last pat and stepped back, once more mistress of herself. She made a production of looking him up and down while he stood grinning at her.

William Spence was a sturdy young gentleman of average height, with his shoulders broad and held proudly. His face was open and boyish except for the thin sliver scar that cut deep across his left brow. Lady Mary was pleased to note that her son appeared as pleasant-natured as ever. She had unconsciously feared that somehow his chosen profession would coarsen his sensitivities.

Her son had inherited her wide gray eyes and his hair was blond, not gold like Abigail's, but wheaten even in the candlelight. Attired as he was in scarlet coat and breeches and Hessian boots, a shako under his arm, he was the very picture of the best of English manhood, she thought with a touch of pride. "It is so good to see you at last, William. I believe you've grown broader than when we saw you last."

William laughed, his audacious grin flashing at his mother. "Put that down to the feed we fellows are getting, Mama. Beer, bread, meat, and gin are cheap in Flanders."

"Really, William!" Lady Mary laughed. "I am serious. I could swear you have grown a full inch. You appear to such fine advantage in all your finery, I assure you."

"Yes, you have become quite the handsome one, William. Or do you pad your shoulders with buckram?" Abigail asked, feeling her brother's upper arm with exaggerated curiosity.

He slapped away her hand and said with dignity, "Indeed I do not, brat. And I'll thank you not to inspect me like a cut of beef offered for sale by the village butcher." Abigail giggled. She threw herself at him to kiss his cheek again. William tolerated the salutation good-naturedly and affectionately tweaked one of her gold curls, remarking that she had improved considerably since he had last seen her. "You've turned into a dashed pretty girl, Abby. If you weren't my own sister I would instantly fall at your feet in admiration."

Abigail blushed hotly at her brother's lavish compliment. "Oh, William, truly? Am I pretty?"

He pretended to study her judiciously, while she stared up at him in anxious suspense. "I doubt that there are more than one or two who can hold a candle to you," he said at last.

Abigail was made speechless with pleasure.

Lady Mary had listened with amusement, but she shook her head in mock reproval at her son. "William, you must not encourage her so. Your sister is already as vain as she can hold."

William's easy smile flashed out. "Is she! Then I shall certainly exercise restraint in future. And I shall warn off my friends by saying that my sister is only passable and not worth their attention."

"Oh, no, no, William! You would not be so beastly!" Abigail exclaimed, horrified. "Why, I would not be asked to dance at all."

William laughed at her. "Silly puss. As though the fellows

don't have eyes in their heads. I promise you that you shall never lack for dance partners.''

Abigail realized that she had been the butt of one of his teases and she pushed him. ''Wretch! I shall revenge myself upon you, see if I don't.'' William immediately threatened her with a turn over his knee for her impertinence. Abigail squealed and put a table between them. ''You would not dare!''

''Wouldn't I just!'' William said, grinning. He feinted a lunge toward her and she squealed again, her eyes reflecting high enjoyment of her brother's company.

''A truce, I pray you!'' Lady Mary protested, laughing. ''Don't you think that we may go in to dinner?''

''Of course. Allow me to escort you properly, Mama,'' William said, holding out his arm to her. He offered his other arm to his sister and proudly escorted both ladies into the dining room.

Dinner was a convivial meal, made pleasant by lighthearted banter and laughter and the familiar teasing between brother and sister. Lady Mary could not remember being happier, when she had the two people dearest to her heart beside her. As she glanced from her son's animated face, with its slender bones and the hint of down on his upper lip, to her daughter, whose blue eyes sparkled with unalloyed pleasure, she wished that her husband had survived long enough to see what fine children they had made between them. She found that she was content merely to watch their expressive faces and listen to their chatter. It was a scene that she knew she would always cherish—the candlelight shedding its soft friendly glow over them, the happy vivacious conversation, even the lingering aroma of roast roebuck and chestnut gravy that they had consumed for dinner.

''I hope that there is a war.''

William's cheerful statement destroyed Lady Mary's contentment. She straightened in her chair. ''I trust you are not serious. There is not a chance of it, is there?''

William looked across the table at his mother, surprised by her abrupt tone. ''Why, Mama, everyone knows that we're going to go head-to-toe with Boney again. It is just a question of when.''

Lady Mary was disturbed. ''Are you certain of this, William?

I had heard of Bonaparte's escape from Elba, of course, but I never imagined that it would mean war again. Everyone, surely, must be sick of war.''

"There you are out, Mama," said William confidently. "There are hundreds just like me who would like nothing better than to test our mettle against one of the greatest generals of our time. Besides, it will mean that I shall have my promotion in no time at all.''

"I think it vastly exciting, don't you, Mama?" Abigail exclaimed, her eyes shining. "Why, it is just like out of a romance. William will charge off against the enemy and return triumphant, with the enemy routed and put to flight, and then kneel to receive a kiss of gratitude on the cheek from his lady.''

"Abigail, how you do go on," Lady Mary said in gentle reproof.

"Quite right. As though I would be so daft as to kneel for some girl or other, whom I've never met, only to be kissed on the cheek," William said scornfully. He arranged his features into a soulful expression and pretended to salute a lady. "My lady, I humbly beg for a token of your esteem from your own marble lips," he lisped.

Abigail shrieked with laughter. Even Lady Mary had to laugh at her son's absurdity, and the conversation passed on to reminiscenses of past Christmas charades and other pleasant memories.

It was not until much later that night, after William had left them to return to his quarters and Abigail had said good night while hiding a yawn behind her hand as she went to her bedroom, that Lady Mary recalled the breezy and knowledge-able manner in which William had declared that there would be another battle.

While the maid brushed out her hair, Lady Mary stared at herself in her mirror. She saw the anxiety reflected in her gray eyes. "Dear God, it cannot happen. It must not happen," she murmured.

"What was that, my lady?" the maid asked.

"Nothing Beatrice. That is enough. Thank you," Lady Mary said, dismissing the maid for the night. She remained sitting at the vanity, fingering a pot of face lotion as though she meant to make use of it. The maid curtsied and quietly exited the bedroom, unaware that she left her mistress prey to disturbing thoughts. Lady Mary was appalled at the mere possibility of her precious son going off into battle again. Abigail's safety could well be jeopardized also, she thought, since the most likely arena for confrontation with Bonaparte's forces was the Low Countries, which were at that moment occupied by the allied troops.

Lady Mary considered herself a practical woman, not easily frightened or given to imagined fears, so she tried to shrug away her misgivings. She would await events, she thought. Undoubtedly she would learn more of what was behind William's extraordinary opinion once she was better connected in society. If her son's easy statement proved to be founded on more than a young boy's hopes for glory and promotion, then possibly there would come the time when she must decide whether to return with Abigail posthaste to England. But she knew even to voice such a possibility to her daughter now was to invite tearful protests, and she decided to keep her own counsel for the time being.

In the meantime she would make discreet inquiries and form her own opinion. Surely there were those in Brussels who were well-informed and who could be expected to know what was most likely to happen, she thought hopefully.

Her decision made, Lady Mary got into bed. She blew out the candle on her bedside table and settled herself against the soft pillows. She was tired and quickly fell asleep. But her night was not entirely restful, being disturbed by half-formed dreams of flashing bayonets and the ominous rolling of drums.

7

THAT FORTNIGHT, while all Brussels waited to hear what Bonaparte was getting up to, the Spence ladies adjusted to their new surroundings. Abigail had never been in such an exciting place, and never in her life had she met so many different people.

Brussels society was truly international in character. Though a surprisingly large number of Belgians spoke English, they heard just as much French and Flemish as well as a heavy sprinkling of German, Spanish, and Russian. There seemed to be a representative of royalty from every European country on the map in residence in the city. During a particularly long introduction of royalty at a ball, Abigail whispered to her mother, "Fancy! I had no notion that those with royal blood in their veins outnumbered their subject populations." Though Lady Mary hushed her impertinent daughter, she could barely stifle a gurgling laugh as the ballroom company again dipped low like so many swaying grasses at the entrance of yet another royal personage.

Lady Mary and Abigail quickly found their feet in society, and they could count a great many cordial acquaintances among the English, many of whom recalled Lady Mary as a pretty, well-bred girl and had welcomed her back to her proper place in the *ton*. The Spence ladies had also a lesser but growing number of friends among the congenial Belgians, whom they had found as a people to be especially courteous, having an incorrigible habit of shaking hands upon meeting or departing.

The ball that evening was hosted by the du Boises, a prominent Belgian family.

Lady Mary had made the acquaintance of Madame Helen du Bois while out shopping only a week previously. Madame du Bois was an Englishwoman who had married a Belgian gentleman of consequence. Lady Mary had immediately liked the

lovely and sociable Madame du Bois, and her liking was recipro-
cated in full. The two ladies promised to visit more formally
and exchanged directions.

That same afternoon Madame du Bois had come to call,
accompanied by her daughter. Mademoiselle Michele du Bois
was of an age with Abigail. She had not inherited her mother's
pale English loveliness, but instead was a striking brunette. Her
black curls, her heavily lashed and sparkling midnight-blue eyes,
her elegant hourglass figure—all served to intimidate Abigail,
who felt pale and childlike by comparison. But Michele's ease
of manner and complete lack of condescension quickly reassured
Abigail, and within minutes the two girls had become instant
friends, each having discovered a kindred spirit in the other as
they talked animatedly of parties, lovely gowns, gentlemanly
admiration, and romantic ideals.

Lady Mary had regarded the two girls, one head gold and
one shining black, as together they looked over a book of fashion
plates. The girls animatedly debated the merits of a certain lace
for an evening gown, completely oblivious of the older women's
more staid conversation.

Lady Mary smiled as she glanced over at her visitor. "I am
glad Abigail has found someone of her own age so soon. I had
feared that she would be horribly homesick for her old friends
at first," she said.

"I am also glad that the girls have hit it off so well. Michele
needs someone besides myself with whom she can practice her
English. I infinitely prefer that a young lady such as Abigail
become her constant companion rather than one of these dashing
young officers," Madame du Bois said with a laugh.

Lady Mary laughed also and nodded. "The young gentlemen
are rascals, are they not? Abigail has heard nothing but compliments since we arrived, and her head is quite turned by the
constant admiration of the soldiers, whom one cannot avoid
meeting everywhere."

"Indeed, one must actually take care not to trip over them,"
Madame du Bois said, her blue eyes twinkling. "Our quiet city
has become very gay since the allied armies have been stationed
in the Low Countries. We have spent the winter very merrily,
and in particular with the arrival of the London Guards, the

cavalry, and the other English troops that have been quartered up and down the country. There is not a young lady in all of Brussels who lacks for admirers.''

"It seems so very odd to me. I cannot help thinking of why all those young gentlemen are in uniform, but it seems not to be of the least importance when placed against the next ball or soiree,'' Lady Mary said.

Madame du Bois shook her head in agreement. ''Indeed, it is odd. Brussels is an open city, quite undefended by battlements or the like. However, my husband says the prevailing attitude of gaiety does not surprise him in the least. It is François's opinion that people are so positive that they may rely upon the Duke of Wellington to protect us that they cannot entertain a thought to the contrary. For myself, though, I cannot but wonder how his grace is to accomplish the thing when he is still in Vienna. I quite fail to understand it.'' Her frown was dispelled when she laughed suddenly. ''François tells me that I am not pragmatic enough, that one has only to realize that the duke is a god and a hero all rolled into one and then it becomes perfectly understandable.''

Lady Mary shared her amusement. ''Why, then, certainly we may all feel perfectly comfortable.''

She was recalling this conversation as she watched the whirling couples on the floor. The majority of the gentlemen were resplendent in uniform, splashes of brilliant scarlet and green and gold and black that quite overshadowed the ladies' paler gowns. Not one countenance displayed the least shade of anxiety, and on everyone's lips was the Duke of Wellington's name, evoked like a talisman against the news of Bonaparte's steady advance across France and the gathering strength of his armies.

"You do not dance, Lady Mary?"

Startled, she turned her head to find the Earl of Kenmare standing beside her chair. He was smiling, and the effect on her was as devastating as it had been the first time they had met, as she was too well aware. She could not recall ever having met a more attractive gentleman, she thought, and she immediately felt a stab of guilt toward her late husband's memory. She set aside the odd feelings to be contemplated later, and responded to the earl's quizzical greeting with a friendly smile that lent warmth to her wide gray eyes. "No, I do not, my lord. I am become too staid for such frivolity," she said with a light laugh as she gave him her hand in greeting.

"Nonsense, my lady. I shall not allow you to pronounce such a sad judgment upon yourself," Lord Kenmare said. He bowed to her. "Pray do me the honor in the next set, ma'am," he said.

With some surprise he regarded the attractive color that rose in Lady Mary's face. She spoke in some confusion. "Really, really, I should not. I do thank you, my lord, but I—"

Recognizing how idiotic she sounded, Lady Mary broke off, laughing at herself. "I have not behaved in such a shatterbrained fashion for years. Do forgive me, my lord! I am not used to such flattering attention. When one joins the dowagers, one does not waltz, you see."

The earl's interest in Lady Mary was sharpened by a notch or two. He had not met many self-effacing ladies, and certainly none who met his eyes with such frankness of gaze. "I believe it is I who must beg forgiveness for placing you in an awkward position. It was certainly never my intention to embarrass you or to press you against your wishes. May I sit with you a few moments and perhaps redeem myself in your eyes?" He gestured at the empty chair beside her.

"Of course, my lord," Lady Mary said, bowing her head in acquiescence. The earl seated himself. Almost instantly she became acutely aware of his nearness when the masculine, clean scent of sandalwood wafted about her. She discovered that her usual self-possession had unaccountably deserted her. She could not imagine what was wrong with her. She hoped that she was not coming down with a fever, for she felt first warm, then cold, then warm again. Her eyes returned to the dancers because her mind had gone completely blank for want of something to say.

Lord Kenmare had followed her gaze, and he thought that he knew what so completely absorbed her attention. "Your daughter is very lovely. I do not think that I have ever seen her without an accompanying crowd of admirers, yet she appears to handle the attention quite modestly," he remarked.

Lady Mary turned toward him, all her inhibitions forgotten in her enthusiasm for her daughter's accomplishment in taking so easily to high society. "She *is* doing well for a first Season, isn't she? I had hoped that she would, though because of her naiveté, I had wondered whether I should bring her out this Season or wait another year." She gave a rueful laugh as her gaze turned once more to the sight of her daughter going gracefully down a country set. "However, I was at a distinct disadvantage in deciding against her come-out this Season, since Abigail is aware that at sixteen I was wedded and already a mother."

Lord Kenmare glanced at the lady beside him, trying to imagine a young girl much like Abigail Spence with a babe in her arms. He found it impossible. With disapprobation he eyed the matron's turban that Lady Mary wore. Lady Mary Spence hardly appeared old enough to be an aunt, let alone the mother of two grown children. On the thought, he said, "I believe that I have recently met your son, Lady Mary. Is he Ensign William Spence? A steady-looking lad with a winning smile that quite appeals to the opposite sex, or so my sister informed me."

Lady Mary laughed. Mischief gleamed in her eyes, and the resemblance to the young gentleman that the earl had remarked on was unmistakable. "That is William, certainly. He is the very likeness of his father, with all his sire's charm. It was that selfsame smile that first attracted me to William and Abigail's father. Roger would have been proud to see them both now." It occurred to her that she must be boring the earl with her prosing. "I do apologize, my lord! I did not mean to drone on about my children, as wonderful as I do think them. Tell me, what do you think of Bonaparte's advances? I hear everywhere that there is not the least cause for worry, and yet I cannot but wonder. The Duke of Wellington is still in Vienna, and though I am certain that we may have every confidence in the Prince of Orange as our acting commander-in-chief, he is young and perhaps rather . . . excitable."

"You are observant, my lady. The prince's experience is slight and his natural confidence leads him to conclude that he can meet Bonaparte on that gentleman's own terms. I understand that General Sir Edward Barnes, the adjutant general, and Sir Hudson Lowe, our quartermaster, have their hands busy in keeping the prince's enthusiasm from running away with him.

But hopefully, his grace the Duke of Wellington will arrive in good time to place a firm guiding rein on his young protégé. Otherwise we may be in for something of a wild ride,'' Lord Kenmare said, only half in jest.

Lady Mary looked at him gravely. ''Then it is your considered opinion that we will soon be at war again, my lord?''

The earl hesitated for the space of a second. ''It is, my lady. As an intimate of the Duke of Brunswick, I am in a position to hear much that is not of general knowledge.''

''I am not thrilled to hear my own private fears confirmed, as you may imagine,'' Lady Mary said quietly.

Lord Kenmare nodded. ''Yes, I understand. I myself have several friends who shall be in the thick of it. It is difficult to bear the impotent knowledge that someone dear to you may soon be in deadly peril. However, I do not think that Ensign Spence would thank you if you could suddenly whisk him away when all of his friends and acquaintances were to remain for the fight.''

Lady Mary laughed at the vision that he had conjured up for her of William's appalled indignation. ''Indeed not, my lord! William would sooner have himself cut up into ribbons than miss an opportunity to prove himself on the battleground.''

''As I feel certain he shall do,'' Lord Kenmare said with a smile.

Lady Mary acknowledged the compliment, and the conversation passed easily on to other things.

The earl stayed beside her for a few minutes more until Monsieur François du Bois came up to greet her, apologizing that he had not before had a chance to speak with her. Then Lord Kenmare rose and made a graceful exit, remarking that he should circulate.

Lady Mary was sorry when he was gone. Once she had recovered from her odd lack of social aplomb, she had enjoyed the conversation between herself and the earl. He was an intelligent gentleman, one of definite opinion but not insistent that another should wholly agree with him. It had been pleasant to talk with someone who listened to and respected her views.

As her eyes followed the earl's departing figure, her gaze

chanced to fall on an elderly couple well-known to her, and she gasped, staring in stunned disbelief.

Monsieur du Bois was made curious by her expression. His heavy black brows shot up, emphasizing his rather prominent and extraordinary blue-black eyes. "My lady, what is it? You look as though you have seen a specter."

"Perhaps I have. I have just now seen my parents, whom I had thought to be in London," she said, giving a shaky laugh.

"Ah? It is a pleasant surprise, then," Monsieur du Bois said.

Only half-attending to her host, Lady Mary blinked to be certain that she was not seeing an apparition. But there was no mistake. The elderly couple rapidly bearing down upon her were her parents, Viscount and Viscountess Catlin. Monsieur du Bois, seeing that her attention was fully trained on the advancing couple, bowed himself off, shaking his head.

The viscount's eyes glittered with an equal measure of malice and amusement as he bowed to his daughter. With a shade of sarcasm he drawled, "Well met, Mary."

Unheeding of any social niceties, Lady Mary asked bluntly, "Whatever are you doing here? I thought you firmly ensconced in London."

"And so we were until we received your letter, dear Mary," Viscountess Catlin said. She smiled, completely impervious to the warring emotions in her daughter's expression. "It was so foresighted of you, my dear, to bring Abigail to the hub of the *ton*. I was quite bowled out by your cleverness. I would not have thought of it; indeed, I did not! I had fretted for weeks that Abigail's first Season would be a shambles, all because of this ludicrous politics one hears too much about, and your letter arrived with the perfect solution. So naturally we began making immediate arrangements to come to Brussels as well."

Viscount Catlin still regarded his daughter with cynical amusement, quite aware of the turmoil in her breast. "You appear astonished, Mary. Surely you must have known that your mother could not have borne to miss Abigail's first Season?"

Lady Mary glanced at her father with the faintest lift of her brows. She noted almost with detachment that he had aged. The viscount was thinner than she remembered, his face more lined, his stature frailer. But time had not dimmed the arrogance inherent in his expression or voice, nor had it granted vulnerability to the unfathomable depths of his cold mocking eyes. "If I do seem astonished, sir, it is scarcely to be wondered at, since I know well how my mother detests travel. Naturally it never crossed my mind that she would be willing to make the long journey from England."

"That is all too true, dear Mary, and indeed the journey was a sore trial to me. But there is no sacrifice too great that I would not willingly endure for my granddaughter's sake," Viscountess Catlin said.

The viscount ignored his wife's comment. He smiled, a bare showing of his teeth. "You underestimate us, Mary. We are not quite yet in our graves, no matter what your secret wishes may be on the matter."

Color rose to Lady Mary's face. She felt the familiar stirring of anger that her father had always been able to provoke in her. The coolness of her voice was a perfect match for the acid tone that he had used. "I have never wished that, my lord, as you must assuredly be aware."

"No? I confess to a twinge of disappointment, my dear. I had thought you a rare hater, but I was mistaken. The commoner rubbed off too well on you," Viscount Catlin said.

As Lady Mary drew in a sharp breath, the viscountess at last chose to become cognizant of the hostility between her husband and their daughter. "Victor, pray do not tease Mary so. Of course she is not common. What an absurd thing to say! As though any daughter of ours could be," she said. She did not understand when the viscount gave a snort of laughter, and so she turned to her daughter, seeking safety in performing the correct protocol. "We shall call upon you and dear Abigail tomorrow, Mary. But do not look for us too early, as I shall sleep in, for I mean to stay until the rooster crows in the dawn. It is all so very exciting, isn't it? Why, I have already counted a score of exquisitely eligible gentlemen that I must immediately begin to cultivate on Abigail's behalf. We shall marry her off in fine style, I promise you! Besides, I have seen so many of our old friends this evening. I do not know why we stayed so

long in dreary London when all the world has come here. Really,
I do not.''

The viscount sketched a bow to his daughter and escorted
away his still-exclaiming wife, who had espied someone else
that she wished to talk to. Lady Mary looked after them, shaken.
She could still hardly believe that her parents were actually in
Brussels. But Viscount Catlin's peculiar brand of mockery was
not easily forgotten, nor her mother's gushing eagerness to
present Abigail to the most eligible *partis* that she possibly could.

Lady Mary knew that Abigail would be delighted by her
grandparents' presence, but as for herself, she could not now
reflect upon the upcoming Season without also being keenly
aware of the difficulties that the viscountess's notions of proper
social advancement would create.

Abigail had already encountered much admiration in the few
days that they had gone about in society. Lady Mary thought
that it would take very little more to turn her daughter's head,
particularly if admiration were to be coupled with the viscountess's unshakable opinion of Abigail's absolute perfection.
Abigail had come back from her last two visits to London
behaving with a spoiled and self-centered air that Lady Mary
had particularly abhorred. Lady Mary shuddered to think how
much greater the effect of Viscountess Catlin's constant strictures on the proper position for a young lady to attain would
be against the glittering backdrop that was Brussels.

8

AS LADY MARY had expected, Abigail anticipated her
grandparents' visit the following day with unconcealed excitement. While Lady Mary calmly embroidered, her daughter kept
dashing to the window to discover whose carriage was stopping
at the curb. Abigail had her hopes dashed several times when

the callers who were ushered into the drawing room proved not to be those whom she awaited with such impatience.

Miss Steepleton observed her former pupil's migration from settee to window and back again with disapproving shakes of her head and a clucking tongue. When it became obvious that these subtle hints would not suffice to curb the girl's behavior, she said to Lady Mary with an anxious air, "I do not know where Abigail could have picked up such restless habits, for I am sure that I must have taught her to behave with more decorum."

"Of course you did, Agatha," Lady Mary said reassuringly. She glanced over at her daughter, wondering what she must think of her former governess's criticism. Abigail had often objected to Miss Steepleton's old-fashioned and stuffy strictures, stating that the retiring woman behaved little better than a cowering rabbit in company and that for her part she would not do so. But for this once Abigail appeared completely oblivious of Miss Steepleton's comments.

It was a very long morning, despite the pleasant intervals with new acquaintances who came to call. Among the visitors were their neighbors Mr. Creevey and his stepdaughters, the Misses Ord. The Misses Ord, having been established in Brussels already for several months, were quite willing to discuss upcoming entertainments and the merits of various young officers, and succeeded in diverting Abigail's attention for the duration of their visit.

Lady Mary discovered in Mr. Creevey a well-informed gentleman who was able to give her some notion what the Bonaparte situation meant, as he apparently possessed an exceptionally wide and illustrious acquaintance. Lady Mary was so much struck by the gentleman's air of certainty that nothing was yet to be feared that she was made more confident of the decision she had made to remain in Brussels for the time being.

Luncheon came and went before at last Abigail's vigil was rewarded. When the viscount and the viscountess were announced, she flew up out of her chair with her hands outstretched. "Grandmama! Grandpapa!" She hugged each of them in turn, and with a stream of cheerful chatter tripping from her tongue, made certain that they were comfortably seated and saw that they were served refreshments.

Viscountess Catlin basked in her granddaughter's attention. She said fondly, ''I am certain that I do not know how I shall go on when you are wedded, Abigail. You have always been such a comfort to me. But I shall manage, as I always have.''

Abigail laughed merrily. ''Oh, Grandmama! As though you haven't a dozen servants hanging about all the day with nothing to do but see to your least whim.''

Viscountess Catlin patted her granddaughter's smooth cheek. ''But none can compare with you, my dearest child, for the very sight of your sweet face lifts my spirits,'' she said. She was rewarded for her sentiment with a quick hug from her happy granddaughter.

Meanwhile, greetings were taking place between the viscount and the other two ladies. Miss Steepleton, who stood in the greatest awe of her mistress's parents, was always flustered in their presence. She uttered what she thought an unexceptionable nicety. ''I hope that we see you well this morning, my lord.'' She was aghast when the viscount swept cold, contemptuous eyes over her.

''My state of health is hardly a topic for public bandying, madam,'' he said bitingly. His response reduced Miss Steepleton to an ineffectual stammer.

Lady Mary had greeted her father even as she listened to the byplay between the viscountess and Abigail. But his acid tone firmly attached her attention and she resignedly came to her companion's rescue. She gave a laugh, saying with an air of easy amusement, ''The viscount's state of health can nearly always be gauged by the degree of his irascibility, Agatha. I judge that today his lordship is in fine fettle.''

Viscount Catlin gave a short bark of laughter. Miss Steepleton was uncertain whether she should also laugh; one could never tell with the viscount. She decided that her best policy would be to efface herself as unobtrusively and as quickly as possible, and she faded into the background behind Lady Mary's chair.

Viscount Catlin was barely aware of the Steepleton woman's

retreat. She was unworthy meat for his ill-humor today. He regarded his daughter's serene expression, relishing the cool expression in her gray eyes. Already she was on the way to climbing on her high ropes, he thought with satisfaction. "Very neatly done, Mary. One day you must explain to me your reasoning in keeping that useless woman hanging from your sleeve," he drawled.

Lady Mary smiled, quite aware of what he was attempting. "I am not to be drawn so easily this day, my lord. I neglected to inquire at the ball, but where are you staying during your sojourn in Brussels?"

Viscountess Catlin heard her query. She leapt in before her husband could draw breath for an acidly phrased reply. "We are at the Hotel d'Angleterre, Mary. I had wished to hire a residence for the term, but alas, none but the meanest hovels were to be had at such short notice. I am very sorry for it, for I shall be unable to get up just the sort of grand entertainments that must launch Abigail into prominence. But never mind, dearest, I shall think of something and we shall all be very gay despite such an unhappy inconvenience," she said, giving her granddaughter's hand a slight squeeze. She turned again to Lady Mary. "Mary, I think it past time to plan Abigail's come-out party. I have several marvelous notions, and though this house is not as large as one could wish for entertaining, we must make do, mustn't we? I shall simply have to trim the guest list to the absolute bare bones, and perhaps hire a quartet rather than full strings, and—"

Lady Mary saw instantly what was transpiring. "It is not at all necessary to put yourself out for Abigail's come-out, Mother. I have already set all the arrangements in motion."

"Mama! You never breathed a word to me," Abigail exclaimed, astonished and pleased.

Lady Mary was aware of her father's cynical smile and she silently cursed her quick falsehood. She managed a credible smile. "I had wished to surprise you, Abigail. I know that this first party is of great moment to you, and I wanted it to be my present to you," she said. Abigail jumped up with a squeak of excitement and ran over to embrace her, causing Lady Mary to laugh in mock protest. "Abby, my cap! Pray . . . !"

Abigail released her mother and helped to readjust Lady Mary's lace cap. "I am so very happy, Mama. And I shall not badger you for a single detail of the arrangements, I promise you. Only, may I please have a new gown? All of my evening gowns are so shabby and old and—"

"Yes, yes, of course," Lady Mary said, giving way without even a pang for the expense to be involved. It would not hurt to have Abigail occupied with a seamstress while she whipped together the arrangements for an instant ball and supper. She only hoped that she could pull off an evening to meet her daughter's undoubtedly giddy expectations.

The viscountess regarded Lady Mary with a somewhat brittle look about her mouth. "Well! It appears that you have not lost any time sitting about since your arrival, Mary. I assume that you have already had introductions to enough suitable *partis* to make up a proper guest list." She raised her thin brows in interrogation.

"Why, Mama and I have already met scores of personages, and all of them are ever so nice. We have received invitations to dinners and balls, and ever so much more, have we not, Mama?" Abigail said, completely oblivious of the undercurrents about her.

"Indeed, I believe that we shall be quite busy in the next several weeks," Lady Mary said, smiling across at her daughter's shining eyes.

Viscountess Catlin smiled also, but with a shade of petulance. The air seemed to have been somehow taken out of her sails. She had envisioned herself as generously bestowing upon her exiled daughter the necessary caveats to reenter polite society. Though she would never admit it, the news that Lady Mary and Abigail had already begun to establish themselves was not altogether welcome to her. She gave a small superior smile. "Oh, I imagine that the invitations are for very genteel amusements, to be sure. But perhaps, with my influence, you shall be presented with the more illustrious sort of invitations that one must have for a truly successful Season," she said.

Abigail was a little awed. "Do you think so, Grandmama?"

Viscount Catlin laughed. He was hugely enjoying himself. The verbal sparring between his wife and his daughter reminded him of nothing less than spitting flames in feud over a particularly nice piece of kindling. He added his own contribution of oil to the fire. "You may rest assured that your grandmother will leave no stone unturned in her ambitions for you, my dear child." He had the satisfaction of seeing a flash of irritation in Lady Mary's eyes and he deemed it the right moment to take leave of her and his granddaughter. He rose, saying, "We have a few other calls to attend to yet. Abigail, pray be good enough to call for our carriage."

Despite the flurry of her parents' departure, Lady Mary did not forget what she had promised Abigail. Immediately after the viscount and viscountess were seen off and Abigail was safely ensconced in the drawing room with the latest fashion plates, Lady Mary called Miss Steepleton to her. When that lady entered with a timid knock, she said, "Agatha, I have gotten myself in a coil and I hope that you might help me out of it. I have promised Abigail a come-out party that must take place in just a few days. I will be so appreciative if you will aid me in the arrangements."

"Of course, Lady Mary. I shall be delighted to do so. I am wholly at your disposal," Miss Steepleton said, gratified to be called upon. It was so lovely to be necessary from time to time in the rendering of her employer's comfort, she thought.

The ball and supper to mark Abigail's come-out was an unqualified success. Lady Mary had consulted with Lady Cecily and Madame du Bois for the names of young officers and of young Bruxellois misses to add to the guest list, so that the company was a varied one, with as many illustrious personages as Viscountess Catlin could wish, as well as a good number of the younger set, which Abigail was certain to enjoy.

William had naturally made an appearance, having solemnly sworn that Bonaparte himself would not have been able to keep him from the scene of his sister's triumph. He brought with him a friend from his division, the Honorable Ferdinand Huxtable-Taylor. "A good chap to have about," William said with his flashing grin. "Wherever he is, Ferdy knows just where one may buy all the best meat pies and beer one could wish."

Mr. Creevey had brought the Misses Ord and their brother,

Charles. When Lady Mary had greeted them all and seen that the young ladies and Charles were well occupied, she asked after Mrs. Creevey, whom she knew to be something of an invalid.

Mr. Creevey thanked her for her kind inquiry. "Mrs. Creevey will be most appreciative when I relay it, my lady. Mrs. Creevey is much in pain and moves with the greatest difficulty to herself, but she remains in cheerful spirits for all that," he said.

"I shall be certain to call upon her one day next week," Lady Mary promised. Mr. Creevey bowed his appreciation and moved on so that Lady Mary was free to greet Lady Georgianna Lennox and her parents, young Lord Hay, and several others who were kind enough to attend and make of Abigail's ball and supper a truly memorable affair.

Lady Mary was extremely gratified by how well the impromptu affair was turning out. It spoke much of her own organizational ability and of Miss Steepleton's indefatigable loyalty that it was so, she thought with a shade of complaisance. The supper that was yet to be served was particularly superb. She had trusted her instinct and relied entirely upon her Belgian cook. The result would be a delectable *sortie* of the country's cuisine: irreproachable mussels redolent of garlic; silken slices of Ardennes ham; eels lovingly encased in aspic; and succulent roast poulet de Bruxelles.

Lady Mary's gaze was caught by the sight of her laughing daughter, and she smiled. Abigail appeared enchanting in a pale pink round gown trimmed with a quantity of blond lace at the modest décolletage, on the small puffed sleeves, and about the hem. Her small matching satin slippers peeped from beneath, discreetly tapping each time the musicians struck up.

Lady Mary was gratified when she saw that her daughter never lacked for a partner and had already danced with a score of gentlemen, including the young Prince of Orange, whom Lady Mary had already learned could be counted upon to amuse himself despite his royal dignity and military responsibilities.

Abigail was at the moment going down a set with a young cavalry officer named Sir Lionel Corbett. The couple made quite a pretty picture, as Abigail laughed gaily up at her partner, a handsome gentleman whose carefully disordered locks glinted gold in the blaze of candlelight and neat uniformed figure owed no debt to buckram padding.

The sight brought back pleasant memories for Lady Mary. She smiled, recalling for a moment herself as a young girl, wildly excited at the prospect of her coming-out party. She had danced all night, she remembered, and had then risen early the following day so as to be sure not to miss the arrival of countless invitations that ensured her of a successful first Season.

Undoubtedly Abigail would spring awake with just exactly the same sort of anticipation, she thought with a hint of rueful amusement for her own dismay. She did not think she would be able to rise nearly as early after this evening, which promised from all the signs to be a drawn-out affair.

With a rustling of train, Viscountess Catlin bore down on Lady Mary. "My dear! Such a triumph, to be sure. I had no notion that you were so well-connected. You have obviously inherited a measure of my own talent for hostessing. Why, it is almost as fine an evening as *I* could have provided for my dearest granddaughter," she said.

Lady Mary was amused by her mother's backhanded compliment. "I am glad that you approve, Mother. I hope to see Abigail well-launched after tonight."

The viscountess was not paying attention. She had spied a tall figure who immeasurably interested her. "Lord Kenmare . . . I had not thought of him before, but certainly he has potential. Only look at how attentively he listens to Abigail's bright chatter. He is just young enough to spoil her a little and yet of a sobriety that must command her respect. And it goes without saying that he has the pocketbook to enable her to live just as well as she ought. Yes, I think that his lordship is a definite possibility!"

Lady Mary had listened to her mother's cataloging of Lord Kenmare's virtues with appalled dismay and some other emotion that she could not quite name. "Mother, pray do not embarrass me in his lordship's eyes. I consider Lady Cecily a friend, and by extention must include Lord Kenmare in that category."

"Embarrass you!" The viscountess was amazed by the very idea. "What an idiotic thing to say, Mary! I hope that I am more subtle than to catch his lordship by the ear and demand a proposal of him!'' She would have said more, but the gentleman in question was making his way to them. She wreathed her face in smiling welcome. ''My lord! How good of you to come to my granddaughter's come-out. Abigail is undoubtedly flattered by your kind attention. Certainly I am most gratified.''

Lord Kenmare bowed to the elderly lady even as he regarded her quizzingly. The viscountess was exuding the sort of friendliness that he was all too familiar with, having been the object of matchmaking dames several times before. After a glance at her daughter's carefully unreadable expression, he wondered whether it was for Lady Mary's benefit or for that of her granddaughter that Viscountess Catlin was making such an effort.

''I have escorted my sister, Lady Cecily Wilson-Jones, who particularly wished to convey her congratulations to Miss Spence upon her entry into society. It is an event that every young miss anticipates, I am told,'' he said, feeling his way. His unasked question was swiftly answered, when Viscountess Catlin made a point of directing his attention to Miss Spence's grace on the dance floor. Obediently he observed the couple going through the country dance, and said, ''Yes, Miss Spence is quite accomplished. I say, Mademoiselle du Bois is particularly graceful, isn't she? She appears to excellent advantage with that young officer. Viscount Callander, is it not?''

''That is Lord Randol, yes,'' Lady Mary said, a quiver of laughter in her voice. She had been very nearly able to read Lord Kenmare's thoughts by the way he had regarded her mother's face. Subsequently his adroit shifting of attention from Abigail to Mademoiselle du Bois greatly amused her.

Viscountess Catlin was not amused. It offended her fond sensibilities that another young lady would be thought to overshadow her own granddaughter's exquisite performance. Quite accomplished, indeed, she thought indignantly. With a sniff for the earl's impertinence, she excused herself by saying that she must greet a close acquaintance.

When the viscountess had moved away, her back held stiff in outrage, Lady Mary dared to look up at the earl's expression. He was smiling, and when he caught her glance, he winked. Lady Mary was taken completely off-guard and she gurgled on a laugh. "The very audacity, sir!" she scolded. "I am the proud mother, after all!"

Lord Kenmare swept a bow. "Forgive me, my lady. I had for a moment forgotten the fact."

Lady Mary shook her head. "Perhaps it is I who should apologize, since it is so obvious my parent has high hopes of you."

The earl smiled and his mouth quirked in the way that Lady Mary found so fascinating. His eyes were warm with humor. "My dear lady, I hope I am sophisticated enough not to take offense at a dash of matchmaking. Indeed, I am quite resigned to being the object of such plotting, for my sister is fiercely committed to pushing me to the altar in the company of some unfortunate lady."

"Is she, indeed?" Lady Mary regarded him with open curiosity. "Forgive me, my lord, but I cannot help asking whether your acknowledged resignation implies that Lady Cecily will be successful in her object."

Lord Kenmare laughed. "One must await the outcome of any such scheme to be certain of success. But certainly I have no intention of falling tamely into line."

When Lady Mary laughed at his wry declaration, he thought that he had rarely been so comfortable with a woman, and he wondered at it. He studied Lady Mary's face, her pleasant features, and the warmth of her expression. She appeared in particularly fine looks that evening, attired in a slim crepe silk gown that fell gracefully about her trim hips. Her only adornments were the pearls about her neck and in her ears and the gold cameo brooch pinned to the center of her discreet décolletage. But he thought that it was something in addition to Lady Mary's physical attributes that he found attractive. There was a complete lack of flirtation or posturing about her that was decidedly different from other ladies of his acquaintance. He decided that it was that lack of artifice which inspired one to confide in her. He found himself to be fascinated by that facet of her character, and for that reason the earl remained near Lady Mary Spence most of the evening.

She was constantly involved in her duties as hostess, of course, greeting her guests and facilitating their enjoyment. But nevertheless Lord Kenmare managed to command much of her time, particularly since he was fortunate enough to claim the honor of escorting her in to supper.

When it came time to take leave of his hostess, Lord Kenmare did so with a measure of regret. He had thoroughly enjoyed his several abbreviated conversations with Lady Mary, and his original good assessment of her had not suffered. She was a lady of intelligence and sense and did not give way in every instance to his opinion. He liked that about her, he thought as he handed Lady Cecily up into their carriage and swung in after her.

He signaled to the driver and shut the carriage door. As the carriage jerked into motion and he sat back against the squabs, he recalled with a faint smile something Lady Mary had said.

He was startled when his sister's voice came out of the shadows. "A penny for them, Robert."

Lord Kenmare turned his head to Lady Cecily, who was seated beside him. "I beg pardon, Cecily? I was not attending."

Lady Cecily laughed. "That is precisely when I meant, dear brother. You have not vouchsafed a word to me since we left the hall. In fact, you have hardly spoken to anyone all evening except Lady Mary Spence." She paused, allowing her expectant silence to speak volumes to him.

Lord Kenmare grimaced. "Pray do not think it, Cecily. I found Lady Mary to be excellent company this evening. But that is hardly the stuff from which a romance may be woven whole."

Lady Cecily smiled. Her eyes gleamed faintly in the shadows of the carriage. "Whoever said anything about romance, Robert?" When her brother swore a good-natured curse at her, she hummed a bright little tune under her breath.

9

AFTER NEARLY a fortnight of great suspense, the city of Brussels finally learned the result of Bonaparte's escape and subsequent landing in France. On March 24 word was brought by various individuals that Bonaparte had passed the preceding night at Lille and might be reasonably expected to be in Brussels in two days' time.

The news spread like wildfire through the British community and set off a panic. The whole day of the twenty-fourth, the English were flying off in all directions, while others arrived who had fled from Paris.

Mr. Creevey and the two Misses Ord came to call on Lady Mary and Abigail late that afternoon. Lady Cecily Wilson-Jones was already sitting with them and she renewed her acquaintance with Mr. Creevey and the Ords. After the quick exchange of greetings, Lady Mary said, "I know that you will forgive me when I immediately broach that topic so prominent in all our thoughts. We have heard such rumors all day, but we have not been certain what to believe. Tell us, Mr. Creevey, have you any news?"

Mr. Creevey's round face looked grave. "It is as bad as you have heard, my lady. Colonel Hamilton, who, as you know, is aide-de-camp to General Barnes and the elder Miss Ord's fiancé, visited us earlier today and confirmed that Bonaparate could indeed be in Brussels in two days' time. I have myself seen the arrival of several personages who have fled Paris, among them the old Prince de Conde and all his suit, as well as Marmont, Victor, and Berthier." At the exclamation of the ladies, he sighed heavily. "Indeed, Lady Cecily, it is very bad. I was sitting earlier today with Lady Charlotte Greville when the Duc de Berri came to call upon her. He expressed his great astonishment to me that any English should remain here, as

Bonaparate was certainly at Lille and will no doubt be here on Wednesday, and that he himself was going to Antwerp, there to catch passage to England.''

"But we shall stay," one of the Misses Ord put in.

Lady Mary glanced at her and then looked at Mr. Creevey, her brows rising. "Indeed! May I inquire why, sir?"

Mr. Creevey shook his head. "Mrs. Creevey's state of health is such that removing her would cause great pain and difficulty to herself. I have consulted some people as to the supposed conduct of the French if they should arrive, and I am encouraged by what I have heard, so that we have resolved to stay.''

"That is something, at least," Lady Cecily said.

"It is so prodigiously exciting, but frightening as well," said Abigail with a shiver. She looked at her mother, whose brows had knit in a slight frown. "Shall we stay too, Mama?"

Lady Mary's expression lightened. "I shall give it a little more thought, but I am inclined to do so. William is here. And I do think that we may rely upon Mr. Creevey's information to guide us in this," Lady Mary said with a nod and a smile at the gentleman. He bowed his acknowledgment of the compliment.

Soon afterward Mr. Creevey and the Misses Ord took their leave, saying that they had another call to make. When they were gone, Lady Cecily turned to her hostess. "Are you and Abigail really staying on in Brussels?"

"I think so, at least for the moment. I have never heard Mr. Creevey convey an intelligence that is unfounded. Perhaps I am mistaken, but I should not wish to leave the city only to learn later that we had done so prematurely. I wish to remain as long as possible so that I will know where William is ordered off to," Lady Mary said.

"Yes, I feel the same. About Reginald, I mean. Robert also shall not wish to leave just now, I know. It is bad enough that he is bound by his oath to Reginald to stand by me, when I suspect that what he would rather do is to join in the fray." Lady Cecily sighed and shook her head. "These are odd times that we live in, are they not?" She began to pull on her gloves in order to take her leave.

After Lady Cecily had left, Lady Mary and Abigail spent the remainder of the day periodically watching the incredible scene of confusion outside in the street as the English left in every type of vehicle available. It was during one of these moments that Abigail exclaimed, "Why, that is Grandmama! And Grandpapa!" She looked around at her mother, her eyes shining, as Lady Mary joined her at the window. "Look, they are just coming up the steps."

"Then come away from the window and deport yourself demurely on the settee. You know that your grandmama thinks it the height of vulgarity for young girls to be caught peeping out of upstairs windows," Lady Mary said, herself going to the wing chair close to the fireplace and taking up her embroidery.

"Pooh! Much I care for that," Abigail said, tossing her head. But she did as her mother suggested, so that when the butler announced her grandparents, she looked the very picture of respectability.

The viscountess swooped down on Abigail, her arms outstretched. "How pretty you look, dear child! I am surprised that you have not a crowd of young officers at your feet, to be sure. Oh, Mary, how are you, my dear? You are looking well as usual."

Lady Mary returned her mother's dutiful kiss of the cheek. "I am well, Mother. We have not seen you or my father for several days. I confess that I am surprised." Her glance traveled to her father, who had held back from the physical exchange of greetings, and the expression in her eyes was questioning.

Viscount Catlin gave his mocking smile. "Your mother insisted upon the visit. We have called to see how you and Abigail are weathering the rumors flying about town. As you may guess, your mother has been ready to depart for hours."

The viscountess tossed an irritated glance at her husband. "Really, Victor, as though anyone with sense would not be anxious! Naturally we must have every confidence in our army, but one must not forget that that horrid little Corsican is a veritable devil. I am certain that Mary is aware of the circumstances. As for our little Abigail, she is such a fragile, sensitive creature that she cannot help the nightmarish thoughts that must be tumbling about in her head. Now, Abigail, you are not to fret."

As Abigail regarded her grandmother in open astonishment, Lady Mary said dryly, "As you have pointed out, Mother, we can trust our army to protect us from Bonaparte. I do not anticipate a hurried flight just yet."

The viscount laughed and addressed his wife with a biting satisfaction. "There, my dear, what did I tell you? Our Mary has ice water in her veins. You will not ever discover her in a distracted swoon." He turned to his daughter. "I am unsurprised, of course. For all your faults, you still have a head on your shoulders. Not like some of these idiots haring off without the sense that God granted them."

Lady Mary inclined her head. "Thank you, my lord."

Abigail finally found her tongue. "But, Grandmama, surely you and Grandpapa are not leaving Brussels!"

"Your grandfather is as stubborn as your own mother, child. He shall not be satisfied that there is any substance to what we have heard until Bonaparte himself knocks at the door," Viscountess Catlin said with asperity. She realized when her husband laughed that she had exposed herself again to his sardonic sense of humor. "But let's not talk about nasty politics. My sweet Abigail, I have the most wonderful news. I have gained an introduction to the Comte l'Buc and he has indicated significant interest in meeting you, my dear! In fact, I am nearly positive that he can be induced to partner you at Lady Charlotte Greville's party this evening."

"But, Grandmama, I have already half-promised myself to Lord Hay for that evening," Abigail said, dismayed. She liked young Lord Hay, who was seventeen like herself and could be counted on for merry talk.

Viscountess Catlin smiled brightly. She patted her granddaughter's cheek. "Indeed, Lord Hay is a very eligible young gentleman. As an elder son he will certainly inherit his father's title; but his lordship is still in his prime, and so that day will be long in coming. The Comte l'Buc, on the other hand, has already come into his own and he has the advantage also of being some years your senior, so he can be counted upon to be a proper guide for a young wife. He will naturally be proud of his wife's social accomplishments and perhaps be more inclined to be lenient of her circle of admirers than would be a gentleman of lesser years, who might exhibit distressing signs of jealousy.''

"Mother, that will be enough," Lady Mary said.

Her tone was such that the viscountess looked up at her in surprise. There was a certain coolness in Lady Mary's wide gray eyes, the slightest rise of her winged brows, that the viscountess recognized from old, and she tightened her lips. "Really, Mary! One would think that you do not *wish* Abigail to make a brilliant match."

"I do not believe marriage to a confirmed old roué to be a *brilliant match*, my lady. Furthermore, I shall not sit quietly by while you intimate to Abigail the mistaken notion that all husbands and wives must expect dalliance from their spouses," Lady Mary said.

The viscountess regarded her daughter with a measure of superiority. "My dear Mary, how can you still be so incredibly naive at your years? Why, I had no notion that sitting about the country for all those years would blind one so completely. If the truth but be known, Sir Roger was probably little different from any other gentleman, and—"

Lady Mary smiled, but the warmth of her expression did not quite reach her eyes. At that moment she looked uncannily like her paternal parent at his most dangerous. "You shall not finish that unworthy thought in my presence, nor ever to my daughter."

Viscountess Catlin rose precipitately, two spots of angry color in her face. "Well! I have never been treated so shabbily! Victor, I think it past time that we leave." She turned away without thought to the social amenities and sailed out of the drawing room.

The viscount was slow to follow his wife's hasty exit. He bowed to Lady Mary, a small sardonic smile playing about his lips. She half-expected him to rebuke her, but he said nothing. Instead, he turned to his granddaughter and raised Abigail's hand to his lips. Her eyes reflected her distress at the scene just ended, and he laughed softly. "Pray do not appear so anxious, dear child. Your grandmother has never understood the nature of your mother's character. Indeed, it took a great many years for me to become reconciled to it. But I do understand your mother, perhaps more than she suspects, and I can assure you that what she says of your father can be believed in whole cloth.''

He left then, leaving Lady Mary and Abigail equally off-balance. It had been a strange speech and, for Lady Mary at least, had hinted at far more than the actual words. She wondered whatever he could have been getting at, but it was a puzzle that must wait. She could see from Abigail's expression that she had not come off in the encounter as well as she could have wished. She held out her hand to her daughter. ''Abigail, come sit beside me a moment.''

Abigail hesitated, then seemed to decide that she should hear her mother out. She took her place on the settee, but before Lady Mary could say anything, she blurted, ''How could you speak so coldly to Grandmama? She was greatly distressed, and so hurt! She only wants what is best for me.''

Lady Mary sighed. ''Indeed, according to your grandmother's notions, I was completely out of line. However, you must realize that the viscountess's ideals are not always what I wish, or what your father would have wished, for you. We had something very precious, Abigail, so precious that its worth cannot be measured by social prominence or wealth or any of the other enticements that you may be offered this Season.''

''I know that you and Papa loved one another. I know that you gave up everything that you were bred to—Grandmama has told me so over and over again. But I do not know why I should be like you. Why shouldn't I encourage a wealthy titled gentleman? Why shouldn't I make a brilliant match if it is what I wish to do?'' Abigail said all in a rush. She had withdrawn from her mother and now sat half-facing her on the settee as though they were antagonists. Her expression was angry, and in her blue eyes was a hint of confusion.

''If it is what *you* wish to do, Abigail. That is the very crux of the matter, is it not? Oh, Abby, don't you see? I wish you to have that choice. I don't care whether you marry at all, as long as you are happy,'' Lady Mary said. She saw at once that she had said the wrong thing.

Abigail flushed and jumped to her feet. Her small hands bunched at her sides. ''*That* is it! You do not wish me to make a splendid match. You do not wish me to marry at all! Grandmama was right. She said you were jealous of me—of my chances. She said you secretly regretted running away with Papa and creating a scandal and living in a lesser society. And now you wish me to share in your misery, so that you can prove to the world that you were right. Well, I shall not do it! Do you hear? I shall not do it!'' She whirled and ran to the door of the drawing room.

Lady Mary had sat stunned and speechless through her daughter's tirade, but Abigail's flight set her in motion. She rose, crying out, ''Abby! Come back! You are so wrong, my dear!''

But Abigail was unheeding. She flew out of the drawing room and slammed the door behind her.

Lady Mary did not pursue her daughter. Indeed, she was at a loss for what she might say. Her thoughts were in a turmoil, and dismay over the argument with her daughter was as nothing to the anger that she felt toward her mother. She had not even suspected that Viscountess Catlin was filling Abigail's head with such idiotic lies. If she had known, she would swiftly have set straight the viscountess's account. But it was rather too late for a simple explanation, she thought with a trace of bitterness.

How Abigail could ever accept such nonsense was in itself astonishing. She had never hidden her past from her children, believing that they should not ever come to feel that there had been anything wrongful in the love between her and their father. It was true that theirs had been a runaway marriage and that she had in consequence been excommunicated from her former place in society. But Lady Mary knew in her heart that she had never for a moment regretted the circumstance, and she had been certain that her children had known of her contentment.

With her reflections, Lady Mary's troubled spirits lightened a little. Abigail was at the moment somewhat spoiled and confused, but she was an intelligent girl. Surely she could not set aside all of her childhood memories of the happy family the three of them had constituted at a few contrary words from her grandmother, Lady Mary thought. She felt confident that after a period of reflection, Abigail would realize how false had been the impressions given her by the viscountess.

Thus it was that Lady Mary went upstairs to begin dressing for dinner with her serene composure once more intact. Later, however, she began to wonder at her earlier confidence. Upon joining her in the front hall to set out for the evening, Abigail had maintained a stony silence toward her which covered the entire distance to Lady Charlotte Greville's residence.

Alighting from the coach, Lady Mary was certain that she had never spent a more unpleasant ride. Ill humor had begun to settle around her shoulders, and it was with an effort that she smilingly greeted their hostess. She glanced toward Abigail and was relieved to see that her daughter's sulky expression had given way to one of anticipation. Surely matters would mend themselves in very short order, she thought. But she was rudely awakened from the last of her complaisance by Abigail's subsequent behavior.

Despite Lady Mary's earlier disapprobation, Viscountess Catlin made a point of introducing the Comte l'Buc to her granddaughter. Abigail greeted him with more warmth than was necessary, even as she tossed a defiant glance in her mother's direction. When he requested her hand in a set, she very prettily accepted and was borne off on the arm of one that Lady Mary had no difficulty in classifying as a predator.

She looked at the viscountess, a distinctly chilly expression in her eyes. "What you have done is unpardonable, my lady. I shall thank you to withdraw your poisonous influence from my daughter's vicinity," she said quietly.

Viscountess Catlin tossed her head, and for a split second Lady Mary saw the ghost of the arrogant, spoiled society beauty that her mother had once been. "What vastly pretty sentiments, upon my word! I wish only the best for my granddaughter, as you would realize if you but put off your blinders, Mary! The Comte l'Buc is a most eligible *parti* and I do not at all regret bringing Abigail to his notice."

"The Comte l'Buc is a known philanderer and it is rumored that he is not above seducing young girls. Abigail is an innocent and you have tossed her straight into the jackal's jaws! But that is only the half of your foolishness, Mother," Lady Mary said. "You have told naught but lies about Sir Roger and myself. You have seen fit to interfere in the relationship between myself and my daughter. I give you fair warning, my lady. I shall not stand idly by while you wreak havoc.''

The viscount came up in time to overhear her last words. His brows rose in exaggerated astonishment. ''What, Mary, do you object to your mother's efforts on Abigail's behalf? How odd, for I seem to recall that as a young girl you liked nothing better than her . . . interference.''

''That was a great many years ago and that naiveté belonged to a very different being,'' Lady Mary retorted. She was watching the set, and by the music she knew that it was coming to an end. ''Pray excuse me. I must snatch my daughter out of her present peril. The *comte* shall not long wish to pay court to your granddaughter, I assure you!'' She swept away, leaving behind the viscountess gasping in outrage.

10

AN AGONY of apprehension and a scuffle of preparation had swept over Europe since Napolean Bonaparte's triumphant entry into France. While the French army continued to rally regiment by regiment to Bonaparte, the dismay escalated among the English residents and holidaymakers in Brussels. Their precipitate flight on the twenty-fourth of March had been accompanied by scenes of undignified confusion and panic, and even though it subsequently became known that there was no foundation to the report of an early invasion of Belgium, and many people who had fled Brussels returned, the incident left a disquieting effect on the minds of the populace.

On April 5 the Duke of Wellington arrived from Vienna to take command of the allied forces. It was widely known that the number of French army already exeeded the allied forces, which would have to act on the defensive if Bonaparte chose to attack. Nevertheless, his grace's arrival was heralded with high relief and an upsurge of renewed optimism.

Lady Mary was as much affected by the times as anyone else, but she was far more concerned over the waywardness of her daughter. Since their falling-out ten days before, Abigail had scarcely spoken more than a dozen words to her. In addition, she had defied her mother's wishes on several occasions when Lady Mary indicated that she preferred Abigail not to attend gatherings that she suspected were not quite respectable. On those occasions Abigail merely turned to her grandmother, who invariably took Abigail's cause as her own and herself escorted Abigail to whatever functions she wished to attend.

Lady Mary recognized that she had lost control of her daughter. She knew from her own observations and the tactful hints dropped by several acquaintances that Abigail was behaving with a wildness that bordered on scandal even in a society that was bent on forgetting the black cloud rising across the frontier in France by indulging in every amusement that could be devised. She felt that her only recourse must be to remove her daughter from Brussels and return with her to England. But she feared that to make such an announcement to Abigail would only push her daughter straight into the viscountess's waiting arms. She had no doubt that if she were to try to take Abigail back to England before the Season was done, Viscountess Catlin would encourage Abigail to move into the Hotel d'Angleterre with herself and the viscount.

Lady Mary felt that her hands were completely tied, and that angered her to such an extent that she was scarcely able to remain civil to her mother. Her temper was not aided by the viscount's caustic observation that he had never seen Abigail in such high spirits, nor by the viscountess's smug expression whenever they chanced to meet.

Lady Mary dreaded that the viscountess's blind encouragement of Abigail's excesses was bound to lead to heartbreak for her daughter, but she could not think of any way to persuade Abigail of it. Whenever she tried to talk to her daughter, the girl refused to listen and accused her anew of petty jealousy and mean-spiritedness. Lady Mary's temper frayed on more than one occasion and she was unable to retain her mild manner. Her unfortunate tendency to cold hauteur overwhelmed her better judgment, with the result that the wedge between herself and her daughter was driven more firmly than ever into place.

William Spence was as alarmed as his mother by Abigail's behavior. He finally spoke up in the course of one of the balls given nightly by Lady Charlotte Greville when he could no longer stand to watch Abigail flirt outrageously with several officers. "Mama, can you not do something? Abby is beginning to be talked about by the fellows, and I do not care for it in the least."

"I have tried, William. But she will not listen to me. Your grandmother has firmly convinced her that I am jealous of her success and therefore determined to bring the Season to naught by dashing any hopes of a good match," Lady Mary said, somewhat bitterly.

"What rot!" William exclaimed, astonished.

Lady Mary attempted a poor imitation of a laugh. "I cannot find it in my heart to altogether blame her. I *do* wish she would stay home from some of the functions, so I suppose one may say that I am in opposition to her. As for her conduct, I *have* told her that at times she has behaved in less than a ladylike fashion. But she does not hear the same criticism from anyone else, not from her score of admirers and certainly not from her grandparents. So what is she to think but that I am mean and disapproving?"

"She'll think somewhat differently when I am done with her," William said grimly. He marched off, bearing down on his sister with determination. Within a very few seconds he had managed to extricate her from the other officers surrounding her by claiming a brother's prerogative to waltz with her.

Abigail was very happy to see her brother. She glanced up at him from under her lashes and said with a note of coquettishness that was new to her nature, "My, you *are* a handsome devil, William! I suspect that there are a dozen young misses heaving regretful sighs that you have chosen to dance with your sister rather than one of them. I pity the poor creatures, I truly do."

"Stop it, Abigail," William said forcefully. "You are making a complete cake of yourself, I shall have you know."

She looked up at him in astonishment, her smiling mask slipping. "Whatever are you talking about, William?"

"I am talking about what a spectacle you have been making of yourself these past several days. Oh, don't look at me in such a hurt and innocent fashion. You know quite well what I am referring to."

Abigail's eyes flashed as she leapt to a hasty conclusion. "Mama has been talking to you, hasn't she? How infamous of her to appeal to you! Well, I shan't listen to anything she may have to say, William, and so you may inform her. She has been mean and—"

"Mama has not uttered one word of complaint to me," William said furiously. "You little fool! I have heard your name bandied about like that of some bawd's by those in my own company. Those same merry fellows that admired you are all fast changing their good opinion of you. And I shall tell you to your face that I do not like to hear my sister's charms compared with those of some fair Cyprian! The next thing I know, I shall have to fight a duel with some rude fellow and likely find myself killed before I ever get onto the battlefield!"

Abigail's face had drained of color, leaving the blue of her wide and fearful eyes the only color in her face. "William? Have I truly lost my reputation?"

William's fury was blunted by her incredulous dismay. "You have been playing hard and fast with more than you know, in the eyes of those officers here tonight, Abby," he said frankly.

"Oh, William!" Distressed tears sprang to her cornflower-blue eyes, making them glisten like precious sapphires. "Whatever am I to do? Grandmama has always told me that one's reputation is one's most prized possession. How can I remain, the butt of everyone's jokes?" She glanced about the ballroom, no longer certain of her unquestioned popularity, and where before she had seen only admiration, now she fancied she saw contempt.

"Silly goose, you needn't make it so dramatic. You haven't quite crossed beyond the pale. But I beg you to pay less heed to Grandmama's advice! She is a dear old lady, of course, but she is completely blind to anything but her unshakable conviction that you can do no wrong. Her lack of good sense is likely to ruin you," William said.

Abigail regarded him with openmouthed astonishment.

"Why, that is just what Mama has said to me." She had always held her brother in hero worship, and that he should convey the same criticism that her mother had struck her most strongly.

"I think it is time that you begin to lend our mother an attentive ear, Abby. She has always been a wise and fair person. Why, only recall that she allowed Grandpapa to buy me a pair of colors even though she was eaten with fear that I would get myself killed first time out."

Abigail thought about it for a few moments. She had been unhappy with the estrangement between herself and her mother, but until this moment she had not been honest enough with herself to allow that she was the party at greatest fault. She said in a low voice, "I . . . I have been less than fair toward her, haven't I, William?"

William grinned down at her bowed head. "Well, yes, I rather think you have. Why do you not tell her so now?"

Abigail cast a wild look up into his pleasant-featured face. "William, I cannot! William, pray . . . !" But her protestations were in vain, for her brother in the course of the dance whirled her over to where their mother sat.

William ended with a flourish. With his arm locked firmly about his sister's waist so that she could not slip free, he drew her with him toward their mother. "Mama, here is Abby. She has decided to sit with you a few moments so that she can explain her conduct these past days," he said.

"How dare you!" Abigail exclaimed, furious and embarrassed. But William only laughed and bowed himself off, whistling a merry tune. She had no alternative but to accept the chair that her mother graciously indicated to her.

Lady Mary could see the turmoil of emotion within her daughter. Abigail's stormy eyes and high color, the trembling of her lips, all attested to it. She said tentatively, "I am sorry for any misunderstanding on my part, Abby. I hope that despite our differences we may become friends again."

"Oh, Mama!" Abigail looked at her mother with appeal and confusion in her gaze. "I have been such a beast to you, I know that I have. And William says that I have gotten myself talked about.'' She swallowed, almost made ill by the appalling thought. ''Mama, what am I to do?''

Lady Mary somberly regarded her. ''My dear child, I shall trust you to discover that for yourself. I know that your instincts are good. My only advice to you is not to put yourself forward at every juncture.''

A young Highlander came up then, somewhat diffidently, and bowed to the ladies. ''Forgive my boldness in approaching without an introduction, my lady,'' he said gravely in a broad accent, addressing Lady Mary in respectful tones. ''I have wished to meet your bonny daughter all the evening, but each time I have gotten up the courage, she is so surrounded by admirers that I have not been able to bring myself to her attention.''

Lady Mary laughed, charmed alike by his frank manners and his laughing eyes. ''I shall forgive you, sir, the moment that I learn your name.''

He flushed slightly. ''I am Captain Bruce McInnes, at your service.''

''Why have we not seen you about before this evening, sir?'' Lady Mary asked curiously. She had thought she knew very nearly all of Abigail's admirers, but she did not recall this particular officer's face.

''I am just recovered from a bout of the influenza, my lady,'' Captain McInnes said apologetically.

Lady Mary held out her hand. ''I am most happy to make your acquaintance, Captain McInnes. I am Lady Mary Spence and this is my daughter, Miss Abigail Spence.''

Captain McInnes turned at last to Abigail. ''May I solicit your hand for this dance, Miss Spence?''

Abigail glanced at her mother. Their just-finished conversation had been an uncomfortable one and had ended on something of an unsatisfactory note. She had expected her mother to read her a stricture for her behavior, but instead Lady Mary had told her to be guided by her own best sense. Abigail was confused, but yet relieved. She did not yet know what her mother meant, but she was glad to be offered an opportunity to escape further reflection on the matter.

Lady Mary misinterpreted her daughter's questioning expression. "If you have not another partner on your card, my dear, I do not know of any reason that you cannot stand up with Captain McInnes."

On the point of refusing, it suddenly occurred to Abigail that Captain McInnes, having been out of circulation with the influenza, was most probably the only gentleman of her acquaintance who had not seen her make a fool of herself for the last several days. So she smiled up at him. "Thank you, Mama. There is no one else that I would prefer as my partner," Abigail said demurely. She rose from her chair and gave her hand to the Highlander. He smiled at his amazing good fortune and drew her onto the floor into a forming set.

Lady Mary moved off to join Lady Cecily, who was sitting on a settee a little removed from the milling crowd. "Good evening, Lady Cecily. I hope that I see you well," she said as she seated herself beside her friend.

Lady Cecily was fanning her flushed face. "Yes, very well—if you discount how miserably hot and unwieldy I feel. I shall be so happy to begin my confinement, simply to have it done with!"

Lady Mary laughed. Her gray eyes twinkled with amused sympathy. "I seem to recall that same devout wish. I believe it is always such toward the end."

"Is it truly?" Lady Cecily asked in hope. "How very kind of you to reassure me that there *is* an end."

Lady Mary laughed again, and that was how the Earl of Kenmare saw her when he came up to the ladies. He had a lemonade in one hand, which he proffered to his sister, and Lady Cecily seized on the glass gratefully. After greeting his sister's companion, Lord Kenmare raised an inquiring brow. "Would you care for refreshment as well, my lady?"

"Not at the moment, thank you, my lord," Lady Mary said.

The three talked companionably for a few moments. Then Major Wilson-Jones, who had managed to arrange leave from his duties in order to escort his wife for the evening, came up. He was of average height and wiry, with keen flashing eyes, and was of a humorous nature that Lady Mary had instantly liked upon their first meeting a few weeks before. He hailed his wife and brother-in-law jauntily and bowed to Lady Mary.

"I hope that you shall not mind it, my lady, but I've come to borrow my wife for a few moments. I have but just this moment discovered the doors into the garden, and—"

"Oh, Reginald! Have you actually?" Lady Cecily exclaimed.

Major Wilson-Jones laughed. He offered his arm to her. "Indeed, I have, Cecy. Pray, will you join me?"

"Shall I, indeed!" Lady Cecily got up from the settee with alacrity. She gave her mischievous smile to Lady Mary. "I do apologize for running away in such a hurried fashion, Lady Mary, but the prospect of being out of this press for a few moments is too enticing to be denied."

Lady Mary smiled. "I am not in the least affronted." She watched the major solicitously escort his wife through the crowd. "Major Wilson-Jones is a thoroughly agreeable gentleman," she said to the earl.

"I could not wish for a better man for my sister," Lord Kenmare agreed. He nodded at the dancers whirling over the floor. "I particularly noticed that Miss Spence appears in exceptionally fine looks this evening. It is no wonder that she is popular with the young officers."

"Yes," Lady Mary said. She watched her daughter for a moment and then glanced up at the gentleman standing beside her. He was still regarding Abigail's gay progress over the floor, with the faintest of smiles on his lips. Not for the first time it crossed Lady Mary's mind that Lord Kenmare displayed an unusual interest in her daughter's social success. Whenever they met, he never failed to convey a compliment to her regarding Abigail. Perhaps the viscountess had not been so far off the mark in considering his lordship as a potential match for Abigail, and certainly to attach him would be a triumph for any young girl.

Lord Kenmare had a great deal to offer besides his wealth and his title. He was in his prime, virile and handsome, and he was a man of intelligence. He was also unfailingly courteous toward herself and to those for whom she cared. William had commented not two days previously that he had run into Lord Kenmare in the park and had been both gratified and astonished at his lordship's friendly manner. Even though Lord Kenmare was at least twenty years Abigail's senior, Abigail could do far worse, reflected Lady Mary. She wondered why the thought did not bring her greater pleasure. She must be the most unnatural mother alive, she thought with an uncharacteristic flash of irritation at herself.

"What do you say to it, my lady?"

Lady Mary abruptly realized that Lord Kenmare had been speaking to her for some seconds and she had not a clue to what he had said. The color stole into her face as she confessed, "Pray forgive me, my lord! I fear that I was not perfectly attending. What was it you were saying?"

Lord Kenmare stared at her, feeling more astonished than insulted. It was a novel experience for him to discover that his presence was so taken for granted that the lady to whom he had been speaking had not heard a word he had said, especially when he had just put forth a suggestion for an outing in his company. Perhaps to ask Lady Mary to go driving with him was not as brilliant a notion as he had originally thought.

Looking up at him, Lady Mary had the most lowering prescience that Lord Kenmare had asked for her permission to pay particular attentions to her daughter. The thought unaccountably filled her with warring emotions of triumph and dismay. The viscountess would have had no difficulty in forming a reply to the earl, but Lady Mary discovered that she was not yet ready to see her daughter seriously courted for her hand. And surely that was what his lordship intended, she thought.

Lord Kenmare found his voice. He was not an uncourageous man, but it did seem rather unfair that he must fly in the face of the lady's apparent disinterest to repeat his invitation. However, he was not one to quail prematurely at an obstacle, and so he decided to plow on. "I merely inquired whether—"

At that instant a mutual acquaintance interrupted their *tête-à-tête*, perhaps fortunately from both Lady Mary's and the earl's standpoint. The moment was lost. Lord Kenmare did not open the issue again. He was beginning to wonder whether his budding interest in Lady Mary might not be entirely misplaced.

He had initially been drawn to her because she seemed less self-absorbed than so many of the ladies of his acquaintance. He had realized early on that Lady Mary was proud of her offspring and he had set himself to make himself agreeable to her by entering into her natural interest in their well-being. He had taken pains to be affable to Ensign Spence whenever he had chanced to meet the boy, when otherwise he might have passed him by with only a polite nod for a slight acquaintance. He had endeavored to convey gentle encouragement to Abigail and had even once or twice brought her to the notice of those who might be expected to take up with a young miss just out. He had thought these unusual efforts must be looked upon with gratitude by Lady Mary and engender in her a wish to further their own friendly relationship, and so was explained his abortive invitation to her, but apparently this was not the case.

As Lord Kenmare watched Lady Mary borne off on the arm of their mutual acquaintance in search of the refreshment table, his mouth turned upward in a faintly quizzical smile. This evening's setback had but firmed his determination. He was attracted to Lady Mary Spence, and by the Lord Harry, he was going to do all in his power to break through that clear wall that she moved so gracefully behind.

11

THE Duke of Wellington held balls continually at his house, which, like the Earl of Kenmare's residence and that of Sir Charles Stuart, the British ambassador, faced on the park. The duke was a jovial host and he enjoyed nothing better than to watch his staff, who were all scions of prominent houses and very accomplished in the social graces and the dance, twirl about with the ladies to the strains of the waltz. His grace was to be seen standing about speaking animatedly, his tall immaculate figure negligent in stance, and occasionally he would break out in his hearty horse's laugh. He seemed not to have a care in the world except to see to the enjoyment of his guests.

It was a wonderment to Brussels society, which watched the allied armies' commander-in-chief with unblinking attention.

The Duke of Wellington displayed not the least perturbation over the continued reports of Napoleon Bonaparte's growing army and its determined advance on the Low Countries, nor the fact that the troops at his disposal were rumored to be outnumbered two to one. His grace's demeanor was such that many who had before expressed alarm were now come to the conclusion that their anxieties were completely unwarranted.

The populace of Brussels was all too eager to forget the ominous signs of war and plunged into a renewed frenzy of gaiety. His grace the Duke of Wellington stood tall among them, and all was well.

The duke was known to have been estranged from his wife for several years, she not once having left England to join him during all the years and all the campaigns. It was not thought surprising, then, that his grace appreciated feminine beauty. When Lady Mary Spence was introduced to him, he swept an approving glance over her, from the incongruous lace cap on her chestnut hair to her neat figure. With a gallantry unsurpassed, he raised her hand to his lips and complimented her. She passed on down the receiving line, flattered but a little embarrassed.

Later in the evening, the Duke of Wellington approached her to stand up with him on the dance floor. When she demurred, pointing out that she sat on the matrons' side of the room, he brushed aside the excuse. "Pooh, madam! What has that to say to anything? You are alive until they put you in the ground," he said with his characteristic forthrightness.

Lady Mary gave a startled laugh. Feeling that she had been left with little choice, and in truth she was very flattered that the hero of the moment desired to dance with her when there were any score of ladies who eagerly awaited the honor, she allowed herself to be drawn from her chair and escorted onto the floor. "I am naturally most happy to accept, your grace," she said. "However, I must warn you that I have not had much practice for years. You may have cause for regret."

The duke's famous horse laugh made others turn in curiosity, among them Lord Kenmare. His brows shot up when he saw who it was that the duke had as his partner. His sleeve was caught in a sharp nip.

"Robert! Do you see?"

He did not turn his head in the direction of his sister's sibilant and astonished whisper. "Indeed, Cecy, I am quite riveted by the sight," he said, starting to grin. "Pray excuse me, dear sister. I have an objective to place in motion." Without paying heed to Lady Cecily's demand of an explanation, he started to make his leisurely way toward Lady Mary's empty chair.

At the end of the set, when the Duke of Wellington escorted Lady Mary back to her place, they found the Earl of Kenmare awaiting them. Lady Mary thanked his grace for his courtesy, expecting that to be the end of his interest in her. But apparently he knew the earl, for he greeted him in a pleased fashion. "Ah, Robert! It is good to see you. I hear good things of you from the Duke of Brunswick. Pity you were not one of my staff."

Lord Kenmare bowed. "That same thought has often occurred to me, your grace," he said dryly.

The duke brayed an appreciative laugh at the compliment. He gestured toward the lady seated beside them. "You are acquainted with Lady Mary, of course?"

Lord Kenmare bowed to Lady Mary and smiled at her. "Indeed, your grace, we are quite old friends by now."

Lady Mary laughed and shook her head. She gave her hand to him in greeting. "Good evening, my lord. Yes, we are indeed old friends."

"Then you already know what a wonderfully light dancer Lady Mary is," Wellington said, raising her hand once more to his lips. "I found no cause for regret in your performance, my lady."

Lady Mary's eyes flew to Lord Kenmare's face. She colored slightly as he regarded her with laughter in his eyes. "I have not had the honor, your grace," he said levelly.

The Duke of Wellington regarded him in astonishment. "Not had the honor? Why ever not, my boy?"

"I . . . I have not danced with Lord Kenmare, nor, indeed, with anyone but yourself, your grace," Lady Mary said, feeling incredibly foolish before the great man's surprise.

The duke turned his keen blue eyes upon her. "My dear ma'am, it is positively criminal to keep such grace as yours bound to a matron's chair," he said bluntly.

Lady Mary flushed, thoroughly out of countenance. The duke's voice was naturally loud, and others were beginning to take notice of the conversation. She felt ready to sink through the floor, when Lord Kenmare came to her rescue. "Your grace, if you will permit, I shall on the instant correct the situation and request Lady Mary's hand in this next waltz."

"Well done, my lord!" Wellington exclaimed. He turned to Lady Mary for a last word. "I leave you in capable hands, my lady." Then he was gone to speak to another guest.

Lord Kenmare held out his hand to Lady Mary, who was obviously struggling with several emotions at once. "In for a penny, in for a pound," he suggested.

She could not help laughing. She laid her hand in his and rose from her seat. "I suppose my days of sitting by in quiet respectability are gone, are they not, my lord?"

"Quite irrevocably," Lord Kenmare agreed. He led her onto the floor and took her into his arms just as the waltz struck up. "Once having seen you take the floor, my lady, all Brussels shall come clamoring for the same honor."

Lady Mary laughed somewhat breathlessly. She had not been held in such intimate fashion for a very long time. She was acutely aware of his light clasp on her right hand, the way that his arm encircled her, and the warmth of his hand against her back. The harmony of their steps and turns gave her a curious sensation of floating.

Lord Kenmare glanced down at the lady in his arms. He was smiling. "I hope that you do not think badly of me, Lady Mary."

She met his gaze with surprise in her eyes. "Whatever do you mean, my lord? Why should I?"

"I made a point of being beside your chair when his grace brought you off the floor," Lord Kenmare said.

"Are you saying that you knew that the duke would insist upon my dancing with you?" Lady Mary said.

"Let us say that I rather hoped he would," Lord Kenmare amended.

"How very enterprising of you," Lady Mary said.

She was then silent for such a long moment that he began to fear that he had indeed angered her. "My lady? Forgive me, it was not my intention to offend you,'' he said anxiously.

She looked up and her gray eyes were exceedingly cool. "Offended, my lord? On the contrary, I am greatly flattered. However, I am having difficulty in understanding your motive.''

The earl saw that she had completely misunderstood. "I have no ulterior motive, my lady, except that I have wished for a great while to have the pleasure of squiring you about the floor,'' he said quietly.

Lady Mary considered him. There was no shifting in his steady blue gaze, nor had there been an evasive note in his voice. Yet she could not but wonder what connection dancing with her had with paying court to her daughter, unless his lordship wished to turn her up sweet on behalf of his future bid for Abigail's hand. If that were the case, he had gone to great lengths for nothing, because she already thought favorably of him as a gentleman.

An insidious part of her mind wanted to know whether she could really accept him as her son-in-law when she was herself so attracted to him, but she ignored the question. She really could not in all conscience stand in the way of Abigail's future happiness, even if it might include this particular gentleman. Therefore she smiled as warmly as she was capable of and said, "Then I am flattered indeed, my lord.''

Lord Kenmare was relieved. For a moment he had wondered whether he had permanently offended her by his successful tactics in getting her out of the matrons' starchy circle and into the limelight, where she undoubtedly belonged. He knew that he and Lady Mary made a graceful couple and that the fact had not gone unnoticed. The corner of his mouth quirked in its characteristic way. He guided his partner into a particularly exuberant turn so that the skirt of her satin gown billowed. Lady Mary did not yet quite realize the change in her social status, he thought, and he had every intention of making certain that the change was permanent.

The sight of Lady Mary being twirled about the floor, first in the Duke of Wellington's arms and then those of the Earl of Kenmare, had created a stir of the first order. It had become accepted for weeks past that Lady Mary did not dance. She had steadfastly refused all solicitations for her hand, seemingly preferring instead to sit on the sidelines with the other matrons and dowagers and letting her daughter shine.

Several gentlemen had considered her sense of duty to be a pity, as she was an attractive woman and said to be quite wealthy in her own right. It was common knowledge that Miss Spence would go to her marriage with a very healthy endowment, and that, along with her vivacious charm, had long since set the caveat to Abigail's success. Abigail had attracted gentlemen close to her own age, but also those who might otherwise have seemed fatherlike to her if it were not for their effusive admiration.

It was to these older gentlemen that this development concerning Lady Mary Spence was of decided interest. A pretty and well-endowed girl was certainly to be considered when one's pockets were to let; but a wealthy widow, for whom that same endowment sprang, was thrice more intriguing. Even the Comte l'Buc, who had been given such short shrift at Lady Mary's hands not long since, stroked his mustache with a thoughtful fingertip as he contemplated the waltzing widow. He could allow himself to forget his smarting pride over that incident; indeed, what was it but an example of a mother's natural attempt to shield her inexperienced daughter from the jaded gentlemen of the world? *Non,* he could quite forgive Lady Mary that, he thought, promptly allowing himself to forget Miss Abigail Spence's existence as he watched the graceful progress of the girl's mother. He would call upon Lady Mary in the not-too-distant future, he decided.

Lady Cecily was delighted by the sight of her brother and Lady Mary waltzing. "I do believe he has been bitten at last, Reginald," she said.

Major Wilson-Jones knew to what she was referring. His eyes, too, followed the elegant couple. "I wouldn't be so certain, Cecy. His lordship is wholly up to the mark. Why, he would be a dunce if he were not, after all the stunts you have pulled with him these last few years."

Lady Cecily tossed her head and laughed, quite incapable of taking offense. "But do you not see, Reginald? It was not at all my doing that Robert has pursued Lady Mary. Indeed, I had no notion of his intention of persuading her to dance until they were already on the floor.''

Major Wilson-Jones glanced down at his wife, much struck. ''I say, that is rather significant.''

''Quite significant,'' Lady Cecily said, nodding. She tapped his arm. ''And don't you go teasing Robert about it or you shall have me to answer to,'' she warned.

Major Wilson-Jones covered her fingers where they lay on his arm. ''Do not fret, my dear. I have a keen sense of self-preservation. One thing I have learned is not to interfere in another man's romances.'' He slanted a glance down at her.

Lady Cecily opened wide her brown eyes in her most guileless expression. ''Oh, certainly, I quite agree with you in a general way. One should never tamper in the lives of one's acquaintances.''

Her husband laughed and shook his head, knowing full well that the earl was considered fair game by his own loving sister.

12

THE BALL at the Duke of Wellington's marked the beginning of Lady Mary's ascendancy in the social realm. She found that Lord Kenmare had been correct. It became something of a coup for a gentleman to be able to claim that he had danced with the retiring Lady Mary Spence, and so she was courted almost as assiduously as her daughter. She was not allowed to remain quietly on the sidelines in the matrons' circle.

Abigail was delighted. ''I think it marvelous, Mama! You have not enjoyed such admiration in years, and now . . . why, you may have your pick of the gentlemen.'' She giggled suddenly and her eyes held a teasing light. ''Perhaps we shall have a double wedding in June. *That* would be amusing, would it not?''

''What a strange notion of fun you have, Abigail. I promise

you, if there is to be a June wedding, you shall have the limelight completely to yourself,'' Lady Mary said, calmly
embroidering.

"For myself, I am quite content that Mama does not remarry
just yet,'' said William, who had come to call upon them that
afternoon. He was standing with his shoulder against the mantel,
his boot resting on the grate.

Lady Mary dropped her hoop into her lap. "Pray, do I have
any say in this matter?'' she asked. Neither of her progeny
appeared to have heard her laughing protest.

"William! How can you be so mean? Mama should not carry
the willow over Papa for the remainder of her life. Oh, she loved
him to distraction and beyond, of course, but only think how
lonely she will be when I have married,'' Abigail said.

"I should think she would enjoy a little peace,'' William said,
grinning at his sister. She threw a sofa pillow at him, which
he easily ducked. It struck a fine porcelain figure on the mantel
and he hastily grabbed it to safety. Cradling the valuable piece
in his hands, he said, "I don't mean to say that Mama should
never wed again. But I have yet to take a liking to any of these
new admirers of hers.''

"I do see what you mean,'' Abigail said, much struck.
"Grandmama will have it that Mama should have the wealthiest
of them, but I really cannot imagine our pretty Mama married
to that decrepit old man that Grandmama introduced to her last
night at the dinner soiree. Why, he doesn't even own his own
teeth, and he hawks in the most disgusting manner just when
one is trying to enjoy one's supper. Of course, I instantly told
Grandmama that she was quite off the mark.''

"Thank you, Abigail. I am glad that you are looking out for
my interests,'' Lady Mary said, once more plying her needle.

"I don't know that it is so much to your interest, but more
mine. I simply could not bear to face that gentleman across the
table until I marry,'' Abigail said with devastating frankness.
Lady Mary and William laughed at her. She looked at them,
wondering at their boisterous amusement. "Well, I couldn't,''
she said candidly.

The door to the drawing room opened and the butler entered
to give Lady Mary a card sent up by a visitor. She looked at

it and exclaimed, "Why, I do not believe it! Whatever does he mean by coming here!" There was a rise of color in her cheeks that had nothing to do with pleasure.

William and Abigail exchanged a swift startled glance. "Whoever is it, Mama?" Abigail asked.

Lady Mary glanced briefly at her daughter. She tapped the card into her palm. "The Comte l'Buc," she said shortly.

Abigail squeaked, her eyes growing wide. "I promise you, Mama, after you related to me what you knew about that man, I never encouraged him again by even a glance! Grandmama was vastly disappointed when I informed her, of course, and I did so hate to disappoint her, so I agreed to go in to dinner with her next choice. Why is it that so many of the most eligible gentlemen are so *old*?"

William had straightened from his negligent pose. He had not paid the least attention to his sister's spate of words. "Shall I deal with the impertinent fellow for you, Mama?" There was a martial light in his eyes and his expression was one of anticipation.

"That will not be necessary, William," Lady Mary said quietly. She nodded to the waiting butler, who bowed and exited, shortly to return with the unwelcome visitor.

The Comte l'Buc entered. He was a gentleman of average height, beginning to lean to corpulence, and affected completely black attire. It was his fond opinion that his favorite color enhanced his black eyes and the luxuriousness of his sweeping mustache. He paused, striking a pose as he raised his glass to his eye. He surveyed the ladies appreciatively, but he regarded the young officer with less approbation. The fellows in their smart uniforms were to be found everywhere and had proved to be harsh competition, indeed, to a middle-aged libertine such as himself.

The *comte* dropped his glass and approached the lady of the house. He held out his gloved hands in effusive greeting. "Ah, Lady Mary. What fine looks you appear in this afternoon. The little cap attaches a certain cachet, certainly."

William made a whooping noise and turned aside his head as though fascinated by the flames in the hearth.

The Comte l'Buc frowned, displeased by the younger man's

rude manners. But almost instantly his expression smoothed.
He had come to make himself agreeable to Lady Mary, so he
turned his shoulder on the officer and thereafter ignored him.
"My dear lady, how gracious you are to receive me," he said,
attempting to capture both her hands.

Lady Mary evaded him, giving him the satisfaction of pressing
only one of her hands. "Comte l'Buc, I must confess to some
puzzlement at your visit. Our last meeting was not precisely
cordial."

The *comte* displayed large white teeth, which appeared in fine
contrast to his black mustache. With an airy gesture he dismissed
such a trifle. He seated himself, preferring to overlook the fact
that he had not been offered a chair upon his arrival. "It was
an unfortunate misunderstanding, certainly, but nothing that
should stand in the way of friendship. I disregard the matter
entirely," he said, making plain that her lapse from good
manners had been quite forgiven.

Lady Mary regarded the gentleman with slightly raised brows.
Her gray eyes held a curiously cool expression, one that the
comte found somewhat disconcerting after his magnanimous-
ness. "Indeed, sir? It is my profound hope that you do not
disregard my wishes."

The Comte l'Buc stared at her ladyship, appalled. He had
managed to anger her, which was the furthest thing from his
intention. He brushed his fingertip across his mustache. Perhaps
his approach needed a slight modification. He insinuated a note
of sincerity into his oily voice. "Lady Mary, I would not
willingly disregard any wish of yours. As regards this dear child,
I assure you that I harbor naught but the most paternal feelings,"
he said with the slightest of bows in Abigail's direction. She
was staring at him with an openmouthed wonder that he found
faintly irritating. He returned the gaze to his somewhat
unfriendly hostess. "Once more misunderstanding has come
between us, my lady. I shall endeavor in future to make of
myself an open book to your eyes." He smiled slowly, putting
all of his charm into it.

There was a short silence. Lady Mary's expression was one
of startled bemusement. The *comte* was not displeased by her
reaction. His ego was such that he accepted Lady Mary's

speechlessness as natural to a lady who has finally been awakened to her desirability by one of his discriminating taste. He was a past master of timing, and so he immediately rose to take his leave, bowing extravagantly to both Lady Mary and Abigail and vouchsafing to the young officer the scarcest of nods.

The drawing-room door closed behind him. William fell into a chair, whooping with laughter. Abigail was shaking her head in astonishment. She said in an affronted tone, "I would not have believed if it I had not been present. Paternal feelings indeed, when it was not above a week ago that he was pressing me to go into the gardens with him! Mama, that man has thrown me over for you!"

William found his voice, his eyes still streaming. "Mama, you should have seen your face when he looked at you just *so*. I was never more entertained in my life!"

"I am glad that I am such a figure of fun for you, William."

William was instantly contrite. "Oh, no, Mama. *You* are not, I assure you. But that pompous little man—believing that he has only to level his sights for you to swoon at his condescension—why, it is truly laughable!"

"I agree, and I cannot imagine what odd notion the gentleman has taken into his head," Lady Mary said. "It is not as though I have ever bestowed more than a civil nod upon him when we have chanced to meet."

"There you are, Mama. You have encouraged the *comte* shamefully," William said, guffawing again.

"William! How can you be so mean?" Abigail asked unsteadily. She was biting her lip against her own laughter, but at her mother's reproachful glance at both her and her brother, she burst into giggles.

"My, but it is a merry party indeed."

The Spences turned quickly, surprised by the voice. The viscount and viscountess stood in the doorway. Viscountess Catlin swept forward to kiss Abigail and William. "You are looking so well, my darlings. William, I demand that you come to call on me. I have told everyone at the hotel what a fine young grandson I have, and never once has anyone seen for himself," she said.

William smiled at his grandmother. He was fond of her in a way, but nothing so strong as his sister's all-encompassing affection for the silly old woman, as he privately thought of her. "Perhaps I shall sometime," he said. His eyes lighted up at sight of his grandfather, however. He held out his hand to the viscount. "Sir! It is a pleasure to see you here."

Viscount Catlin took hold of his grandson's hand and returned the boy's smile. His cold eyes had lost a measure of their usual frost. "William. You do well by that uniform."

Viscountess Catlin had at last come around to noticing her daughter. "Oh, Mary. That is quite a fetching cap. You must give me the name of your milliner, to be sure."

Lady Mary smiled slightly. She was beginning to wonder whether Abigail had not been right in insisting that her caps were not quite the syle for her. First the Comte l'Buc and now her mother! She held out her hand to the viscountess. "Good afternoon, my lady. We shall be taking tea in a few minutes. Will you and my father not join us?"

The viscount heard her and turned around. "No, we shall not. We but stopped for a moment."

"We are on our way to tea with Lady Charlotte Greville, actually. I only wished to see my dear Abigail, and I am very happy that William chances to be here as well. Abigail, I have brought a little trifle for you that I found whilst shopping today." Viscountess Catlin pulled open her reticule and gave a small beribboned box into her granddaughter's hand.

"Oh, Grandmama, you should not have," Abigail said, throwing a quick glance at her mother's face, half-fearful that the viscountess's favoritism would anger her mother. But Lady Mary's expression was only one of mild interest, and, reassured, Abigail opened the jeweler's box. Her eyes rounded and she gasped. "Oh, oh, oh!"

William bent forward. His brows shot up, and when he glanced at his grandmother, there was a curiously censuring light in his eyes. "Diamond studs, Grandmama? My sister is a bit young to wear something so extravagant, I think."

Viscountess Catlin laughed a little and waved aside her grandson's quiet objection. "You are as conservative as your mother, dear William." She did not sound as though she were conveying a compliment. "Try them on, Abigail, so that I might see how well they look on you."

Abigail gently closed the box. She might chafe still at her mother's opinion, but she listened very closely to all that her brother ever said. "Thank you, Grandmama. They are truly beautiful, and so special that I shall save them for my marriage day," she said quietly.

Viscount Catlin smiled faintly. His eyes mocked his wife's startled expression. "You have been rolled up, my dear wife," he said softly.

The viscountess trembled, scarcely able to contain the smarting of her pride. But she was not one to openly counter the convention of reserve with an outburst of emotion. She tinkled a little laugh. "Was that not the Comte l'Buc that I saw leaving when we arrived, Victor? It was a pleasant surprise to discover that he had come to call upon you, Abigail, to be sure."

"Oh, the *comte* did not come to call upon me, but on Mama." Abigail saw at once by the slightest change in her mother's expression that she had said the wrong thing, but she did not understand why.

Viscountess Catlin was rendered speechless. It was the viscount's sardonic laughter that freed her tongue. Two spots of angry color appeared in her cheeks. "Well, Mary! You have stooped rather low, have you not? I would not have suspected you capable of stealing your own daughter's beaux!"

"Really, Mother," Lady Mary said, her sangfroid shaken for once.

"Why, it is no such thing, Grandmama!" Abigail exclaimed, astonished by such a ludicrous suggestion.

William turned to the viscount. His countenance had grown surprisingly stern. "Sir, I must object. My grandmother is obviously laboring under some misguided notion of her own that leads her to an insult of my mother. I shall not stand by while she does so."

Viscount Catlin regarded his grandson for several seconds. He respected strength above all else, and he was at once surprised and pleased to discover that his grandson should apparently possess it in full measure. The eager boy had grown into a man of determination, he thought. He bowed. "I agree that it is time for us to take our leave, William."

"I am not ready to leave, husband," Viscountess Catlin's eyes glittered. "There are yet a few choice words I wish to say, and—"

The viscount's hand fell upon her arm. The pressure of his fingers was unmistakable. "Tea awaits us, my dear." The viscountess had no choice but to submit to her husband's wishes. She did so with a miffed air, tossing her head. Viscount Catlin gazed at Lady Mary for just a second before he escorted the viscountess from the drawing room.

"Well! I have never, *never* heard Grandmama utter such nonsense in my life. As though you would—or, if it comes to that, *could*—steal my beaux," Abigail said with quite unconscious vanity. She looked earnestly at her mother. "I do not in the least regard anything that Grandmama said, Mama."

"I am glad of it, Abby," Lady Mary said. She was seething with anger, but little sign of it appeared in her expression. Only the slightest quiver in her voice betrayed her. Deliberately she changed the subject. "Shall I ring for tea?"

"Do that, Mama. I should like to wash the taste of this entire afternoon out of my mouth," William said. He twitched one of his sister's glossy curls. "By the by, I am glad that you do not mean to wear those earrings just yet, Abby. They belong on a married woman, not on a miss who has not yet cut all of her teeth."

"William, you can be so disgustingly earthy," Abigail complained, but she was smiling. She handed the jeweler's box to her mother. "I should like you to safeguard this for me, Mama. I might be tempted otherwise. They are such *pretty* earrings."

Pulling on the bell rope for tea to be brought in, Lady Mary smiled at her daughter as she slipped the box into her pocket. "I shall be honored to do so, Abigail."

13

LADY MARY forgot the viscountess's accusation very quickly. The fact that Abigail had not seemed to be affected by the poisonous suggestion made it easy for her to do so.

The whirl of social obligations contributed much to her sanguine attitude, centering as it did around the Earl of Kenmare. At whatever of the numerous functions that she chaperoned Abigail to, Lord Kenmare never failed to request her to dance with him, and often reserved her hand for supper. Lady Mary was always happy in his company and she never questioned the wisdom of being seen so much with him. After all, Lord Kenmare paid charming compliments to her daughter, and as far as anyone knew, he was interested in Abigail. That was a thought on which Lady Mary preferred not to dwell. Instead she accepted his lordship's most flattering attentions as part and parcel of the high gaiety of the Season.

The prospect of war seemed to have been all but forgotten. Napoleon Bonaparte's astonishing welcome in France was still a topic of interest—that could not be denied. But everyone preferred to think of him as a bad dream that one vaguely recalls upon waking. Lady Mary herself had at some point stopped noticing the ubiquitous uniforms as anything more than a smart form of attire that admirably suited the young gentlemen.

Lady Mary's enhanced enjoyment of the Season was high the evening that she attended a party at Lady Charlotte Greville's toward the end of April. She had just seen Abigail off on the arm of an admirer and had herself returned to her seat after a set and begun to fan her warm face when she overheard Mr. Creevey address the Duke of Wellington.

"Your grace, what is your opinion of Napoleon Bonaparte's chances?" Mr. Creevey asked.

Lady Mary was not the only one who turned an interested

ear to hear the duke's reply. Those around immediately abandoned their own conversations to listen.

"Why, Creevey, Bonaparte will not fight the allies. No, I believe a republic is about to be got up in Paris by Carnot, Lucien Bonaparte, and the rest," Wellington said.

Lady Mary noted that Mr. Creevey's expression was one of greatest surprise. She slowly closed her fan, waiting for the gentleman to speak. Mr. Creevey chose to use a broad allusion to the theater. "If it is with the consent of Manager Bonaparte, then of what nature will the piece be?" he said.

Wellington brayed his trademark horse's laugh. "No doubt it will be a tragedy by Bonaparte's standards. They will be at him by stiletto or otherwise in a very few weeks," he said confidently.

Mr. Creevey frowned. "I would have thought the odds to be in favor of the old performer against the new ones, your grace."

"No such thing, Creevey, no such thing," the duke answered. He passed on, and those standing about resumed their own conversations, which now inevitably included much repeating of Wellington's opinion.

As Mr. Creevey passed her, Lady Mary quietly hailed him. "Mr. Creevey, I could not but overhear your conversation with the duke. What do you think of his grace's words? Why, it sounded as though he did not think we are to go to war at all, as we have all heard before to be a certainty. How glad I would be if that were truly the case!"

"You have asked my opinion, my lady, and I shall give it to you frankly." Mr. Creevey was apparently in the throes of some disturbing emotion. "I think that his grace must be drunk! Anyone of plain common sense must see that we are shaping up for a fight. Indeed, I believe it to be inevitable."

After a very few words more, Lady Mary allowed Mr. Creevey to depart. With a tiny frown between her brows, she thought over what he had told her. She knew him to be a truthful gentleman of impeccable intelligence, being himself a barrister and a member of the Whig party in Parliament. Mr. Creevey was known by everyone and was acknowledged by even the highest-placed personages. It was extremely doubtful that Mr. Creevey should ever be misled by false information.

In light of all that she knew about Mr. Creevey, the Duke of Wellington's assertion to the contrary just a few moments before seemed extremely odd, especially coming as it did from a military man of some genius.

Lady Mary began to have an inkling of suspicion that the duke was playing a very deep game indeed. As she thought over the past month since Wellington's arrival in Brussels, she recalled that his grace had always brushed aside the gloomier predictions and had maintained an imperturbable joviality, whether he was in attendance at someone else's function or while entertaining at his own residence. The duke's demeanor had served to spread calm over the sense of panic that had begun to grip the entire populace of Brussels. Indeed, if he had shown the least degree of worry in the face of the rumors, Lady Mary had not a single doubt that the social Season would be far less enjoyable.

Lady Mary thought the conclusion inescapable. The Duke of Wellington was deliberately maintaining a facade of unconcern in order to keep panic among the populace at bay. Therefore, war was indeed hovering on the horizon.

It was not a comforting thought, and did much to destroy the ambience that had recently fallen upon her during the past few weeks.

Lady Mary glanced about her, and suddenly to her eyes the laughing people and the gay music and the dancing seemed but a caricature of reality. She began to feel stifled. She abruptly rose from her chair and began to walk across the room towards the doors leading out to the garden and the cool of the night air.

The Comte l'Buc watched Lady Mary slip out of the ballroom in the direction of the gardens. He stroked his mustache, his teeth white beneath it. The opportunity to discover a lady alone in the gardens was one that should not be lightly dismissed. It was true that Lady Mary had not seemed particularly receptive to his offerings of nosegays and candies since he had called upon her. But his black eyes gleamed at the thought of a tryst in the garden. He flattered himself that there were few his equal at initiating lovemaking by moonlight. The *comte* sauntered after

Lady Mary, glancing once behind him at the oblivious crowd before he exited.

The garden was lovely, drenched with plays of shadow and silver moonlight. Lady Mary walked leisurely between the hedges and rosebeds, stopping now and again to bend to the fragrance of a bloom. Already her nerves had steadied. She wondered at herself, but supposed that it was simply the shattering of the fantasy that they all lived in that had so unsettled her. She would do better now that she was prepared for the worst, she thought, rather than have it come upon her with no other warning than the call to arms. She shuddered, knowing that she would never become resigned to the thought of her son going off to war. But at least William was safer than many others. His division had been given the task of garrisoning the town, and so she imagined that the Fifth Division would probably be the last ordered up.

Discovering herself to be standing beside a stone bench, Lady Mary sat down. She was not quite ready to return to the fantasy world of laughter and amusements. She contemplated the blooming roses, allowing the cool breeze sighing among the hedges to complete the job of soothing her nerves.

Lady Mary had no inkling that she was stalked until a heavy arm slipped over her shoulders. She gasped, startling away, but found that she was lightly pinned against a broad expanse of waistcoat. The man's wide hand had come lightly down over her eyes. His breath was unpleasantly close on her neck.

"I give you three guesses, my lady," he breathed in her ear.

"Whoever you are, release me this instant," Lady Mary exclaimed furiously. She was too angry to be afraid. The house with its windows shining elongated panes of blazing light was but a few steps distant. She could distinctly hear the laughter and the indistinguishable commotion of conversation. It was absurd to be frightened, yet her heart beat wildly in her breast.

Soft laughter brushed her ears. "Naughty, naughty. One must play the game or pay a forfeit." The arm over her shoulders shifted. The hand blinding her left her eyes only to capture her chin. There was a blur of motion, then heavy lips came down on hers. The kiss was expert and forceful.

Lady Mary struggled. The man's arm pressed into her back

like steel and he held her with apparent ease, arched and captive against his wide torso. Lady Mary twisted her head, wrenching her mouth momentarily free. Soft bristles slid over her cheek. "No . . ."

He recaptured her mouth, cutting her off in mid-cry. Her lips were still parted. The *comte* took instant advantage, pushing past her resistance like a knife through butter, pillaging her mouth. Lady Mary felt wavering on a swoon with that greedy and yet not entirely unpleasant stroking. Triggered memories of turbulent emotions, long-buried passions, stirred, and she was abruptly acquiescent under the deepened and prolonged kiss.

The hand was no longer imprisoning her chin. Instead her breast was warmly encompassed.

The shocking touch tore Lady Mary out of the seductive trance to which she had unwittingly fallen prey. She twisted and fought like a wild thing, and suddenly she was free. The warmth of the man was replaced by a cold slap of night air. She heard a muffled curse, the crack of bone on bone.

Dazed, she sat up. As she did so she realized that she had been lying prone on the stone bench, that her gown was disarranged. She pulled up her gown, which had been pulled off one shoulder, and stood up to shake the creases out of her skirt. It was then that she saw a figure staggering off through the hedges. "But who . . . ?"

"It was the Comte l'Buc."

Lady Mary whirled on a gasp.

The Earl of Kenmare stood behind the bench. There was a grim set to his expression that was made starker by the moonlight. In his hand dangled a lace cap. Lady Mary's hands flew to her head, but her questing fingers discovered her hair bare of adornment. "I believe that cap to be mine," she said inanely.

He came around the stone bench to give it to her.

Her hands were shaking so that she could not take hold of the cap, she discovered. "I . . . I am sorry, my lord. But I seem quite incapable of helping myself," Lady Mary said, holding out her hands in attestment. "Could . . . could you possibly put it on for me?"

Without a word, Lord Kenmare stepped closer and reached up to settle the lace cap on her soft hair. The faintest scent of sandalwood surrounded her. Lady Mary was watching his face, when he suddenly glanced down and met her gaze. The pulse fluttered in her throat at what she saw in his eyes. She wanted desperately to look elsewhere, but she could not.

The earl slowly dropped his hands to her shoulders. Slowly, gently, he shook his head. "Foolish, idiotic woman, coming into the gardens without escort," he murmured.

"How did you know?" she whispered.

The corner of Lord Kenmare's mouth quirked upward. "I, too, had designs on your virtue, my lady," he said quietly. "But the *comte* was before me. I was never more enraged in my life to be so upstaged."

"And so you hit him," Lady Mary said, recalling that peculiar sound of cracked bone. She gave a faint smile. "I thank you for your chivalric instincts, my lord." He laughed and his hands tightened momentarily on her shoulders.

The beginning strains of a waltz came distinctly across the hedges and rosebeds. Lord Kenmare lifted his head to listen a few seconds, then glanced down at the lady with him. He stepped back from her so that he could make a low bow. "Pray, will the lady honor me?" he asked.

Lady Mary was enchanted by the suggestion. The roses drenched with moonlight, the handsome gentleman awaiting her answer, appealed to her sensitive and heightened emotions. She curtsied, and without a word went into his arms.

They danced in elegant splendor, alone in the moonlit garden. As they turned again and again, Lady Mary's gown stood out, brushing against the blooming roses until the delicate heady perfume filled the night air. The cool breeze of their movement brushed their faces, stirred their hair.

Lady Mary felt the warmth of his hand on hers, the strength of the arm that held her so near to him. Her eyes never strayed from his, nor did his gaze waver from her face. She had not a thought in her head, having given her soul away to the melody of the waltz that had entered her very blood.

When at last the waltz ended, Lord Kenmare did not immediately release her. There was something spellbinding in her wide eyes, perhaps the hint of a question, that held him. She swayed toward him and his arms of themselves gathered her closer. He reached up to touch her face. For several seconds they stayed thus, caught in a poignant, intimate moment that teetered on the brink of passion.

He ached to kiss her, to crush her to him and possess her. Lord Kenmare took a shuddering breath and gently set her from him. Lady Mary stared up at him, wondering at the earl's distracted air.

He looked distantly at the pretty cap that graced her soft hair. "Why the devil do you wear the silly things at all?" he said. Without another word, afraid of what he might betray to her, he walked off.

Lady Mary stood abandoned in the middle of the walkway. A fiery blush suffused her face. She pressed her palms against her hot cheeks.

14

LADY MARY never spoke of that evening to anyone. She did not need to, however. For days afterward, Abigail was full of exclamations over the Comte l'Buc's abrupt disappearance from her mother's circle of admirers.

"Say what you like, Mama, but I think it incredibly rude of a gentleman to pay assiduous court to a lady and then without explanation simply forget her existence!" She was affronted not so much by the *comte's* desertion as by his bad taste in losing interest in the pursuit of her attractive mother.

Lady Mary did not appear in the least put out. "My dear Abigail, what would you have me do?" she asked dryly. "If I had known how much you liked the *comte*, perhaps I would have looked upon him with a kindlier eye."

Abigail grimaced. "Pray, Mama! As though I would wish such a hypocrite for my stepfather! I was never in my life more shocked!"

"Indeed, Miss Abigail! Such manners are those of a rag-dog,'' Miss Steepleton said. She was quite prepared to believe any scurrilous tale told of the *comte*. His handsome features and black mustache had always reminded her of the dangerous heroes in the romantic novels to which she was addicted.

''Yes, we have had a singular escape indeed,'' Lady Mary said. She directed her companions' attention away from discussion of the *comte*'s perfidy to the incredible tapesty before them. ''Is it not stunning? I had no notion that such artistry could survive the centuries so perfectly intact.''

The ladies were touring the galleries of the Château de Boloeil.

The visiting British, in unending pursuit of amusement, had been fascinated by distant glimpses of the huge and beautiful edifice of the château. Upon inquiry, the owner had graciously agreed to open a portion of his home to parties interested in seeing the inside of the sixteenth-century château, which was known as the ''Belgian Versailles'' for its 240 windows and extensive gardens.

That summer day, Lady Mary and Abigail, with their companion Miss Steepleton, had chosen to join such a group, and now lingered before one of the several original Arras and Tournai tapestries that decorated the château.

''Beautiful indeed, my lady,'' Miss Steepleton said, nodding in true appreciation. She had brought her sketchbook with her and now she clutched it in hopeful anticipation. ''My lady, should you mind it so very much if I remained a few moments to put my poor efforts to paper?''

''You are far too humble for your own good, Aggie,'' Abigail said, shaking her head reprovingly at her former governess. ''Your drawings put anyone else's efforts all to shame.''

Miss Steepleton blushed, immensely pleased by the compliment. She thought that it was amazing how much good the sojourn in Brussels had done for Miss Abigail. The girl's once-thoughtless kindnesses had become more habitual to her and in Miss Steepleton's opinion greatly made up for the months that Abigail had been so completely under Viscountess Catlin's sway.

''Of course you may tarry, Agatha. You may catch up with us in the chapel,'' Lady Mary said.

"Very well, my lady," Miss Steepleton said, settling happily to her task.

Lady Mary and Abigail walked on slowly, now and again stopping to examine some new treasure that appeared to their eyes. Their slow progress eventually led them to the chapel, where they found Lady Cecily and her brother.

The chapel inspired reverence in the visitors. There was a pervasive sense of peace in the small room that had not been present elsewhere in any of the sumptuously furnished rooms that Lady Mary and Abigail had just finished passing through.

Lady Cecily was seated on one of the richly cushioned pews, fanning herself in a leisurely fashion. She beckoned to Lady Mary and Abigail when she saw them. They joined her, greeting her in the hushed tones that their surroundings seemed to demand.

Lady Mary glanced toward the earl, whose back was toward them as he concentrated on something before him. "Whatever is his lordship doing?" she asked quietly.

"I have persuaded Robert to take a brass rubbing for me," Lady Cecily said, the laughter in her brown eyes belying the completely sober tone in which she uttered the explanation.

Abigail giggled, but at once clapped a hand over her mouth when the sound of her merriment echoed in the vaults above their heads. When the echoes had ceased, she removed her hand from her mouth. "I am most sorry," she whispered in contrite apology.

"Never mind, my dear," Lady Mary said. "I am certain that through the ages these walls have embraced laughter and tears with equal serenity."

"How very true, my lady."

Lady Mary turned to find that the earl had completed his task and joined them. Her eyes danced as she met his gaze. "My lord, I understand that you have been taking a rubbing. I should like to see it, if I may."

"Yes, Robert, and so should I," Lady Cecily said. She gave a playful grin as she slanted a glance up at his face. "I hope that it is properly done, or I shall be resigned to the necessity of requesting a second try at it."

Lord Kenmare held up the sheet, upon which had been

blacked the image of a brass altarpiece. "As you can see, Cecily, I have been quite proficient at the unfamiliar task," he said. Lady Cecily laughingly agreed to it and thanked him for indulging her wish for the rubbing.

A small group of individuals entered the chapel, among them being Miss Steepleton. She saw the rest of her party immediately and came over to join them. "I am done with my sketching, Lady Mary," she said.

"And I am finished with any more brass rubbings for the day. In light of this, I offer the suggestion that we exit this fine château and get on to our picnic luncheon," Lord Kenmare said. The ladies agreed that it was a fine suggestion indeed, and the company spent considerably less time in leaving the Château de Boloeil than they had in traipsing through it.

Once outside in the warm June afternoon, Lord Kenmare handed his sister and Lady Mary into the waiting landau before helping Abigail to mount her horse. Then he swung up onto his gelding and, with Abigail cantering beside him, set the pace for the carriage driver.

Their destination was a high knoll from which the country-side could be seen for miles around. Lady Mary stepped out of the landau and crossed the grass to a better vantage point. She heard the clop of hooves behind her and turned her head. The earl had walked over to join her, holding his reins in his hand. Lady Mary smiled in greeting and then turned back to the view before them. As far as the eye could see was field upon field of corn, rippling and waving with the breeze. Beyond were the forested hills, which she knew sheltered rushing streams and small villages and noble châteaus cousin to the one they had just left. "It is a beautiful country, is it not?" she asked.

"Quite beautiful," agreed the earl.

The breeze freshened and pulled at her straw bonnet. Lady Mary caught hold of the brim, wondering as she did so whether his lordship had taken note that she was not wearing a matron's cap beneath it. She had put away all of her caps and not worn a single one since the night that he had so bluntly made known his dislike of them.

Lady Mary had received several compliments on the improvement in her dress, though none had been so mannerless as to actually mention the disappearance of her caps. None but her children, she amended with a wry smile. Abigail and William had both teased her mercilessly, her son going so far as to insist that she had broken free of an imprisoning chrysalis and was at last trying her wings. "Now you cannot sit with the dowagers and matrons, for they shall be far too envious of you to allow it," William had said with great satisfaction.

But Lord Kenmare, the author of her freedom from the stuffy matrons' circle, had not by word or gesture ever alluded to her capless state. It was really quite provoking, she decided.

The earl's expression was frowning and distant as he surveyed the countryside. Lady Mary wondered at it, for she saw nothing untoward in the bucolic scene before them. "My lord? What is it?" she asked.

Lord Kenmare glanced at her. "I was but thinking. The frontier and France are not so far distant from this point."

With Lady Mary's understanding of his meaning, a haze seemed to cross the face of the sun. She shivered. At once his lordship offered his arm to her, saying that they should return to the others. Their party had chosen a good patch of ground upon which to set out a picnic luncheon, both sunny and yet sheltered from the quickening wind by the tall trees that bordered the small meadow. A cloth had already been laid out with a small feast of fried chicken, tender *marcassin,* tomatoes stuffed with small sweet North Sea shrimp, various cheeses, bread and butter, and grapes. Bottles of wine stood waiting to be opened.

Lady Mary's and his lordship's return was greeted with enthusiasm by Abigail. "My lord, pray tether your horse at once and come to join us, for Lady Cecily promises us that we do not eat until you have seen what she has had prepared," she said.

Lord Kenmare raised his brows. He directed an inquiring look at his sister, who was seated on a small chair that had been toted in the landau along with the other picnic paraphernalia. "Cecily? What is this mystery?" he asked with mock sternness.

Lady Cecily laughed and shook her head at him. "Oh, no, Robert. You shall not browbeat me so easily, I assure you. Now, do as Abigail has bidden you and you shall have your curiosity answered."

Lady Mary settled beside her daughter on the ground cover,

a smile curving her lips for Abigail's barely suppressed anticipation. "One would think it is your own surprise that you are awaiting, Abby," she teased.

"But I have already peeked, so it is not at all a surprise to me," Abigail confided in a loud whisper.

"Miss Abigail, surely you did not!" Miss Steepleton exclaimed, astonished at such forwardness.

Lady Cecily laughed and reached over to pat that lady on the shoulder. "It is quite all right, Miss Steepleton. You mustn't scold, for I invited Abigail to do so. It is so much more fun when one can share the excitement of the moment," she said.

Miss Steepleton uttered an incoherence, completely overset by Lady Cecily's kind condescension. But her lack of sophistication was generally overlooked in the wake of the earl's arrival.

"Well, Cecily? What is this mystery?" he demanded.

Lady Cecily signaled the carriage driver, who had been standing patiently to one side ready to serve. With a flourish the man opened a picnic basket and brought out a finely iced and decorated cake. Lady Cecily grinned at her brother. "Have you an inkling yet, Robert?"

He stared flabbergasted at the cake. "You never brought it with you!" he exclaimed. "I thought myself safe at least until the evening."

Lady Cecily pealed in laughter, swiftly joined by the other ladies when they saw the earl's expression. "Yes, Robert, I brought your cake with me. Surely you did not expect me to forget your birthday, even with this convenient little outing, which, by the by, was most suspiciously proposed by you for this date," she said.

"I should have expected it, of course," Lord Kenmare said, grinning in acknowledgment.

"Many happy returns," Lady Mary said sincerely. Miss Steepleton and Abigail added their voices to hers, though Abigail quite confounded her mother and former governess by inquiring his lordship's age. "Abigail, pray!" exclaimed Lady Mary in rueful amusement.

Lord Kenmare waved aside Lady Mary's intervention. Quite

soberly he said, "I am all of six-and-thirty, Miss Spence, a great age indeed."

"That is not such a very great age. Why, Mama is herself four-and-thirty," Abigail said. She at once flushed, realizing that she had committed a definite *faux pas*. "I *do* apologize, Mama!"

Lord Kenmare regarded with intent interest the becoming color that flew into Lady Mary's face. He smiled faintly. "I might possibly have doubted your word on that before, Miss Spence. But now that I have seen her without her caps, your mother appears just as youthful as her years."

"My word!" Miss Steepleton exclaimed faintly. The earl's compliment had rendered Abigail momentary speechless and had made a surprised but satisfied smile appear on Lady Cecily's face.

As for Lady Mary, she gravely thanked his lordship for his compliment, richly warmed by the fact that he had noticed after all. She glanced up at the sunlight above. The bright blue sky was completely devoid of clouds.

15

LADY MARY and Abigail attended a party at Lady Conyngham's on Wednesday evening. William, looking very smart in his regimentals, was their escort. They arrived early, but already there were several people who were known to them in evidence. William glanced about and predicted, "It will be a proper squeeze tonight."

William found chairs for his mother and sister before wandering off to find his own cronies, assuring himself that his filial duty was done for the moment. He had no doubt that his mother and sister would soon have a score of partners and would hardly need him to entertain them.

Indeed, it was not many minutes before Lady Mary and Abigail were noticed and several acquaintances came up to greet them. The ladies' dance cards were soon filled, but they had arrived in the middle of a set and so were able to visit and to observe those already indulging in the exercise. Abigail directed her mother's attention. "Look, Mama, there is Michele. Does she not look stunning tonight?"

Lady Mary looked in the direction of Abigail's interest. Michele du Bois was dancing with Viscount Callander and the couple were easily the most magnificent on the floor. They seemed to have eyes for no one but each other as they whirled past, completely unheeding of Abigail's wave.

Lady Mary noted that Sir Lionel Corbett, though he had come up to greet them and lingered beside Abigail, was always faced so that he could keep a jealous eye on Mademoiselle du Bois. She thought the young cavalry officer seemed rather possessive of a young lady whose affections were generally thought to have been firmly engaged by another.

Monsieur and Madame du Bois joined Lady Mary and her circle. "A pleasant evening, *non*?" Monsieur du Bois said, after making his bows.

"Quite pleasant indeed, *monsieur,* after the day's heat," Lady Mary said. "Why, Helen, you look as satisfied as a fat cat with a bowl of cream. What has occurred?"

Madame du Bois looked particularly gay that evening. She glanced after her daughter and the viscount as they danced past. "I suppose it will do no harm to make an informal announcement among friends, will it, François?"

Monsieur du Bois raised his shoulders in a Gallic shrug. "I do not see why that it should. All the world will know tomorrow."

Madame du Bois laughed and said, "This very evening Michele and Lord Randol have plighted their troth. I was never more happy in my life than to see their genuine happiness."

"Why, that is wonderful news indeed!" Lady Mary exclaimed.

Abigail clapped her hands and exulted. "I knew that it could not be long before Lord Randol offered for Michele. They are such a perfect couple. Why, one can see it in how wonderfully they waltz together. I cannot wait to tell her how happy I am for her!''

The du Boises accepted the congratulations of the others. Sir Lionel Corbett, once he had said all that was proper, excused himself and swiftly strode away. His face was white and stiff with shock, and as Lady Mary watched him go, she could not but pity his acute disappointment.

The Duke of Wellington arrived and as usual was immediately surrounded, much like a candle flame is by moths. For two days rumors had circulated that the French had crossed the border into Belgium, and someone inquired anxiously of his grace for the truth of the matter.

''Yes, it is so,'' he said gravely. There was instant consternation, for it was understood that Bonaparte's forces completely outnumbered the allied troops. The duke disregarded the gloomier statements, saying that he would trust his fellows to do the job. ''When other generals commit errors, their armies are lost by them, and they are sure to be beaten. When I get into a scrape, my army gets me out of it,'' he stated firmly. His witticism sparked general laughter and the tension at once faded.

While Lady Mary was still smiling over the duke's answer, Captain McInnes approached to request permission to stand up with Abigail. She looked upon him warmly, appreciating his respectful manners. It was one of the things that she particularly liked about the officer. She knew that his name was scrawled on her daughter's card more than once and that he actually had no need of her permission. ''Of course you may do so, Captain.''

Abigail gave her hand to Captain McInnes. ''I am most honored,'' she said. Without hesitation she went with the young officer, her spirits at their most sparkling and vivacious. She had learned to like Captain McInnes very much; indeed, more than any other of her admirers.

From across the room Viscountess Catlin saw that her granddaughter was singled out by a young officer unknown to her. Upon inquiring, she learned the officer was a Captain McInnes, who was said to be a laird of some sort. The viscountess was not blind to the radiant expression on Abigail's face when the girl looked at the Highlander, and warning bells went off in her head.

Viscountess Catlin's thin lips tightened as she watched her granddaughter and the upstart go down the set. She decided it was urgent that she drop a small word of guidance into her granddaughter's ear. It would not do to have the girl take it into her head that she had fallen in love and toss aside all of her brilliant chances for a splendid match so that she could throw herself away on some obscure Scottish laird, she thought. Her nails dug into her palms with the strength of her determination. Abigail must be prevented from making the same mistake that her willful mother had.

Viscountess Catlin awaited her opportunity. Since the debacle over the Comte l'Buc and Lady Mary's resulting fury, she was more careful in how she approached her granddaughter. So she waited impatiently for the set to end, poised to intercept Abigail and her partner as they left the floor and before they had returned to Lady Mary's vicinity.

Captain McInnes and Abigail slowly neared, their conversation and laughter meant only for each other. The viscountess swept down upon them. She caught her granddaughter's arm. In the process, the viscountess had managed to draw the girl a little apart from Captain McInnes so that he had perforce to allow Abigail's hand to slide away from his arm. "My dearest Abigail! How perfectly lovely you look this evening. That rose pink is truly one of your better colors," she said, completely ignoring the young officer.

"Grandmama! I did not know you had come tonight. Where is Grandpapa?"

"Your grandfather has decided to take a turn at cards. I do not understand why, for he is too easily bored to enjoy it. But then, he is easily bored by every amusement." Viscountess Catlin still had not glanced at Captain McInnes, and from the corner of her eye she saw a dawning expression of understanding cross his craggy face. The Highlander was not a complete fool, then, she thought with satisfaction.

But Abigail did not fall into the proper place in the viscountess's little game. She put out her free hand to the young officer and he automatically caught her fingers. Abigail smiled radiantly at him and said, "Grandmama, I should like you to meet Captain Bruce McInnes. He is of the Ninety-fifth and has become a particular friend of mine."

The viscountess was forced at last to acknowledge the officer's presence. She smiled brightly, but her eyes did not reflect a friendly light. "Ah, Captain McInnes. I have not met you previously, I believe." Without waiting for his reply, she turned her head again to her granddaughter. "Abigail, there is almost interesting gentleman that I wish you to speak with. I think that you will find him quite eligible in all degrees."

Abigail was bewildered by her grandmother's rude manner. She looked up at Captain McInnes, who had lost his former laughing expression and whose face had become closed against her. He met her eyes and smiled. "I shall call upon you tomorrow, Miss Spence," he promised. Lifting her fingers to his lips, he took gentle leave of her. He spared a cool glance for the viscountess, and instead of making a respectful bow, he saluted her in a negligent fashion that was calculated to incur her wrath.

The viscountess's eyes flashed at the young officer's audacity. But he was already striding away and therefore safe from her haughty set-down. "Come, Abigail. We shall find a settee and compose ourselves for a private chat," she said.

Abigail hung back. "But I thought you wished me to meet someone," she said.

"That was just a ruse, my dear. You must see that it was necessary in order to pry you loose from that most inopportune gentleman."

Abigail freed herself from her grandmother's fingers. "What do you mean? Captain McInnes is decidedly one of the nicest gentlemen I have met this Season."

"Abigail, I would prefer to discuss this in a more private fashion," Viscountess Catlin said, aware that Lady Mary was not so distant that she could not read her daughter's expression and feel obliged to join them. Certainly she did not need interference from that quarter, she thought.

"No. I wish to hear now what you have against Captain

McInnes. Why, you have only just met him. How could you treat him so rudely, Grandmama?'' Abigail asked, very much bewildered and hurt and angry.

"Oh, very well. It is of no great moment, after all," Viscountess Catlin said, giving away with a petulant gesture. "It is only my concern for you that motivates me to speak to you at all, Abigail. I but wished you to understand that gentlemen such as Captain McInnes, while very charming and amusing, are not at all those upon whom you should bestow your attentions. My dear, it is the middle of June! I have yet to be informed of your engagement, when I had held such high hopes for a wedding. The Season is almost over, Abigail. And you have thus far failed to attract the offer that will guarantee your position in this life." She smiled pityingly at her granddaughter, whose eyes had filled with startled tears. "Think over what I have said, Abigail. You are a clever and ambitious girl. I suspect that when you have thought about it, your mind must rule that too-romantic heart of yours."

The viscountess swept away, leaving her granddaughter stunned by her cruelty. Abigail's mind was in a confused whirl. She did not know what to think. Her grandmother's lecture had rung true in her ears. It was true that she had not received the brilliant offer that she had been led to covet. Oh, there had been a few offers, but for one reason or another she had decided against each. It was true that the Season was almost done. The return to England suddenly loomed before her, a journey that she realized now must be made either in triumph or in disgrace. It was unthinkable that she should return without a glittering ring upon her finger and jewels about her neck. She, Abigail Spence, the prettiest girl of the county, to return home in ignoble defeat. Abigail shuddered.

But Captain McInnes . . . She could not shake the memory of his laughing eyes or the gentleness of his smile when he gazed at her. He appealed to her in ways that no other gentleman had ever come close to doing. She suspected that if he had offered for her, she would not have thought twice about her answer.

But now ugly reality, in the guise of her grandmother's professed concern for her future, had intruded upon her starry-eyed world. Captain McInnes was not a brilliant match. Though a

Scottish laird, he held no position in the English *ton*. She had gathered a foggy notion that his family holdings were extensive, but Abigail was quite certain that Captain McInnes was not what was referred to as well off.

Torn by loyalty and love, Abigail thought she was going to be ill.

She was startled by a touch at her elbow, and leapt nearly out of her skin. Her heart pounding, she saw that it was his lordship, the Earl of Kenmare. "My lord! How . . . how you frightened me," she said breathlessly.

Lord Kenmare looked keenly at her, taking note of the strained expression she wore. "Are you quite all right, Miss Spence?" he asked quietly.

Abigail gave a small unconvincing laugh. "Why, of course! Why shouldn't I be?" When he did not say anything, but merely regarded her steadily with a gaze that she felt certain could read her mind, Abigail gave a sob. "Oh, my lord." She pressed her hand to her mouth as though to stop herself from saying more.

Lord Kenmare slipped her arm into his and guided her through the crowd to a settee against the wall. He seated her and then sat down himself. She averted her face, but not before he had seen the tears in her eyes. Without a word, he offered his hand-kerchief to her.

Abigail accepted it with a mewling cry and ducked her face into the linen. After a moment she had managed to regain enough control of herself that she could meet his waiting gaze. "It . . . it is my grandmother, my lord. She has only my best interests at heart, but . . ." She stopped, biting her lip, then burst out, "My lord, I cannot but think that there must be more to a match than dowries and position and titles."

The earl realized at once what the problem was. Apparently Miss Spence had grown fond of someone who did not meet with her grandmother's high standards. "Indeed, I believe that there should be. However, many have chosen their spouses on the basis of those other things and have ended quite happily."

Abigail held his eyes, her own very unhappy. "Did you, my lord? I have heard Lady Cecily mention that you were once married."

Lord Kenmare was silent a moment, remembering. He had

met Miss Madeline Haverton at a dress function and had instantly fallen in love with her. But it had been his position and title that had made him unexceptionable in the eyes of her parents. "Yes. My wife and I were very happy."

"I see." Abigail's lashes swept down. She realized that she still had his handkerchief, and she returned it to him with a wavering smile. "You have been most kind, my lord, and most helpful. May I impinge on your courtesy for a moment longer and ask for your escort in returning to my mother? I should like to sit out the next few sets, I think." Lord Kenmare assured her that he would be honored, and he took her back to Lady Mary.

That lady's eyes were keen and she took in her daughter's pale expression with the faintest lift of her brows. With a fleeting glance at Lord Kenmare she asked, "Abigail, are you feeling unwell?"

"I do have a bit of the headache, Mama. I should like to simply rest for a few moments, if that is all right."

"Of course you may, my dear. I am certain that the gentlemen to whom you are promised for the next few sets will understand." Once Abigail had sunk down in the chair beside her, Lady Mary looked up again into the earl's eyes. "I have not seen Lady Cecily tonight, my lord. Is she well?"

"She was rather more tired than usual when she rose from supper, and she urged me to come alone." Lord Kenmare gestured at Lady Mary's dance card. "I hope that I am not come too late to stand up with you, my lady."

Lady Mary smiled, and her eyes twinkled. "I made sure of saving a waltz for you, my lord." She had grown accustomed to his invariable habit of inviting her to stand up with him, and truth to tell, she would have been very regretful if he had not asked her to dance with him this evening. She turned again to her daughter. "Abigail?"

At once understanding her mother's unspoken question, Abigail waved her hand. "Of course I shall be all right, Mama. Pray feel free to enjoy yourself." She watched as Lady Mary and Lord Kenmare went onto the floor. She saw how easily they danced together and that her mother's eyes could be seen to sparkle even from a distance. It occurred to Abigail that perhaps Lord Kenmare could mean more to her mother than simply a good friend. She gave a laugh that ended abruptly in something suspiciously like a sob. It would be the height of irony if Lady Mary were to be offered just the kind of suit that the viscountess wished so demandingly for her.

16

ON THURSDAY, the fifteenth of June, everything appeared so perfectly quiet that the Duchess of Richmond gave a ball and supper to which all the world was invited. The ball took place in a large room on the ground floor, on the left of the entrance, connected with the rest of the house by an anteroom. The room itself was stunningly decorated and a blaze of candles.

"It is very beautiful," Abigail said, admiringly to the daughter of the house, Lady Georgianna Lennox.

"You would never believe it now, but this room had been used by the coachbuilder, from whom the house was hired, to put carriages in; but it was papered before we came here. My sisters use the room as a schoolroom, and we play battledore and shuttlecock here on wet days," Lady Georgianna said.

The usual plethora of royals gathered, and upon the entrance of King William, the Belgians gave such enthusiastic shouts of *"Vive le roi!"* that the crystal chandeliers shook. When all royalty had been duly acknowledged and honored, the company turned to the business of the evening, which was to be both amused and amusing. The ladies flirted and the gentlemen were quite willing to accommodate them. The splash of bright uniforms formed a pleasing contrast to pale gowns and the more somber evening clothes that a minority of gentlemen had attired themselves in. That night no one gave a thought to what the uniforms represented. The merriment continued unabated as the company chose to forget that scarcely twenty-four hours before, Bonaparte had crossed the frontier.

It was not until near ten o'clock that rumors of an action between the French and Prussians were circulated through the room in whispers. Lady Cecily put her hand on her husband's sleeve. "Reginald!"

Major Wilson-Jones smiled down at her in a reassuring fashion. "We'll know soon enough, Cecy. But I'll wager it is but another false report." He was not alone in his estimation, for no credit was given the rumors for some time.

Then an officer arrived from Marshal von Blücher and the dispatches he carried were delivered to the Duke of Wellington in the ballroom. While his grace read them, he seemed to be completely absorbed by their contents.

After he had finished, for some minutes he remained in the same attitude of deep reflection, totally abstracted from every surrounding object and totally unaware that he was the focus of all eyes. Virtual silence reigned in the ballroom, even the musicians having stopped playing. His grace's countenance was expressive of fixed and intense thought and he was heard to say to himself, "It is Marshal von Blücher's opinion . . ." He remained thus a few minutes, and after having apparently formed his decision, he gave his usual clear and concise orders to one of his staff officers, who instantly left the room. The duke became again as gay and animated as ever, his loud horse laugh distinguishable above the heightened buzz of conversation that had resumed with the departure of the officer.

Lady Mary regarded the Duke of Wellington from the vantage point of a short distance. "I cannot believe that all is so sanguine as his grace's joviality seems to indicate," she said, disturbed.

"I wholeheartedly agree with you," Lady Cecily said. "His grace has always possessed a soft spot for a pretty female, and though I am as large as a frigate these days, I shall endeavor to play upon his cordiality and find out the round tale." She determinedly swept forward to bring herself to the Duke of Wellington's attention. Soon afterward Lady Mary had occasion to see that the duke and Lady Cecily were ensconced on a sofa. While they were seated there, and as Lady Mary took note when her attention was not claimed by an acquaintance, several other dispatches were brought to the duke.

Lady Cecily eventually parted from the duke. Immediately she returned to Lady Mary to report.

"Tell me quickly," Lady Mary was scarce able to contain her anxious curiosity.

"I could not wring a word out of him," Lady Cecily said, shaking her head. "He affected great gaiety and cheerfulness, but it struck me that I have never seen him with such an expression of care and anxiety upon his countenance." Lady Cecily paused as she considered the matter. "His mind seemed quite preoccupied, although he spoke to me in the kindest manner possible. Frequently in the middle of a sentence he stopped abruptly in order to call to some officer to give him directions, in particular to the Duke of Brunswick and the Prince of Orange." Lady Cecily looked at Lady Mary with eyes that had darkened with dread. "I very much fear that it is nearly upon us, Mary."

Lady Mary stood immobile, sternly quelling the sudden drumming of her heart. Her eyes sought and found the upright proud figure of her wheaten-haired son. She took a deep breath and smiled tentatively at Lady Cecily. "We shall be brave when the time comes, will we not?"

Lady Cecily snatched at Lady Mary's hand for a quick squeeze. "I admire your high courage, my dearest of friends. Yes, we shall be brave. As brave as are our men."

The Duke of Wellington stayed to supper and then went home. Several of the guests looked upon his grace's calm manner as reassuring. Surely the duke would not be so sanguine if he were going to fight a battle. But when orders were passed for individuals to repair to their regiments, matters began to be considered in a different light. Officers began quietly to leave the ballroom. There were still couples dancing on the floor, and young misses feverishly flirted with their beaux, but a coldness had insinuated itself slowly over the gathering, and the gaiety had become forced and leaden.

The full-throated commanding notes of a bugle sounded, to be echoed by others at regular intervals throughout the city.

In the ballroom, the music faltered, died away, and the dancing stopped. Faces drained of color, eyes glazed, desperate expressions entered countenances as the meaning of the bugles' short, sharp calls penetrated even through the walls.

It was eleven o'clock.

Drums began to beat. The Highland pibroch sounded.

"The call to arms," Lord Kenmare said, appearing suddenly beside his sister and Lady Mary. His quiet tone did not quite mask the unusual tremor in his voice. He could not but think of his friends, his brother-in-law, all of his acquaintances who would be grim players in the coming drama.

Lady Cecily clutched her brother's arm, having nowhere else to turn. Some minutes before, Major Wilson-Jones had quietly come up to take his leave and to tell her that he was ordered to report to bivouac in the park. He had slipped away, as had several others, and she had thought herself strong enough to carry off a brave front.

But now her veneer of bravery was not needed because everyone now knew the horrible reality. The Prussians had been driven out of Charleroi and the British army was being set in motion to meet the enemy.

Lady Cecily watched as, all around, soldiers took leave of their dancing partners, their sweethearts, their mothers. Some would not have time to change out of their evening clothes, but would fight in their froths of lace. "All of them going, just like that." She was struck by a thought and she swiftly looked around for Lady Mary, only to find that her friend had vanished.

Lady Mary swiftly crossed the floor to her son. Her entire being was beating with her fear for him. William met her with a wide grin and merry eyes, exclaiming, "Mama, isn't it glorious? We are going at last!"

Lady Mary swallowed convulsively and tried to steady a wavering smile. "Yes, yes, you are going at last." Tears rushed to her eyes. She threw her arms around him, uncaring that she might embarrass him or that she had lost her brave front. "My dearest boy!" She felt his arms come up about her and enfold her in a swift hard hug.

"Mama, you mustn't cry," William said. "I shall make you proud of me, I promise."

She made herself drag her arms down from about him and step back. She looked up at him, smiling tremulously. "Of course you shall. My, don't you look the fine one! I wish your father could have seen how well you have turned out.''

William laughed. He hugged her again, obscurely grateful that she had regained her composure. "Thank you, Mama. Now I must go. But where is Abigail? I have not seen her yet.''

"I . . . I saw her last near the anteroom,'' Lady Mary said, having difficulty keeping her fright and her tears under control. "I shall come with you, perhaps even walk with you to the Place Royale, if you should not mind it, William.''

His gray eyes alight with anticipation, he flashed another wide grin. "Of course not, Mama. We shall go find Abigail and walk out together.'' He offered his arm to his mother and with a flourish escorted her toward the ballroom door.

Abigail had been dancing with Captain McInnes when the call to arms came. She had started violently, and the confusion and trepidation of her thoughts led her to blurt, "The French! They have come!''

The captain shook his head, his countenance growing grave on the instant. But there was a fierce burning light in his eyes. "Nay, 'tis only the call to arms. We shall meet Bonaparte on common ground, I wager,'' he said in his lilting brogue.

Abigail was immensely relieved, only to be immediately filled with dismay again. She stared up at her partner, having grasped at last what was happening. "But that means that you—'' She stopped on an incoherent gasp. Her hands twisted together. "Oh, no, no!''

Captain McInnes smiled down at her. "My dear girl,'' he said, drawing the words out with tender care. He glanced about before he drew her out of the stream of hurrying passersby and close to the wall beside the door. "Abigail, I must speak now, whilst the moment is still mine.''

Abigail could but stare up at him, at the intense blue eyes and the craggy dark face that had become so unsettling to her dreams. She was scarcely able to believe in her senses, that all the rasied voices and the drums were real. She was almost inclined to think it all a dream.

But the din of war that resounded in her ears could not be brushed aside so easily, nor could the hard grip that Captain McInnes had on her hands. She could not banish from her mind the impression that in a few seconds she must part, perhaps forever, from Captain Bruce McInnes, and that this hurried moment might well prove to be their last together. "I do not want you to go," she whispered intensely, hardly aware of what it was she said.

His smile faded abruptly. Without a single hesitation, he caught her up in his arms and kissed her deeply.

Abigail had never been kissed in such a fashion. Before, she had been treated to mere sweet nothings by gallants who whispered delicious compliments. But this was an onslaught to her senses, drowning her in feelings that she had never been aware of possessing. When he at last released her, she felt she would have fallen but for the fact that his arms were still about her. She scarcely heard what he was saying, being more aware of his breath ruffling warm against her hair, but gradually understanding came to her.

"Ah, my dear girl, you can have no notion how I have longed to do that. Abigail, I wish you to wait for me. Will you, my dear girl? Will you wait for me to come back and make you mine?"

"Wait for you?" Her voice sounded strange in her own ears, and apparently it did to him as well, for he set her away from him slightly so that he could search her eyes. Her face flamed and she stepped out of his arms. "Captain, I am sorry! I did not mean to tease you, truly I did not."

He caught her hands. "Abigail, you have not teased me. I have fallen in love with you, you silly lass. Of course I wished to kiss you."

"Oh, oh, oh!" Abigail was beside herself with agitation. Awhirl in her head were all of her grandmother's warnings and her own doubts and desires. "But I cannot . . . Oh, I do not know what to say, what to do!"

Captain McInnes laughed at her softly. "My dear Abigail, say that you will wait for me and we shall wed. Say that you love me in the full measure that my heart holds for you."

Abigail stared up at him in consternation, her breast rising and falling rapidly with the turbulence of her emotions. At her silence, the tender glad light in his eyes faded a little. "Abigail,

I know full well that you feel something for me. I have seen it in your bonny eyes. I have felt it in the trembling of your body when we have danced.''

"I cannot admit what I do not know," Abigail said desperately, holding to that shred of her mind that believed everything that her grandparents had told her about what she should expect of life. The choice had come too quickly. Captain McInnes was not a titled gentleman, not particularly wealthy. But he haunted her dreams so. Oh, why, why did she feel so queer? she wondered wildly.

Captain McInnes gazed at her. There was a growing realization, coupled with sad pity, in his eyes. "I see. At last I understand." He took her hand, raising it to his lips for a lingering salute. "Always remember that I carry you in my heart, lass." Then he stepped away from her.

Abigail's eyes widened. She put out her hand. "Bruce!" But it was too late. He did not look back, but went out of the ballroom, to mingle and disappear into the flowing crowd of uniforms and gowns.

Abigail fell back against the papered wall, noticing with a dazed segment of her mind the pretty trellis and rose pattern. She felt strangely empty and ill, and her limbs shook as though with ague.

That was how her mother and her brother found her. She spoke mechanically to them, her listlessness giving way only when she realized that William, too, was going to join his division. She instantly agreed to accompany them both to the Place Royale, in order to be with her brother as long as possible, but also because she was driven to see Captain McInnes again.

17

ABOUT TWELVE o'clock at night the soldiers turned out. There was not a house in which the military were not quartered, and consequently the whole town was one universal scene of bustle. The soldiers assembled from all parts in the Place Royale, with knapsacks upon their backs, some taking leave of their wives and children. Others sat down unconcernedly upon the hard pavement to wait for their comrades. Still others snatched what sleep they could upon packs of straw, surrounded by all the din of war.

William was flushed and his eyes gleamed with high excitement as he took in the frenetic activity. "Isn't it marvelous, Mama?"

It was fortunate that he did not expect an answer, for Lady Mary found that she could not speak. The martial scene was overwhelming in its noise and confusion. Bat horses and baggage wagons were loaded, artillery and commissariary trains were harnessing, officers rode in all directions, carts clattered, chargers neighed, bugles sounded, drums beat. High above all the frenzied activity, the colors flew.

In contrast, a long procession of carts was coming quietly in as usual from the country to the market, filled with old Flemish women, who looked comic seated among their piles of cabbages, baskets of green peas, early potatoes and strawberries, totally ignorant of the cause of all the warlike preparations. Gazing at the scene around them with wonder, they jogged merrily along one after another through the Place Royale amidst the crowds of soldiers and the confusion of baggage wagons.

Yet there was order amidst all the apparent confusion. Regiment after regiment formed with the utmost regularity, and at two o'clock A.M., they began to march from the city.

William stood beside Lady Mary and Abigail, impatient and eager to be gone. But when at last his regiment was called, he was abruptly reluctant to part from his mother and his sister.

They, too, had heard the call, and reflected in their eyes and their clinging hands was his own fear of the unknown.

William looked down into his mother's white face. "Mama, it is time for me to go." He felt her fingers tighten about his before she nodded and slowly, reluctantly released his hand. She reached up to kiss him, and in his ear whispered, "Come back to us safely, dear William." A lump rose in his throat. He nodded and smiled.

Then Abigail was in his arms, unrestrained tears streaming down her face. "Oh, William!"

William awkwardly patted her. He swallowed past the constriction in his throat and said gruffly, "I will be quite safe, I promise you. Come, there's a good girl. You'll ruin your fine looks if you keep this up." He gently set his sister aside. Flashing a last cocky grin for his family, he ran to join his forming regiment.

About four o'clock in the morning the Forty-second and Ninety-second Highland regiments marched through the Place Royale and the park, their steady step firm and collected. Their military demeanor, with the skirling strains of the bagpipes playing before them as they went rejoicing to battle, and the beams of the rising sun shining upon their glittering arms, brought tears to the eyes of the watching spectators.

Lady Mary, though really not taking particular note of anything but the bustle of the forming army and William's leave-taking, was nevertheless aware that here and there about her and Abigail were several acquaintances, most come, like themselves, directly from the Richmond ballroom. Lord Kenmare and Lady Cecily had come up to stand beside them. "One cannot but admire their fine appearance," Lady Cecily murmured, brushing her wet eyes clear as she watched the Highlanders depart.

Lady Mary glanced at her daughter, who had said nothing for several minutes since Willliam had torn himself free of them and run to join his regiment. She thought compassionately that Abigail had never been subjected to a harsher separation. Sir

Roger had died while she was still in arms and so she had never known her father; but she practically worshiped William, and Lady Mary knew that she must be suffering.

Abigail was oblivious of her mother's gaze. She stood quite still, a strained expression on her face, twisting her fingers against her breast as the Ninety-second passed. Her desperate gaze did not waver from the stern mustached countenance of one particular Highlander.

As though he felt himself stared at, he glanced in Abigail's direction. Their eyes met and locked for one brief poignant, agonized second. Then he was nearly past her. Abigail gave an inarticulate cry, flinging out her hands after him. But her gesture came too late; he could not possibly have seen her appeal. She turned to her mother, the tears streaming down her cheeks, her eyes full of misery. "I never said . . . I never told him . . . Oh, Mama!" She clung to Lady Mary, hiding her face against her mother's neck and sobbed as though her heart was breaking.

Lady Mary stood, fighting to breathe past the tears locked in her own throat, her arms clasped hard about her daughter. She vaguely realized that Abigail must have formed an attachment to some officer that she had not been aware of, but the half-formed thought was swiftly forgotten. Her eyes were on another segment of departing soldiers. The Fifth Division, which had garrisoned Brussels and which she, in her ignorance, had felt to be the safest place in the army for William, after having bivouacked in the park until daylight, was at last setting forward toward the frontier.

Among them was her beloved son.

William caught her fixed gaze and he broke into a spontaneous grin. His eyes were alight with excitement. He waved, and in response Lady Mary raised her hand to him. "Abigail, look quickly! William is going!" Abigail twisted with a cry, her staring eyes searching desperately for sight of her beloved brother.

William swung jauntily into the march. As he passed, above the tramp of boots and the other noise, Lady Mary could have sworn she heard the high, sweet notes of William's whistle. It very nearly and completely undid her.

The cavalry of the Third and Fifth Divisions passed. Major Wilson-Jones blew a kiss to his wife, and a somber and particularly sweet smile lit his face as he looked over the heads in the crowd to her white, still face. "Have faith, my girl!" he called, and then his white charger pranced past and he, too, was quickly gone.

Lord Kenmare glanced down at his sister, who had several minutes before begun to clutch at his arm for support and now leaned heavily against him. "Do you wish to return to the house now, Cecily?" he asked quietly.

She shook her head. Her eyes did not lift from the scene before her. "No. I wish to see it all," she said.

He did not argue with her. For nearly four more hours he and the ladies and hundreds of other spectators remained in the Place Royale to see the rest of the army move out.

Before eight o'clock in the morning the streets, which had been filled with busy crowds of soldiers and officers, had fallen empty and silent. The great square of the Place Royale, which had been filled with armed men with all the appurtenances and paraphernalia of war, was now virtually deserted. The Flemish drivers were asleep in the titled carts that were destined to convey the wounded. The heavy baggage wagons, ranged in order and ready to move when occasion might require, stood under the guard of a few sentinels. Only some officers were still to be seen riding out of town to join the army.

The spectators looked at one another with dazed, exhausted eyes. Then with barely a word to anyone, singly or in small parties they walked slowly out of the Place Royale to make for their lodgings and cold beds.

Lady Cecily leaned heavily against her brother as they walked, her head against his side. His arm was about her shoulders to steady her. Lady Mary and Abigail walked side by side, their arms about each other's waists. In the park in front of the Kenmare residence, they all stopped to take leave of each other. "You will allow me to order out a conveyance for you, Lady Mary," Lord Kenmare said.

Lady Mary shook her head. "It is but a step more, my lord. And I think Abigail and I would benefit from the short walk,"

she said. Understanding at once, Lady Cecily mutely reached
out to catch her hand and press her fingers.

"Of course. Only stay one moment and I shall myself escort
you," Lord Kenmare said. None felt much like speaking. Lady
Mary and Abigail merely nodded and smiled their good-nights
to Lady Cecily. While Lady Mary and Abigail stood waiting
below, Lord Kenmare and Lady Cecily walked up their front
steps. Lord Kenmare placed his sister into the solicitous hands
of a footman and then returned to Lady Mary and Abigail so
that he could conduct the ladies to their own residence in la Rue
du Musée. He parted from them at their front door.

But he did not go directly home, instead returning to the Place
Royale. Along with several others, he was in time to witness
the departure on horseback of the Duke of Wellington with his
staff.

The duke was in good spirits, observing that as von Blücher
had most likely settled the business himself by this time, he
should perhaps be back in time for dinner.

The Earl of Kenmare opened his watch. It was eight o'clock
A.M.

18

AFTER THE ARMY was gone, Brussels seemed a perfect
desert.

The populace was without news the better part of the day.
Sometime during the long tense hours of waiting it began to
rain gently, which only served to accentuate the general
oppression of spirits. Every countenance was marked with
anxiety or melancholy. Every heart was filled with anxious
expectation. However, it was not supposed that any action would
take place that day, because surely it would take some time
before the French forces were discovered and engaged.

There was then general and sweeping consternation when

about three o'clock in the afternoon a furious cannonading began, originating in the direction that the army had taken.

Upon hearing the first dull boom, Abigail started up from the settee. "Mama, do you hear it?" She rushed to the window, pressing close to the glass panes to peer up and down the street below.

Lady Mary joined her daughter at the window. "Yes, Abigail, I do. And I very much fear what it portends." They looked out at the street but saw only others like themselves who were without news. Lady Mary threw open the window in order to catch snatches of what was being said. Hurrying to and fro, those in the street met and gesticulated, and parted, no wiser than before. Had the British troops encountered the French before they had joined the Prussians? Were they separately engaged? Where? When? How? In vain did everyone ask questions which none could answer.

The anxious babel did not abate, and Lady Mary eventually closed the window against it. "Surely we shall hear something soon," she said, to reassure both her daughter and herself. She and Abigail continued to watch through the window as numbers of people in carriages and on horseback set off toward the pounding of the cannon.

In the evening, having heard nothing all day, Lady Mary and Abigail set out walking toward the park. Miss Steepleton had been invited to join them, but she had declined with a nervousness that she could not conceal.

On all sides, the ladies heard different stories from those who had earlier set out and had now returned no wiser than when they had gone. A thousand absurd reports, totally devoid of foundation, were circulated.

Lady Mary and Abigail found the ramparts crowded by others like themselves. Speculation among the waiting citizens and the British was intense. It was known that only thirteen thousand British troops had marched out of Brussels that morning and that the rest of the army was unconcentrated. Rumors flew about that the French were thirty- or forty-thousand strong. Under such circumstances it was impossible, even with the fullest confidence in British valor, not to feel extreme anxiety for the army.

At length intelligence came from the army, brought by an officer who had left the field after five o'clock. The British in their march encountered the enemy on the plains of Fleurs, about fifteen miles from Brussels. The Highland regiments had received the furious onset of the whole French army without yielding one inch of ground. According to the officer's account, the Highlanders had fought to the last with resolute, unshaken valor, and fell upon the very spot where they first drew their swords.

When she heard it, Abigail moaned and covered her face with her hands. "Hush, Abigail," Lady Mary said, straining to hear the rest of the reported intelligence.

The combat was terrible, said the officer. The enemy were in much more formidable force than had been represented, and, deriving confidence from their immense superiority, they fought most furiously. Yet the brave handful of British had stood their ground, repulsed every attack, and were still fighting.

Even after hearing the officer's report, Lady Mary and Abigail could not bring themselves to return to the townhouse and they remained at the ramparts to listen to the heavy cannonade. In the course of the evening the cannonading became perfectly distinct and regular. Abigail clutched her mother's hand tighter. "Mama, it is coming closer," she said tensely.

Lady Mary thought for a moment that her daughter was right; then she shook her head. "It is the stillness of the evening that makes it seem so," she said with a show of confidence. She sensed the tension ease a little in Abigail's body. "Let us go home for dinner," she said coolly. She and Abigail left the ramparts; their places were immediately taken by others.

In the park, people wandered about with restless, aimless steps, and Lady Mary hurried Abigail across, not wanting her daughter to have a good look at the expressions on the faces of those they passed.

The dull boom of the French cannon could be heard even through the walls of the town house. During dinner, Miss Steepleton shook so from nerves that her glass rattled against her teeth each time she sought to drink.

The cannonade continued for five hours after the last accounts came away. After picking listlessly at their plates, the ladies retired to the drawing room to spend the long tense evening, all unwilling to go upstairs to bed while the oppressive noise continued. The anxiety to know the result of the battle was maddening, but there was no relief. Toward ten o'clock the regularly resounding thunder became fainter and soon afterward entirely died away.

Lady Mary, Abigail, and Miss Steepleton looked at one another, each wearing much the same expression that teetered between dread and hope. But the cannon did not begin again. "Thank God," Lady Mary breathed. With one accord the ladies went up to bed. But sleep was to elude them, for scarcely an hour after their heads touched their pillows, there began a new noise.

Between midnight and one o'clock, Lady Mary was startled up out of her fitful sleep by a rumbling noise. She leapt from her bed to rush to the window. She saw that heavy carriages were rolling rapidly in long succession down the street toward the Place Royale. Up and down la Rue de Musée doors opened, windows were thrown up, and the loud querying cries and exclamations of her neighbors filled the air as people hung out their windows or clattered into the streets.

The bedroom door was thrown open. She whirled, startled, as Abigail rushed in.

"Mama! Have you seen them? Oh, what does it mean?" She joined her mother at the window. Her arms were wrapped tightly about herself and she was shivering uncontrollably.

"I do not know, Abigail," Lady Mary said, her heart pounding. For some minutes they listened in silence.

Faster and faster, louder and louder, the long train of artillery continued to roll over the cobbled streets. The frightened cries of the people increased.

"We must find out what is happening!" Lady Mary exclaimed, unable to stand it any longer. She snatched up a dressing gown, plunged her arms into it, and belted it even as she and Abigail ran hastily out of the bedroom.

The first person they encountered was a scared *fille-de-chambre,* who exclaimed upon seeing them, "*Les Français sont touts près—dans une petite demi-heure ils seront ici. Que ferons-nous, que ferons-nous! Ils faut partir toute de suite.*"

"What are you saying?" Lady Mary gasped, alarmed. "How do you know this? Who told you that the French are but a half-hour's march away?" She grasped the hysterical girl's shoulders and shook her. "Speak girl!"

But the *fille-de-chambre* was past reaching. She could only moan again and again, "*Les Français sont touts près.*"

Abigail stared at her mother, her eyes huge in her white face. "Mama, I am so frightened."

"As I am, Abigail. But I do not think we should panic just yet," Lady Mary said. She flew down the stairs, her daughter close behind her.

Lady Mary was struck of a sudden by the eeriness of the place. The house seemed deserted. Every room door was standing open. The candles were left burning on the tables. There was not another soul in evidence.

The street door stood wide. The solitude and silence which reigned within formed a fearful contrast to the increasing tumult without. Lady Mary and Abigail stepped outside onto the front steps. At the bottom of the stairs they discovered their servants, some of whom had just returned from the Place Royale. Consternation was plain on every countenance and the shrill edge of fear vibrated in their voices. Lady Mary stepped forward and said sharply, "What is the meaning of this?"

Her authoritative tone served to cut across the swift talk and wild gesticulations. The butler came up the steps. His voice shaking, he said, "My lady, we have but this moment learned. A large body of French have been seen advancing through the woods, only half an hour's march from the city, which, as you know, is wholly undefended. The English army . . ." His voice broke. "The English army is said to be in full retreat."

Lady Mary was stunned. She could hardly take it in. It was one thing to dismiss the ravings of the hysterical maid, but quite another to have the impossible confirmed by a man whom she had come to think of as immovable. "I do not believe it," she said.

Her flat statement seemed to release the voices of the others. From every side was repeated, "*C'est trop vrai—c'est trop vrai.*"

However, they all soon had the satisfaction of being assured by a passing officer that the artillery were moving through to join the army, that they were not retreating, but advancing. Completely reassured, Lady Mary and Abigail reentered the house, whereupon they were struck by the incongruous sight of their companion standing *en déshabillé* at the head of the stairs. Miss Steepleton waved a smelling salt in one hand and clutched the top of her dressing gown to her skinny throat with the other. She asked shrilly, "Have they come? The French— have they come?"

Lady Mary realized that the woman was on the edge of hysteria. She went quickly up the stairs, Abigail following closely behind. When she reached Miss Steepleton, she said soothingly, "It is a false alarm only, Agatha. We may all return to our beds now."

Miss Steepleton was not so easily reassured. "But I heard the shouts. They shouted that the French are but a half hour's march away. My lady! What are we to do?"

Lady Mary firmly led the woman back to the door of her bedroom and gave her a gentle push. "You are going to lie down and rest, Agatha, as are Abigail and I. It was a false report, as I told you. In the morning this will all seem but a bad dream, I promise you." Even as Miss Steepleton still exclaimed in fearful conjecture, she shut the door and then she and Abigail separated to find their own cold beds.

The alarm of the British community gradually subsided. Some people did take their departure, but as the French didn't make their appearance, some went to bed, while others merely lay down in their clothes, by no means assured that their slumbers might not be broken by the entrance of the French.

On Saturday, the seventeenth of June, between five o'clock and six o'clock in the morning, those in Brussels were roused by a loud knocking at the door and cries of "*Les Français sont ici! Les Français sont ici!*"

The inhabitants started up from their beds and rushed to their windows. The first sight they beheld was a troop of cavalry covered in mud galloping through the town at full speed as if the enemy were at their heels. The troops shouted of rout, of slaughter, of Bonaparte.

Immediately upon the troops' passing, the heavy baggage wagons in the Place Royale, which had been harnessed from the moment of the first alarm, set off at full gallop down la Montagne de la Cour and through every street by which it was possible to effect their escape. In less than two minutes the great square of the Place Royale, which had been crowded with men and horses, carts and baggage wagons, was completely cleared of everything and entirely deserted.

Apprehension held the city in suspense; only gradually did the uneasy inhabitants return to their beds.

Again were the cries repeated of *"Les Français sont ici! . . . Ils s'emparent de la porte de la ville!"*

Once more the doors of all the bedrooms were thrown open and the people flew out with their nightcaps on, scarcely half-dressed. Distracted, they ran about pale and trembling they knew not where, with packages under their arms. Some carried huge heterogeneous collections of things down to the cellars and others loaded with their property went flying up to the garrets.

It was impossible for the people of Brussels, who were wholly ignorant of the event of the battle and acquainted only with the unequal numbers under which it was being fought, not to fear that the enemy might at last have succeeded in breaking through the British or at least the Prussian lines, or that Bonaparte, ever fertile in expedients, might have contrived to elude their vigilance and sent a detachment under cover of night by a circuitous route to seize the unguarded city.

The news of the advance of the French, the alarming reports which had been brought in from all quarters during the night, the flight of the troops, and above all the failure of any intelligence from the British army, tended to corroborate this last alarm, and it seemed but too certain that the enemy were actually at hand. This time the panic did not die down.

At the Hotel d'Angleterre, Viscountess Catlin clutched her husband's arm. She was white of face and her voice was hoarse with fear. "Victor! We must go! We must!" He covered her tight fingers with his, squeezing hard, and nodded abruptly.

Coatless and without his cravat, Viscount Catlin threw open

the door to their rooms. Aghast, Viscountess Catlin tried to catch him back even as he stepped into the hall. "Victor!"

He threw over his shoulder, "For God's sake, finish your dressing! I shall return in an instant." He sharply closed the door, cutting off the viscountess's wail.

A *fille-de-chambre* was running past, and the viscount shot out his hand to detain her. "What news?" he demanded. The poor *fille-de-chambre* was nearly frightened out of her wits. She stood wringing her hands, unable to articulate anything until the viscount urgently shook her. Her eyes rolled wildly at him. She gasped, *"Les Français! Les Français!"*

He was unable to get anything more out of her and he let her go in disgust. She stumbled away as the viscount clattered quickly downstairs past the taproom to the hotel entrance. He paused in the doorway, staring in startled disbelief at the scene of dreadful confusion in the courtyard.

People of all classes milled about shoulder to shoulder, knocking one another aside, or engaged in heated exchanges. There was frantic scuffling to get at the horses and carriages. The air was rent with the squabbling of masters and servants, ostlers, chambermaids, coachmen, and gentlemen, all scolding at once, and swearing in French, English, and Flemish. Some made use of supplication and others had recourse to force. Words were followed by blows. One half of the Belgian drivers refused either to go themselves or to let their beasts go, and neither love nor money, nor threats nor entreaties, could induce them to alter their determination.

At the far side of the courtyard stood one of the coachmen that the viscount had employed during his and his wife's stay in the Low Countries. The viscount's thin lips tightened at sight of the man, and he swung abruptly back into the hotel.

Returning to his rooms, he assured his fearful wife that they would shortly be leaving and he advised her to have her maid finish the packing. She returned to the other bedroom, twisting her hands and exclaiming worriedly under her breath.

Viscount Catlin shouted for his manservant. He dressed hurriedly with the help of his valet, who glanced frequently toward the windows through which the shouts of alarm clearly penetrated. Once the viscount had made his appearance impeccable and shrugged on an overcoat, he turned to a portmanteau and from its depths withdrew a long flat case. Opening the case, he took out two dueling pistols.

The valet's eyes bulged. He swallowed convulsively as he watched his master coolly inspect the priming of the pistols before thrusting them deep in the overcoat pockets.

The viscount felt his servant's gaze on him and he glanced round at the valet's appalled expression. His eyes grew cold. "Pray do not permit me to keep you from your task, Vincent," he said softly.

The valet started nervously, then hurried to pull the remaining items of the viscount's attire from the wardrobe. He cast a frightened glance after his master, who calmly went out of the bedroom.

The viscount crossed the private parlor and rapped sharply at his wife's bedroom door. There was a frightened gasp, then silence, from the other side of the door. Viscount Catlin ground out an expletive. "It is hardly credible that the French would be so courteous as to knock, my dear," he said bitingly.

The door flew open and the viscountess fell into his arms. "Victor! Thank God it is really you!"

He set her back on her feet. "Have done, my dear. I came to inquire whether you have finished with your packing," he said.

"Yes. At least . . . I am not certain," the viscountess said, completely distracted.

"Pray inquire of your maid, then. I shall await you in the parlor."

Viscount Catlin waited impatiently for his household to assemble. When they did so, his wife and her maid carrying portmanteaus and the valet bringing up the rear with the rest of the baggage, the viscount cautioned them all to stay close behind him. He led the way downstairs and the party was crossing the entry when the hotelier caught sight of them. Immediately the man gathered from their manner of dress and the baggage they carried that they were leaving. The hotelier hurried over, speaking agitatedly. "Ah, my lord! You too are going away. I am much saddened at the loss of your company, but . . . My lord! My lord, your bill!''

Without so much as pausing, the viscount reached into his coat pocket and tossed a tied leather bag at the hotelier's face. The man flinched and the bag fell to the wooden floor with the unmistakable sound of silver. The viscountess gasped and swung startled eyes to her husband's face. "Victor, you have given him too much!" He was unheeding, but swept to the door of the hotel, the others hurrying to keep up with him.

The situation in the courtyard had not changed. Viscount Catlin viewed the scene with a fainty contemptuous expression. Then he plunged into the melee to make his way over to the coachman he had earlier spied. He stared at the man on the carriage box. "I wish to depart immediately for Antwerp," he said, his voice rising clearly above the frantic and furious clamor all around.

The coachman shook his head rapidly. "*Non,* my lord. I do not take my animals out in such a panic. Not this day or any other. It would be madness to set out in this. I will not do it. I do not lose my animals, *non.*"

The viscount smiled, a mere parting of his thin lips. His pale blue eyes were cold. "I do not give you a choice, my man."

With many gesticulations, the coachman called upon all the saints and angels in heaven to witness that he would not set out—"*Non,* not to save the Prince of Orange himself!" he declared.

The viscount withdrew from his pocket one of the loaded pistols. He cocked it, and the click was amazingly clear even in the tumult about them. "I am perfectly capable of handling the team myself," he said in a hard voice.

The coachman looked at the silver-haired gentleman, at his lean wolfish face and cold, cold eyes. He shivered, crossing himself hastily. The Français were one kind of devil, and this Anglais another. "It shall be as you wish, my lord," he said hoarsely. He was a practical man. One dealt with the devil at one's door before wasting a thought on the one who was still to come.

Viscount Catlin allowed a thin smile to flit across his lips.

"Very good. We depart immediately," he said. The baggage was made secure and he told the valet and the maid to enter the carriage. He started to hand up the viscountess, but she hung back with a perturbed expression. "What is it, my dear?" the viscount asked irascibly.

"Victor, should we not procure a second coach?" she asked, plucking at his sleeve. "This one will be rather too crowded with the servants, do you not think?"

Viscount Catlin barked a laugh. "My dear lady, you must steel yourself. I fear that the French have scuttled any chance of traveling in our usual style."

"Really, it is most inconvenient," Viscountess Catlin complained, getting into the carriage. The viscount gave a short order to the driver before swinging up into the carriage and shutting the door. The carriage started with a jerk and then rattled out of the courtyard of the hotel.

19

WAGONS FILLED with wounded began to arrive, and the melancholy spectacle increased the general despondency. The streets were filled with the most pitiable sights. Numbers of wounded who were able to walk wandered upon every road, their bloodstained clothes and pale, haggard countenances giving testimony of the sufferings they had sustained.

The leaden skies wept misting rain as the wounded sprawled helter-skelter along the sidewalks where they had dropped from loss of blood and exhaustion, and numerous were the sorrowful groups standing round the dead bodies of those who had died of their wounds on the way home.

From their drawing-room window Lady Mary and Abigail witnessed a Belgian soldier dying at the door of his own home, surrounded by his relatives, who wept brokenheartedly over him. It was a moment too private and too painful for the public walkway, and with one accord they left the window, greatly affected.

Lady Mary's eyes glittered with tears, but her expression was one of settled determination. "I know that we had planned to go to the church to scrape lint for bandages, Abigail, but if you think that you can stand it, I believe we must do what we can to minister as best we might to those poor wretched men outside in our own street," she said.

"Oh, indeed, Mama!" Abigail exclaimed, her eyes shining with both dread and excitement.

"We can do little for their wounds, but at least we may ease their distress with something to drink or even perhaps to eat," Lady Mary said. She pulled on the bell rope, and to the footman who answered the summons she gave swift orders. The kitchen was galvanized into preparing soup and weak tea while Lady Mary and Abigail went upstairs to change into pelisses and bonnets that would help protect them from the rain.

When the soup and tea urns were ready, Lady Mary and Abigail left the town house to begin their small effort. The soldiers were parched beyond endurance, having not had any nourishment since they had marched out of Brussels, and were exceedingly grateful for the sips that they received.

Lady Mary and Abigail were not the only ones engaged on such errands of mercy. Others directed their servants to carry those sprawled on the pavement into their homes. Still others offered blankets and pillows to those not yet housed.

But for some, even such meager assistance came too late.

"It is so utterly horrible," Abigail said, tears coursing down her face as a man died in her mother's arms. She watched as Lady Mary gently laid the man down on the pavement and brushed her fingers over his eyes to close the lids. There was a smear of bright blood on her mother's skirt, and Abigail shuddered. "Mama, how can you bear it so calmly?"

Lady Mary drew a steadying breath, not quite as unaffected as her daughter thought her. "It is a trick of the mind, Abigail. To give any one of these poor sufferers access to your feelings is to allow yourself to be unmanned for the performance of your duty. It is less painful to look upon the whole than to contemplate even one of these men. Abigail, you must learn this truth quickly, for I fear that this is but the beginning of the monstrous consequences,'' she said quietly, rising to her feet. She looked compassionately at her daughter, but she did not touch her. She was aware of the horror that Abigail would feel to be touched by hands that had just left a dead man's face.

Without a word, Abigail moved on to the next man and Lady Mary followed her. They labored without ceasing until the soup and tea were gone, whereupon they returned to the town house to replenish their supply.

They had already seen some of their servants moving up and down the street also doing what little they could, and so they were unsurprised to find that the town house was very nearly deserted. However, the housekeeper caught them by surprise when she rushed up to Lady Mary and threw out her hands in agitated appeal for understanding. ''Madame! My nephew— he is wounded, he has nowhere else to go, no one to care for him but me—''

Lady Mary held up her hand to slow the woman's swift tumble of words. ''Slowly, Berthe, I pray you.'' The housekeeper was encouraged to tell her story, still disjointed and with great distress, but at last the ladies understood that she had without authority brought her nephew into the house and put him in an empty bedroom and that at that very moment a physician was expected.

''Of course it is all right, Berthe! I would not have had you do anything else,'' Lady Mary said warmly. Struck by a thought, she asked, ''You did say that a physician is coming, did you not?'' Assured that this was so, she smiled suddenly. ''Very good indeed, Berthe. We shall have a few more patients for the doctor to look at, I think.''

''Madame?'' Berthe said, not understanding. But as Lady Mary outlined what she wanted, she nodded in voluble appreciation. ''*Oui*, madame. It shall be attended to at once.''

As the housekeeper went to seek reinforcements to carry out Lady Mary's wishes, Abigail regarded her mother with a dubious expression. ''Are you certain it is truly what you wish, Mama? We have only let the place, after all.''

Lady Mary brushed aside such a consideration. ''I do not think that the owner himself would do less than to offer the sanctuary of his home to his fellow countrymen, especially when it does not appear that the weather will improve anytime soon. Come, Abigail, let us put off our bonnets and change out of these soiled and damp pelisses. There is much to be done if we are to turn this place into a house for the wounded,'' she said, only half in jest.

The ladies did not have far to look for patients. Close to their own door were several wounded. Lady Mary had the footmen carry four soldiers into the garden house. Berthe's nephew occupied one of the spare rooms, and so they were able to bivouc only three more wounded men in the other spare rooms.

When the wounded had been settled comfortably and had been seen by a physician, Lady Mary and Abigail settled in the drawing room. They were exhausted by their exertions and had been promised an early tea by Berthe to warm them.

Scarcely had Lady Mary and Abigail seated themselves when the butler showed in Viscount and Viscountess Catlin. Lady Mary received her parents without reserve, alarmed by the strange and early hour of their visit. But when she saw that they were dressed for travel, she suddenly knew why they had come.

Abigail was less perceptive, and she felt only gladness to see her grandparents. She ran to them with outstretched hands. ''Grandpapa! Grandmama, how happy I am to see you.''

Viscountess Catlin wrapped her arms tightly about the girl. ''Ah, my sweet dear little Abigail,'' she said, tears starting to her eyes.

Lady Mary greeted her father with more restraint. ''It is good to see you, as always, my lord. You have chosen an odd hour to call, and an odder attire,'' she said, sweeping her hand at her father's mode of dress.

The viscount laughed shortly. ''You've wit enough to see, Mary. Yes, your mother and I are leaving Brussels. The rumors are alarming. I will not take the chance of remaining until it is too late to escape Bonaparte's triumphant arrival.''

Viscountess Catlin turned to her daughter. ''We are leaving for Antwerp at once.''

''Leaving?'' exclaimed Abigail. She looked from one to the other of her grandparents. Her fingers tightened on her grandmother's hand. ''Oh, Grandmama!''

The viscountess patted her granddaughter's arm. "Yes, my dear. I am made too fearful by these dreadful rumors. It is all too much for me. I want to be safe in my own dear England."

Viscount Catlin stared somberly at his daughter. "Mary, I want you and Abigail well away from this place also. I want you to come back with us to London."

Though Lady Mary was pale, her composure remained intact. She hardly needed a moment to reflect before she answered. "I am truly sorry, sir. I cannot do as you wish. Until I know for certain what happens to William, I intend to remain her in Brussels."

"Mary! Even you cannot be such a fool!" Viscountess Catlin exclaimed, her voice cracking with astonishment. She began to admonish her daughter with a rapidity that bordered on hysteria.

The viscount threw up his hand to silence his wife's torrent of scolding. "A moment, my dear." His hard eyes studied his daughter's face. "You mean that you will not do as I wish, isn't that it, Mary?"

Lady Mary sighed. She steeled herself for the usual tide of wrath that her defiance had always provoked. "Our past differences have nothing to do with my decision, sir. I hope that you can understand my reason, which is simply as I have already stated to you," she said quietly.

Again the viscountess exclaimed. But Viscount Catlin silenced her, much to his wife's unwelcome surprise. "You have always been a stubborn and difficult young woman, Mary. At times you remind me most forcibly of myself," he said with a rare flash of humor. He nodded in reluctant acceptance. "Very well, Mary. I honor your decision. I trust that you will not come to bitterly regret it."

The viscountess's cheeks became suffused with bright patches of angry color. She demanded shrilly, "What are you saying, husband? Have you gone completely mad as well?"

Viscount Catlin spoke with a hint of coldness. "Not at all, my dear. I am merely respecting our daughter's right to exercise her own judgment and to choose her own fate."

Lady Mary's smile wavered. She was completely taken aback by her father's unexpected understanding. "Thank you, Papa."

The viscount smiled also, but it was a mere showing of the teeth and no warmth reached his eyes. "Pray do not thank me quite as soon, my lady. I demand that same right be granted to your own daughter and that you do not presume to speak for her. Abigail, too, must make her own choice in this."

Viscountess Catlin seized upon his demand with almost frenzied insistence. She turned to her granddaughter. "Yes, yes! Abigail, you must come with us. Your mother has completely lost her mind, you must see that. I shall not allow you, at least, to fall into the hands of those mad rapining French dogs." Her hands tightened on her granddaughter's arm. "Come with me now and I shall help you to pack your prettiest things."

The viscount stared at his granddaughter, his expression unreadable. "Which is it to be, Abigail? Shall you choose flight to safety with us, or uncertainty, perhaps even death, if you should stay?"

Horrified, Abigail stood rooted to the carpet. Her wide frightened eyes traveled from her grandmother's adamant expression to her grandfather's grim countenance. Her gaze finally came to rest on her mother's calm face. "Mama . . ."

Lady Mary smiled faintly. She glanced at her father, who met her eyes with something akin to triumph in his cold gaze. "Your grandfather knows me too well, Abigail. I cannot in all conscience make this choice for you. Often enough you have told me that you are a woman grown. Abide by that, Abigail," she said quietly.

Though her heart was hammering in her ears, she did not allow her feelings to be revealed in her expression. She was not certain how she wished for Abigail to decide. On the one hand, she would bitterly miss her daughter and regret the inevitable strengthening of the viscountess's influence. But if her faith in the Duke of Wellington and the British troops was misplaced, the marauding French would indeed descend on Brussels. She would infinitely prefer that Abigail be spared any such fate.

The vision conjured up by her imagination was so appalling and so frightening that she involuntarily threw up her hand against it. The words to urge her daughter to go trembled upon her lips.

But Abigail, after struggling with her own helplessness and doubt, had already made up her mind. "I shall stay with Mama," she said, somewhat pale but speaking bravely.

"My darling, you do not know what you are saying!" Viscountess Catlin exclaimed. She captured both of her granddaughter's hands. "Abigail, you must attend to me in this and be guided by one much older and wiser in life!"

Abigail gently disengaged herself. She wore an expression that for all its sweetness bespoke firm determination. "But I do know, Grandmama. I am choosing to be foolish and brave and perhaps a bit mad. So many of us are, I think. I, too, wish to know about William. And there are others." With the last admission, she suddenly flushed.

The gathering of tears in her grandmother's eyes shook her resolve and she appealed for understanding. "Oh, don't you see, Grandmama? I must stay, or otherwise I should regret it all my life."

But the viscountess was beyond understanding. "You may well regret it, in the very instant of losing your life," she said bitterly.

Viscount Catlin, on the point of sarcastically congratulating Lady Mary on her victory, was struck to silence when he saw his daughter's closed eyes and pained expression. "My dear Mary!" he exclaimed, alarmed by her uncharacteristic betrayal of weakness.

Lady Mary at once recovered herself. She shook her head against him and she looked somberly at her daughter. "Be very certain of what you do, Abigail. I do not think that the chance to leave Brussels in safety will come again."

"I know, Mama. But I have thought it over and I realize that I must stay," Abigail said softly.

Mother and daughter exchanged quiet smiles, in that moment their spirits having a full comprehension of one another. When the viscount saw their complete agreement, his shoulders sagged. He was defeated. He had gambled upon his daughter's innate sense of fairness and he had lost both her and his granddaughter. His sense of honor would not allow him to go back upon the lines he had himself drawn. He took hold of his wife's elbow. "Come, my dear. There is nothing more that we can do here," he said gruffly.

The viscountess stared up at him in bewilderment. Then she glanced at her daughter and her granddaughter. "But we cannot simply *leave* them like this!"

"Of course you cannot. You must stay for tea," Lady Mary said, deliberately misunderstanding her mother's meaning.

Abigail at once placed a detaining hand on her grandfather's tensely held arm. "Yes, you must stay. I insist upon it. After all, it may be the last time that I . . . that we . . ."

Her voice broke as she choked on sudden tears. With a strangled sound the viscountess fell into her granddaughter's arms and they both started to cry. "Oh, Grandmama! I shall miss you so dreadfully!" Viscountess Catlin but wailed and sobbed harder.

Lady Mary turned away to brush at the tears that were falling down her own cheeks. A handkerchief appeared before her watering sight and she took it, putting it to good use. She turned to look up at her father and tried to smile.

"Somehow I never thought to see you in tears, Mary," he said.

The lack of his customary sarcasm was obvious. Lady Mary winced. "I am not so unfeeling as that, Papa," she said quietly. She went to pull the bell, and upon the entrance of a footman, requested that tea be brought to the drawing room. She glanced at the viscount. "I have a favor to ask of you, sir."

Viscount Catlin allowed himself a sardonic smile. He could not banish the sudden leap of his heart as he thought that perhaps she was having second thoughts. "You've the cold nerve of the true aristocrat, daughter. You do not lose your coolness of thought, whatever the moment. What is it you wish of me?"

"I wish you to offer seats to any of our English servants who may wish to leave us to return to England," Lady Mary said.

After the slightest hesitation as an expression almost of pain crossed his face, the viscount acceded to her request with an abrupt nod. He turned away to stare out of the window, his hands clasped tightly behind him.

Overhearing, Viscountess Catlin exclaimed, "Mary!"

But upon meeting her daughter's cool steady gaze, she said nothing more to urge Lady Mary and Abigail to change their decision, understanding at last that it was useless. She sighed and said only, ''We have but the one carriage. How shall we manage it, Victor?''

The viscount did not turn around. He spoke over his shoulder. ''I assume since Mary wishes it, she will also turn out another carriage to handle the business.''

''Of course. I shall order out the horses at once,'' Lady Mary said, going again to the bell rope to call in the footman. She sent a quiet message by the footman to those of the household who had accompanied her and Abigail to the Continent that the opportunity to return to England was available. There was nothing more to say then, and the four waited in awkward silence for the tea tray.

20

WHEN TEA was brought in, Viscountess Catlin at once offered to pour. Lady Mary allowed her to do so, understanding that her mother was desperate for something to occupy herself and even that simple act would be of help to her. She turned her attention to the ritual of a proper tea, calmly offering biscuits to her companions and accepting a cup of tea from her mother's trembling hands.

The half-hour spent over tea was uncommonly subdued, as each was preoccupied with private thoughts. Occasionally one or another would recall his or her social obligations and leap in with some comment or other that would cause a momentary flurry of vivacious speech, which would then wither away as quickly as it had arisen.

After the tea was done there was no more reason to delay. The viscount and viscountess rose to take their leave. It was a painful farewell. Viscountess Catlin clung to her daughter and granddaughter while slow tears slid down her lined face. Even the good-bye said between Lady Mary and Viscount Catlin was a lingering one, punctuated by his clearing of his throat.

As she looked up into her father's face, she was stabbed to the heart by the suddenly haggard look in eyes that she had always thought of as unfathomable. "You must not be anxious on my account, Papa," she said softly.

Viscount Catlin forced his habitual mocking smile to his lips. "Allow me my moment of fatherly concern, Mary. It is not often that I indulge in such weakness."

Lady Mary and Abigail accompanied the viscount and viscountess from the drawing room. In the entry hall stood those who had traveled with the Spences to the Continent.

Miss Steepleton was dressed in her traveling pelisse and two battered portmanteaus rested beside her feet. She looked at her mistress, her pasty face marked by dull red patches of shame. "I do not know what to say, my lady. It is true. I am deserting you. But the chance to leave this place—not to have that horrible cannonade again pounding away at me or fear the French at the door at any moment . . . oh, my lady! Pray say that you forgive me!"

Lady Mary took Miss Steepleton's cold hands in hers. She was not particularly surprised by the woman's decision, since Miss Steepleton had suffered progressively worsening of her nerves from the hour that the cannonade had begun, and at every panic had become visibly fainter at heart and more hysterical. "Nonsense, there is nothing to forgive. You must go back to England and recover from your ordeal here."

"You are too, too kind, my lady!" Miss Steepleton gasped. She disentangled herself from Lady Mary's light hold and fumbled in her reticule for a handkerchief, which she used to blow her reddened nose.

Lady Mary's maid came forward to pay her respects to the viscount and viscountess and wish the travelers well. Abigail's maid hovered, looking frightened and confused. She was obviously torn between her duty to her mistress and an evident desire to be able to join Miss Steepleton. The maid, Beatrice, told her gruffly, "Get your things, there's a good girl. No one will be thinking poorly of you, least of all Miss Abigail."

"Indeed not, Molly," Abigail said immediately. She hooked her hand through the maid's trembling arm. "Come, I shall myself help you to gather your belongings."

Viscount Catlin had observed the proceedings with increasing annoyance. His irascible demand not to be kept standing about hurried the two girls upstairs. He brought out his watch and muttered to himself.

Within a very few minutes all of the travelers were re-assembled on the front steps and the good-byes started all over again. The viscount exchanged a hard embrace with his grand-daughter. "I am depending upon you to take care of yourself and of your mother, who is an extremely foolish woman," he said gruffly. Abigail nodded mutely, fearing to trust her voice.

While the viscountess took affectionate and morose leave of Abigail, the viscount turned to his daughter. He raised her cold fingers to his lips. "My dear Mary, I have often been angered by your obstinacy, but perhaps never more than I am today," he said gratingly.

"I know, my lord. But I shall never be other than I am," Lady Mary said. She reached up on her toes to kiss his hard cheek. "The grace of God be with you and me and my mother."

He smiled in a wintry fashion. "Better, perhaps, that He remain here with you and Abigail." He looked at her a long moment, then said, "I have never told you this before. Though I have often been infuriated by your decisions, I have come to respect and admire your strength of character."

Lady Mary regarded him with genuine surprise. "My dear sir, you astonish me. However, I shall always be careful to recall the stress of the moment under which you confessed such weakness to me, so that I will not hold you to that good opinion."

The viscount smiled faintly, for once completely without mockery. He touched her cheek with a light finger. "My very dear daughter," he said softly. As surprised tears sprang to Lady Mary's eyes, he turned away to sharply remind his wife that time was wasting. "At this rate we shall still be on the road through the night," he complained.

The Catlin servants, Abigail's maid, and Miss Steepleton got into the carriage that Lady Mary had ordered brought around.

The viscountess clung to Abigail and Mary until the last possible moment before the viscount urged her with ungentle hands up into their carriage. The viscount started to follow his wife, but hesitated on the carriage step to look up at Lady Mary standing above him on the town house steps. "Have you got another team of horses, Mary?" he asked harshly.

Lady Mary smiled faintly, and there was a gleam of understanding in her gray eyes. "Yes, my lord. I am not wholly without a sense of preservation."

"I am most happy to hear it," the viscount said, at his most sarcastic. He swung himself up into the carriage, signaling the driver with a wave of his arm before he firmly shut the door. The carriage started off with a jolt and rattled away. The window was thrown open and the viscountess's head appeared. She waved and blew kisses to Lady Mary and Abigail, only withdrawing back into the carriage as the corner was reached. The carriage carrying Miss Steepleton and the servants followed close after its leader.

Lady Mary and Abigail had stood on the front steps, continuing to wave until both carriages had turned out of la Rue du Musée and become lost to sight.

Lady Mary dropped her hand. She felt at once saddened and content. It had been many years since she had felt so close to her parents, and it had taken a second wrenching separation to bring it about. She touched her daughter's elbow. "Come, Abigail. We should go in out of the rain," she said quietly.

Still staring down the crowded street, Abigail said in a low voice, "Do you think we shall ever see them again?"

"I hope so. Indeed, I pray so," Lady Mary said. She put her arm around her daughter's slim waist and an instant later she felt Abigail's arm slide around her. They smiled tremulously at each other. Together, their arms still about each other, they reentered the house.

Before the ladies had a chance to go up and change out of their damp day dresses, the Earl of Kenmare arrived. Lady Mary immediately ushered his lordship into the drawing room and inquired whether he would like refreshment. Abigail quietly joined her mother and the earl, not wanting to miss anything of possible interest.

Lord Kenmare declined Lady Mary's offer. He spent little time on preliminaries, but came straight to the point. "I called on you to tell you what I have learned from an aide-de-camp of the Duke of Wellington's, who left the army at four o'clock to carry news of the action to us here in Brussels."

Lady Mary gestured urgently for him to be seated. "Of course, my lord! We have been anxiously awaiting just such news," she said.

Lord Kenmare said gravely, "Bonaparte beat von Blücher so soundly last night that all communication between the latter and his grace the Duke of Wellington was cut off. Under the circumstances the duke was obliged to fall back and take up another position."

"Thank God! We had heard that our troops were routed and hotly pursued by the French." Lady Mary gave a small laugh. "Most of the night Abigail and I half-expected at any moment to be interrupted in our slumbers by the enemy, while all our household kept wringing their hands over the report of our defeat."

Lord Kenmare grimaced slightly. "The Belgians apparently cannot be brought to an understanding of the difference in a total rout and an orderly retreat."

"We had heard also that the French were less than a half-hour's march away," Abigail said.

Lord Kenmare smiled reassuringly at her still-anxious expression. "It appears that a foraging party of French came bravadoing to the gates of the city, demanding its surrender. So you see, it was indeed all a false alarm. Actually, the news is more encouraging than not. Though our troops were attacked by such tremendous superiority of numbers and fought under every possible disadvantage, they completely repulsed the enemy and remained masters of the field."

"Then Grandpapa and Grandmama need not have left so precipitately as they did!" Abigail exclaimed in regret.

"There will be a desperate battle on the morrow, will there not?" Lady Mary asked quietly.

The earl nodded in reply, but his frowning attention was focused on Abigail. "Miss Spence, did you say that the viscount and viscountess have fled Brussels?"

Abigail nodded, not noticing her mother's warning shake of her head. "Yes, they left us just before your own arrival."

Lord Kenmare looked at Lady Mary. "And will you and your daughter also be leaving Brussels, my lady?"

"I wish to stay at least until the battle tomorrow is thoroughly joined. I hope to hear news of my son, you see," Lady Mary said.

The earl nodded his understanding. He appeared to reflect deeply for a moment before he said abruptly, "Lady Mary, I am uneasy that you and Miss Spence are now without someone who may be trusted to look after your protection. In view of the viscount's absence, I offer myself and my household in that capacity."

Lady Mary was touched by his concern. "I do thank you for your most kind consideration, my lord. Abigail and I shall rest easier in the knowledge that we may call upon you."

"You do not precisely take my meaning, my lady. I feel most strongly that you and Miss Spence should come to the safety of my roof," Lord Kenmare said. He saw from her expression that he had greatly startled her, and he bent forward to take her hand. "Pray do not misunderstand me, Lady Mary. There is nothing improper in what I propose. I simply believe that my staff, who are all my own and traveled with me from England, may be better relied upon than a household in a leased residence."

Abigail sat as though struck to stone by the extraordinary conversation. She had never heard a gentleman voice such an invitation. She was quite positive that her grandmother would have summarily dismissed the earl's suggestion as the grossest impropriety, and she waited curiously and with bated breath for her mother's reaction. She thought, judging from her mother's expression, she was not to be disappointed.

Lady Mary's delicately winged brows had risen a fraction. She withdrew her fingers from Lord Kenmare's light hold. When she spoke, her voice, though friendly, was cool. "Perhaps there is something in what you say regarding the loyalty of one's own staff, my lord. However, I hardly think such a step to be necessary, and though I do thank you for your concern, I must decline your most obliging invitation."

Lord Kenmare knew himself to be firmly rebuffed. He bowed stiffly from the waist. "I must accede to your wishes, of course," he said. He left soon afterward.

A short time later, a note was brought in by the butler. Lady Mary took it, wondering aloud from whom it could be. She unfolded the note and read it quickly. Then she sat frowning, her eyes unseeing.

Abigail could scarcely bear her own curiosity. "Well, Mama? What does it say?"

Lady Mary came out of her reverie. She said quietly, "Lady Cecily begs me to reconsider my decision and to come to them. She says that with her time approaching so soon, she would feel less anxious with us there in the house."

Abigail thought about it. "Lord Kenmare is rather clever, isn't he?"

"Yes, quite clever," Lady Mary said. She did not sound as though she was entirely admiring of his lordship. However, a rueful smile suddenly lit her gray eyes. "Well, Abby, it appears that we shall be removing to the earl's house in the park after all."

"Most improper," Abigail said primly.

"Yes, most," Lady Mary agreed.

Abigail giggled. "I shan't ever breathe a word about it to Grandmama, I promise."

"I do hope that you won't. The viscountess has very clear notions on what makes and unmakes a lady's reputation. I do not think she would approve at all of this little aberration from propriety," Lady Mary said, pulling the bell rope.

Upon the footman's entrance, she requested that he carry a reply to Lady Cecily Wilson-Jones, informing her ladyship that she and Abigail would come. Then Lady Mary alerted the staff of her plans and asked her maid to oversee the packing for both herself and Miss Abigail. They would naturally precede the arrival of the maid and their belongings at the Kenmare town house.

Lady Mary and Abigail attended to their toilets, to meet again in the front hall a little over an hour later. Lady Mary had changed into a fresh gown, putting on over it an ankle-length carriage dress to protect her gown from the rain. She wore a lavishly trimmed poke bonnet, and kid gloves completed her outfit. Abigail was similarly attired.

The porter respectfully informed the ladies that the carriage was at the curb. The servant ran ahead of them down the front steps so that he could open the carriage door and hand them in. Lady Mary and Abigail settled themselves on the carriage seat, the door was firmly closed, and the carriage jerked into motion.

21

UPON THEIR ARRIVAL at the town house in the park, the ladies were shown immediately into the drawing room, where Lady Cecily awaited them. She was reclining on a settee and her expression appeared more tired than either lady had ever before seen on her countenance. She held out her hand first to Lady Mary, then to Abigail, and gestured for them to make themselves comfortable.

"I am so glad that you felt able to come to us after all," she said. "I was never more annoyed in my life when Robert related to me how he had botched things with you."

Lady Mary gave her hostess an inquiring look. "Am I to understand that it was originally your wish to have us here?"

"I must confess that it was not. I shan't disguise that from you. But I saw instantly how wonderful it would be and so I sent off my note posthaste. His lordship shall be both surprised and pleased to find that you and Abigail have taken advantage of our hospitality after all," Lady Cecily said.

The door opened and the butler stepped inside. "Yes, Briggs? What is it?" Lady Cecily asked. She was informed that luncheon was waiting to be served and she nodded. She smiled at Lady Mary and Abigail as she rose from the settee. "I know that you shall wish to put off your bonnets and carriage dresses first, so I shall have a footman show you up to your rooms. I assume that your baggage is not long behind you?"

"My maid should arrive with it shortly," Lady Mary said, rising as well.

Lady Cecily glanced at Abigail as she walked with her visitors to the drawing-room door. "And your maid, Miss Spence?"

"Pray call me Abigail, my lady," Abigail invited, and was rewarded with a nodding smile from Lady Cecily. She shook her head. "My maid left Brussels with my grandparents this morning, so I suppose that I shall be sharing Beatrice for the moment."

"My brother naturally told me that the viscount and viscountess had fled. I imagine that it was a most painful parting," Lady Cecily said. She glanced quickly at Lady Mary's face, expecting to discover some hint of lingering distress. But Lady Mary only shook her head, a faint smile curving her lips.

Abigail nodded in agreement. "Oh, indeed, my lady! When they came to tell us, we had just come in from tending the wounded in the street. Mama, it has only just occurred to me how fortunate it was that you had time to change out of your bloodied gown before Grandmama—"

"Bloodied gown?" Lady Cecily threw up her hands. "Not another word, I pray you. I can see that you have much to relate to me. Believe me, I shall await you in the dining room positively agog with curiosity."

Their conversation had long since carried them into the entry hall. The ladies parted, Lady Mary and Abigail to follow a footman upstairs while Lady Cecily entered the dining room. She did not have long to wait, as Lady Mary and Abigail returned almost immediately and took their own places at the table.

While the barley soup was served, Lady Cecily demanded to know all that her friends had done since she had seen them last. Lady Mary allowed Abigail to tell Lady Cecily of their morning, putting in only a few words here and there. The soup bowls had been taken away and the second course of thick-backed here in its own rich brown gravy was served before Abigail was done.

"And so you have turned your house into a hospital," Lady Cecily said, shaking her head in admiration.

"So many are doing the same. One cannot but do other than

what one can, when those poor young men are lying about helpless and bleeding. It quite wrung my heart to see it. But there is really so very little that we can do," Lady Mary said quietly.

"I know precisely what you mean. I have been frustrated beyond measure by my silly spells of weakness these past few days. I have but once managed to go to the church to scrape lint. It quite makes one feel positively useless," Lady Cecily said. "But at least I have had the garden house opened up and put to use for the wounded. We have also been able to put up some officers in two of the spare rooms. None of ours are seriously wounded, being simply more worn out with fatigue and lack of nourishment, I think, and it is a good thing, too, since we do not have a physician calling upon us regularly."

The door closed. The Earl of Kenmare stood on the threshold a moment, his glance encompassing all three ladies. He slowly entered the dining room. He was white about the mouth and there was such a haggard look in his eyes that Lady Mary at once knew something was terribly, terribly wrong.

Lady Cecily also realized it. She asked sharply, "Robert, what is it?"

The earl glanced at his sister. In a flat, cold voice he said, "Young Lord Hay and the Duke of Brunswick are dead. Their bodies were brought through the town last night."

Lady Cecily stretched out her hand to him. "Oh, Robert, no!"

Lady Mary recalled that Lord Kenmare had once mentioned a close friendship with the Duke of Brunswick, and she felt deep pity for his loss. But at the same time she was caught up in terror for her son, William. With each new report of casualties, or at the sight of yet another wounded soldier, her heart had constricted with the always-present fear. She had told her daughter that it was easier not to think of the wounded as individuals, and it was; but that did not stop her from dreading that each hour might bring news of the death of her own son.

Abigail sat transfixed, staring at the earl. She could not seem to grasp the reality of his words. Her merry companion and admirer, Lord Hay, was dead. Then other faces crowded into her mind—William; Captain McInnes; Sir Lionel Corbett; Lord Randol; and all the rest. For the first time in her life she knew what it was to be truly afraid. She felt as though she was going to be ill. With revulsion she pushed away her plate. She said faintly, "Mama . . ."

Lady Mary turned her head quickly at the queer note in her daughter's voice. Abigail had gone starkly white. At once Lady Mary rose from her place and went around to Abigail's side, putting her own glass of wine to the girl's lips. "Drink, Abby," she said firmly.

Abigail swallowed a small amount of the wine and it seemed to help the horrible spinning in her head. She gasped, "Mama! Lord Hay—he was but seventeen! And William! What if he, too—?"

Lady Mary said fiercely, "Do not even consider it, Abigail. Until we hear otherwise, William is in perfect health. Do you understand?"

"Yes . . . yes." Abigail was illogically relieved by her mother's firm command.

"Robert, did you hear anything about . . . anything else at all?" Lady Cecily asked, clutching her brother's fingers tightly.

He held her hand between both of his in a hard grip. "Nothing of Wilson-Jones, Cecily. But as Lady Mary has said, until we do, then we must assume that he is alive and well."

"Of course he is all right," Lady Cecily said staunchly. Her game smile flickered past the fear in her brown eyes.

"That is my girl," Lord Kenmare said.

Lady Cecily urged him to sit down and eat with them; but he said that he had to go out again. Lady Cecily did not attempt to detain him. There was a fierceness in his expression that she recognized. While he was in that particular frame of mind, she knew that it would be futile to point out to him that the rain had already darkened his coat and that he ran the danger of becoming ill with renewed soakings.

As the earl went to the door, Abigail started up from the table. "My lord! Pray allow me a moment," she begged.

Lord Kenmare raised his brows, a hint of impatience in his face. But he nodded courteously enough. "Of course, Miss Spence."

He held the door for her to precede him, and before it fell

shut again, Lady Mary was startled to behold her daughter catching urgent hold of the earl's hands, obviously in some sort of appeal. The earl shook his head at something Abigail said and then the door closed to shut off her view. Lady Mary wondered, with a queer feeling in her breast, what her daughter could possibly have to say to the Earl of Kenmare that was of such an intimate nature, for there had been no doubt that Abigail had spoken quite familiarly to him.

A few minutes later Abigail returned to the dining room, wiping crystal tears from her cheeks. She did not volunteer anything regarding her conversation with Lord Kenmare. Instead, she asked for permission to excuse herself so that she could go up to her bedroom. "Of course, Abigail," Lady Mary said. She suspected that Abigail was in need of a good cry, if her own state of emotions was anything to judge from.

Lady Cecily and Lady Mary made an effort to do justice to the well-prepared dishes before them, but they failed miserably. Almost with one accord they rose from the table and repaired to the drawing room. Neither of them mentioned it, but they awaited the earl's return and to hear whatever news he might have gathered.

Lady Cecily and Lady Mary passed the time by rolling bandages, embroidering, and flipping through a ladies' magazine. There was very little significant conversation between them. Several times when their glances crossed it was because one had just looked away from the clock when the other chanced to look up at it.

There was the strong warning rumble of thunder. The ladies started, looking at each other fearfully. For an appalled instant Lady Mary thought the cannonading had begun again. But then lightning cracked, filling the drawing room with wild flickering light. Torrents of violent rain sheeted the drawing-room windowpanes and the day grew instantly darker. "I shall ask for extra candles to be brought in, shall I?" Lady Cecily said, reaching for the bell rope. Her request was swiftly attended to and the extra candles were soon blazing. But the light only served to provide a greater contrast to the wild darkness outside the windows, which did nothing to soothe the ladies' restlessness.

It was two hours before the Earl of Kenmare returned, and he was not alone.

The first intimation that the ladies had of his lordship's arrival was the crashing open of the outer door and his furious voice demanding assistance. Lady Mary and Lady Cecily stared at each other, for an instant transfixed with dread.

Lady Cecily recovered first, and as awkward as her pregnancy had made her, she moved swiftly to throw open the drawing-room door. "Robert, whatever are you bellowing . . . ?" The sight that greeted her eyes drove the color from her face.

The porter was struggling to close the street door against the driving rain, while a footman attempted to relieve Lord Kenmare of the wounded man that he had slung over one shoulder. "Get away from me, man! I have him," his lordship was saying irascibly. "Run have a bed made up. We'll need hot water, clean clothes, a nightshirt—just get my valet on it, there's a good man!"

"Dear Lord, is it Reginald?" Lady Cecily clung to the edge of the drawing-room door, her brown eyes appearing too prominent in her white face. Lady Mary had come up beside her, and she clutched convulsively at her friend's arm.

Lord Kenmare cast a harassed glance at his sister. He hoped that she was not going to faint, as she loooked to do at any second. "Get Lady Cecily's maid, damn you!" he shouted at a servant. "Think, Cecily! Is the uniform Wilson-Jones's?" he asked unkindly, at the end of his rope.

His harshness served its purpose. Lady Cecily looked closer. "No, no, of course it isn't," she said, regaining her composure. She brushed a hand across her eyes. "I am sorry, Robert. It came as such a shock. Even when one expects . . . Actually, I don't know what to expect anymore!" She burst into tears.

Lady Mary put her arms about her and urged her gently away from the doorway, saying soothingly, "Come, my lady. Come back to the settee. You must lie down after sustaining such a shock." She supported Lady Cecily's faltering steps back into the drawing room and over to the settee. She was just making Lady Cecily comfortable on the pillows when her ladyship's maid rushed in. Lady Mary reassured the concerned maid and then withdrew to allow the woman to tend to her mistress, closing the drawing-room door quietly behind her.

Inquiring of the porter for the whereabouts of the earl and his burden, Lady Mary glanced up at the balcony above. She lifted her skirts and started up the stairs.

22

LORD KENMARE laid the wounded man on the bed. The officer was unconscious and he lay quite still. His countenance was unnaturally pale, the eyes in their sockets somewhat hollowed. Lord Kenmare frowned as he studied the man. He didn't like the sound of the man's breathing. It was too rapid, too ragged.

He was still contemplating the officer when Lady Mary walked into the room. She glanced at the earl, taking swift note that his hair was plastered to his skull and his coat and trousers were soaked, before her eyes went to the young man lying sprawled on the bed. "Why, I recognize this officer. He is an admirer of Abigail's—a Captain McInnes."

"Yes, I found him lying outside a hospital tent in the rain," Lord Kenmare said.

Lady Mary went to the bedside and looked down on the young officer with compassion. "It appears to be a very bad wound," she said quietly.

"Yes," Lord Kenmare said briefly. His valet came into the bedroom carrying a small stack of clothing that Lord Kenmare recognized as having been pillaged from his own drawers. He grunted in approval. The officer's uniform was soaked through and torn and filthy where he had bled. Lord Kenmare told his manservant to help him get the wounded man undressed, as an indirect notice to the lady in the room.

Lord Kenmare glanced in Lady Mary's direction when she

did not seem to hear. She was matter-of-factly pouring water from the pitcher into the basin on the table beside the bed. She picked up a cloth and began to dampen it. "You may wish to wait outside until we are done, my lady. It looks to be an ugly sight," Lord Kenmare suggested.

She glanced across the occupied bed at him. Her brows rose slightly and she smiled. "My dear sir, I have seen already so many distressing sights today that I do not think this one more shall overset me."

Lord Kenmare shrugged, and with the help of his valet set to the task of divesting Captain McInnes of his ruined coat and shirt. The officer muttered unintelligibly, swinging his head restlessly from side to side on the pillow. The valet managed to remove the wounded man's boots by using a sharp knife to slit the leather.

Lady Mary sat down on the edge of the bed and began to remove the filthy, blood-soaked bandage that covered the officer's left shoulder. The bandage didn't come off easily, having stuck to the flesh beneath, but eventually Lady Mary managed to work it loose and pull it completely away.

Lord Kenmare swallowed at his first sight of the wound. The gaping flesh had been hurriedly stitched closed. It was alarmingly puffed and red.

Lady Mary gently touched the wounded flesh. "It is feverish and infected. I fear that gangrene cannot be far behind," she said quietly.

Lord Kenmare nodded. "I will send for a doctor at once."

Lady Mary looked up at him. "And will the doctor come?" He could not answer her. With all the wounded needing assistance, it might be a day or more before a physician could be persuaded to come. She shook her head. "I fear the doctor will come too late. We must reopen the wound and clean it ourselves now, before the infection becomes worse." She took a deep breath. "I shall do it myself, if you will assist me, my lord."

Lord Kenmare stared at her. "Do you know what it is you are proposing, my lady?"

Lady Mary looked up at him with a steady gaze. "Yes, my lord. I do."

The earl stared a moment longer into her clear gray eyes. Abruptly he nodded. "Very well. Send for what you will need. Fitz and I will assist you."

The valet looked rather green at his master's pronouncement, but he did not demur several minutes later when the earl requested him to sit upon Captain McInnes's legs. Lord Kenmare himself held the wounded man's shoulders. Lady Mary had quickly been supplied with a knife, scissors, and a needle and thread that had been boiled in water. She had also a quantity of knitbone boiled up into a poultice ready at her fingertips, kept hot between towels set into a covered pan.

Taking up the scissors, Lady Mary took a long steady breath. At the first touch of steel against flesh, Captain McInnes came up off the bed with a hoarse strangled cry. Lady Mary started back, appalled. Then she saw that the officer's half-open eyes were unfocused, unseeing. "He is still not quite awake. He cannot feel it all. We must go on," she said, more to herself than for the benefit of the two men watching her.

The earl gritted his teeth and hung on to the man with all his strength while Lady Mary continued with her difficult task. He watched as with all apparent calm she cut the original stitches, cleaned out the infection, splashed the area liberally with antiseptic powder, restitched, applied the poultice, and rebandaged. All the while, the wounded officer thrashed and cried out. Once he twisted an arm free and his flailing fist connected solidly with the earl's chin. Lord Kenmare bit off a curse. "I am sorry, my lady," he panted, fighting to recapture the man's arm. He was sweating with exertion and horror when he at last regained control. He did not know how much more the officer could possibly endure, but mercifully, before the end, Captain McInnes gave himself up to complete unconsciousness.

When it was all done with, Lady Mary straightened slowly. She did not appear to be aware that her gown was soiled here and there with blood. As she surveyed her handiwork, she brushed her disheveled hair back from her brow.

Her hands were shaking, Lord Kenmare noticed. There was

strain about her mouth and she was pale; but her expression retained the calm that he was coming to recognize as characteristic of her. He had never admired her more than at that moment.

He went around the bed and slipped his hand under his elbow. She looked up, startled, as he drew her to her feet. "You look in need of some wine, Lady Mary."

"I . . . Yes, my lord. That would be most welcome," she said. The tremor in her voice betrayed that she was not so unaffected as she would have liked him to believe.

The earl told his valet to clean up the signs of the operation. He escorted Lady Mary out of the sickroom to his own sitting room. He steered her to a chair and then went to an occasional table to pour a liberal amount of brandy for both her and himself. He handed one of the glasses to her and toasted her, saying, "To your good health, my lady. I have never in my life witnessed such fortitude."

The color was slowly returning to Lady Mary's face. She took too large a swallow and choked on the strong drink, falling into a coughing spasm. The earl set aside his glass and was instantly beside her, exclaiming in concern as he pounded on her back. She was flushed and tears were streaming down her cheeks before at last she mastered herself. "Forgive me. I did not intend to make such a spectacle of myself," she said hoarsely, trying to laugh.

Lord Kenmare smiled slightly, but in his blue eyes there was an emotion quite different from amusement. He still stood very near to her, and his hand still touched her back. With his other hand he gently brushed away the wetness from one of her soft cheeks. His fingers lingered along the contours of her face.

The tenderness in his eyes and the warmth of his hand against her skin mesmerized Lady Mary. It was for a second only that they stood thus, and then he bent his head to find her lips. Lady Mary held herself absolutely still.

At first his lips moved warmly, almost lazily, against hers, sending little shivers down her spine. Then his hand slipped past her ear into her soft hair, to cradle her head and to hold her for his deepening pleasure. As he gently drew her close to him, her breasts flattened against his broad chest.

She moaned against his mouth, unconsciously arching into his provocative kiss. His lips instantly hardened and demanded more of her. Lady Mary's lips began to part beneath his hunger. His tongue thrust inside, exploring her soft mouth, tasting, building, with every stroke, sweet fire.

Of their own accord, her arms slipped over his shoulders and wound about his neck. Her fingers caught in his damp curling hair, drawing him even closer. A growl of satisfaction sounded deep in his throat. The hand pressing against her back left its place to run the length of her spine. The heated blood pounded harder in Lady Mary's veins. When his hand curved over her firm rounded flesh, he pulled her against him into such intimacy that there was no mistaking his arousal. She gasped, her whole body shuddering. She had not needed a man for a very long time. It had always been good with Roger.

The thought was like a dash of icy water.

Lady Mary's eyes opened. Her hands let loose of his hair and slipped down to push urgently against his chest. Her mouth broke free of his. "I cannot!"

He had instantly sensed her abrupt withdrawal, felt the stiffening of her body. Lord Kenmare breathed rapidly, staring down into her wide eyes. The woman in his arms was very, very desirable. His body ached for release.

Anger burned in him. He knew that he could take her now. But he would not, he realized, almost with disgust. Exerting every ounce of his control, he forced himself to relax the hold he had on her.

She slipped from his loosened embrace and turned away, one trembling hand going to her throat. She was shaking from head to toe. Her heart pounded. She was confused. She did not know why she had stopped his making love to her. Never in her life had she felt more vulnerable. It frightened her out of her wits.

"I should go change out of this gown," she said inadequately. She felt his lordship step closer. She stiffened, fearing that he would touch her and fearing that he would not. She did not know what she would do if he turned her back into his arms. She did not think that she would have the sense to resist, nor did she really wish to. Lady Mary swallowed, her pulse beating erratically in her throat in dread expectation. But she was not to discover what she would or would not do, after all.

"Of course, my lady." His voice was low in her sensitive ears.

Lady Mary slowly turned to face him. Lord Kenmare's voice had vibrated with some indefinable emotion; but his words were perfectly polite, to the point of banality. She looked closely at his face, but his expression was unreadable as he gestured for her to precede him out of the sitting room.

She lowered her eyes and went quickly through the door. As she went down the hall to her bedroom, she knew without glancing around that Lord Kenmare stood watching her retreat until she had closed the bedroom door between them.

She crossed the room slowly toward the bell rope hanging beside the bed to call her maid. The unmistakable crash of a slammed door made her jump nearly out of her skin. Lady Mary stood in the middle of her room, her unblinking gaze fixed on the undisturbed bed. She suddenly flushed to the roots of her hair. "What an utter fool I have been," she breathed.

23

ABIGAIL HEARD about the wounded Highlander from the maid lent to her by Lady Cecily. When she heard his name, she gasped and the color was driven from her face. She flew from her own bedroom to that where she had been told Captain McInnes had been settled.

She started to knock on the door, but thought that the noise would waken him if he were asleep. So instead she stole inside quietly, strangely afraid, though of what, she was not certain. No one was then in attendance and Captain McInnes still lay unconscious.

Abigail looked at his white, haggard face. She hardly recognized him as the same young officer who had kissed her so sweetly. She reached out to touch his hair, and her hand froze. She had at last seen his shoulder, wrapped tight with white bandages through which had seeped a thin streak of bright blood.

Abigail couldn't breath. Her heart seemed to be pounding in her ears. She backed away one hesitant step after another, nearly to the door, before she whirled and ran out of the bedroom.

Abigail ran downstairs to the drawing room, instinctively seeking her mother, but the room was empty. She sank down on the settee, trembling. She was deeply shaken by her abortive visit to Captain McInnes. Seeing him lying there had set up a chain of thoughts that she would far rather have done without. She shuddered, hugging herself.

It had been so difficult for her to help tend the wounded on the street. Time and again she had had to swallow back her nausea. But that had been quite different from what she was now feeling. She had not known those wounded soldiers. But she did know the unconscious gentleman lying abovestairs, and when she thought about what must be happening to others that she knew, she was certain that she must faint with horror.

Lady Mary came downstairs and entered the drawing room. She stopped short at sight of her daughter sitting so still and pale on the settee. She went swiftly across the room, exclaiming, "Abigail! What has happened?"

Her daughter's face was abnormally white and strained in appearance and Abigail clasped and unclasped her hands in an uncharacteristically nervous fashion. Lady Mary sat down beside Abigail and took her fidgeting hands into her own, trying to still them with the comfort of her grasp.

But Abigail hardly noticed. Her whole being was concentrated on the man lying upstairs. "I had heard that Lord Kenmare brought in Captain Bruce McInnes. Surely you recall him . . . must have guessed how I felt about him."

Lady Mary was astonished. Certainly she had known that her daughter liked the young officer, but she had not known that there was anything deeper between them. She suddenly recalled how affected Abigail had been when the Highlanders had marched out of Brussels, and again when word had come of their valiant stand against the French. "Oh, Abigail . . ."

Abigail shuddered, caught up in her own thoughts and deaf to the sympathetic inflection in her mother's voice. "He was so proud, so beautiful. And now . . . " Her entire body shook violently. "Now he looks as though he is dying! I tell you, I don't know that I can accept it. No, I won't, I won't!" Her voice climbed to the edge of hysteria and broke on a sob.

"Abby, my dear!"

Abigail turned and threw herself into her mother's arms. She sobbed as though her heart would break. "Oh, Mama! I was stupid, so very stupid! But I did not know! I assumed that they would all come back, every one of them."

Lady Mary drew her weeping daughter close. The drawing-room door opened and Briggs appeared. Lady Mary quietly requested of the staring butler that tea be served in the drawing room and then she said, "Now, Abigail, you will tell me what has passed through your mind that has so upset you."

Abigail raised her head. Her eyes were swimming with tears. "I know it was improper of me, but I . . . I had gone in to see Captain McInnes. I knew he had been hurt, but I didn't know how he would appear. I was so shocked. Oh, Mama, it was perfectly horrible! I saw Captain McInnes lying there, as though at his own wake, and the blood! And then all of a sudden I was thinking about William and all the rest."

The tea was brought in and at a sign from Lady Mary, the ladies were left alone. Lady Mary handed a cup of hot tea to Abigail. "First of all, it is true that Captain McInnes has been gravely wounded. But I have hopes that he will not die. As for the others, you must simply keep faith for William and for the rest." She saw Abigail shudder and she said gently, "I know it seems an impossibility to do so, Abby. Believe me, I wrestle with my own fears for William hourly. But I truly believe that he must be alive and well."

"Mama, do you truly think so?" The color was beginning to return to Abigail's face with the dual comforts of the hot soothing tea and her mother's quiet confidence.

"Of course I do," Lady Mary said staunchly. She pushed deep her own conflicting emotions in her effort to reassure her daughter. Nothing must be allowed to show in her expression or her manner that might hint at her own fear to Abigail.

"I so wish that I could cut out this faint heart of mine," Abigail said with self-revulsion.

"I doubt that is the sort of catharsis which would best soothe your exacerbated feelings," Lady Mary said dryly.

"Oh, Mama! I was not speaking in a literal sense," Abigail said, the shadow of a smile beginning to creep back into her eyes.

Lady Mary was glad to see the easing of her daughter's bleak expression. A faint smile flitted across her face. "You are braver than you know, Abby."

Abigail leapt up to throw her arms about her mother. "I do thank you for that, Mama." When she had straightened up, she said hesitantly, "I shall try to stop hanging about your apron strings so tightly, Mama."

Lady Mary's eyes misted with tears. She smiled at her daughter and said quietly. "Already you have loosened your fingers, my dear."

Abigail left her mother than, her spirits already recovering.

Lady Mary was not nearly so sanguine. She was glad that Abigail was attempting to take such a responsible attitude about her own fears. It boded well for the maturing tenor of her character, and to that extent the war and its horrible consequences had been beneficial. She had watched Abigail hourly casting aside a bit more of her frivolity and selfishness.

But as for herself, after the earlier trauma of dealing with Captain McInnes's wound and the buffeting by a riot of emotions engendered by Lord Kenmare, being brought face-fo-face with Abigail's realization of the nightmare very nearly completed the fraying of her own control. The constant fears that she held at bay swelled to an almost unbearable clamor. She still did not know how her son was faring. She could do no more than sit anxiously awaiting news of him.

Her thoughts were still so full of William that when Lord Kenmare entered the drawing room with an expression more somber than she was used to seeing upon his countenance, Lady Mary immediately leapt to the conclusion that he had had bad news of her own. Her face paled and she jumped up from the settee. "My lord! What is it? You appear so grave."

Lord Kenmare looked at her in surprise, and the heavy frown

between his strongly marked brows eased slightly. "Do I, my lady? Forgive me, I did not mean to frighten you. I have been out again. These nearly hourly conflicting reports have me in such a suspended state that I scarcely know how to respond to them anymore."

Lady Mary sent a startled glance at the mantel clock, and was shocked at how late it had become. She had apparently sat idle, without awareness of the passing time, for more than an hour.

As Lord Kenmare had spoken, he had gone to the side table to open a decanter of wine. He offered to pour a glass for Lady Mary, but she declined it. Instead she watched him with sharpened eyes, seeing how deeply the lines had become carved in his face and how the grim set of his jaw seemed to have settled into permanence. "Is it worse?" she asked quietly. Some part of her mind wondered at her lack of embarrassment in facing his lordship, but what had passed between them seemed totally irrelevant beside the news that it was obvious he had brought back with him.

The earl waved her back to her former comfortable position and seated himself opposite. Before replying to her question, he swirled the wine in his glass, observing it with a peculiar concentration. He said abruptly, "The alarm is so great this evening that I have myself witnessed one hundred napoleons offered in vain for a pair of horses to leave Brussels. In addition, I have heard that numbers of our friends and acquaintances have actually set off in this weather on foot to walk the nearly thirty miles to Antwerp or else have embarked in boats upon the canal."

"My God, has it come at last, then?" Lady Mary whispered. Her hand rose to her throat in a betraying gesture. Her thoughts sped swiftly, and she gasped, appalled by the enormity of the situation that they faced. "But what of Lady Cecily? She can scarcely be expected to flee in her condition. It would be certain to bring on the babe. And those poor young men lying wounded upstairs and in your garden house—they cannot be left to the French!"

Lord Kenmore threw himself almost violently out of his chair and dashed his wineglass into the open fireplace. Glass splinters flew, and wine sizzled in the heat of the fire. "Dash it, do you not think I know it?'' he asked savagely. He smashed his fist against the mantel. ''I have gone over it a thousand times. We've horses and carriages enough for ourselves, the servants, and perhaps three of the wounded men. We should have to leave most of the baggage behind at that, and all of it if we are to accommodate any more of the men under our care.''

''Then that is what we must be prepared to do.''

At the perfect calm in Lady Mary's voice, Lord Kenmare looked around at her. He was held astounded by sheer amazement, and then he threw back his head to laugh.

When he met her gaze again, his expression had lost its awful savagery. ''As usual you have cut to the chaste of the matter, Lady Mary.'' He went over to raise her fingers to his lips. ''Thank you, my lady. You are an anchor in this cursed maelstrom,'' he said somberly.

Lady Mary's face suddenly flushed with soft color. She was made unusually agitated by his praise, especially as she felt it was undeserved. ''I am hardly that, my lord! Indeed, I would not be quite sane if I were unaffected by this experience. But I hope that I am practical enough to do what must be done.'' She found that he still held her hand, and she gently withdrew it from his warm clasp. ''I should see to things now, my lord.''

He stepped back immediately. ''Of course, and I shall see that the carriages are made ready in the event that we shall need them.'' He walked her to the door of the drawing room.

Lady Mary hesitated a moment before going through the door. She looked up into his lordship's handsome face with a certain stillness in her expression. ''Shall we be going away tonight, my lord?''

Lord Kenmare was on the point of answering in the affirmative when he was stopped by the near-pleading look in her eyes. He realized that she still did not know what had happened to her son, and nor did they know what had occurred to his brother-in-law, Wilson-Jones. ''I think not, my lady,'' he said slowly. ''The French, if they are victorious, as is so greatly feared at this hour, will hardly enter Brussels in this weather and at night. If the news is no better in the morning, we shall leave then.''

She smiled, a blazing expression of relief and gratitude. ''Thank you, my lord,'' she said in a low voice. She started to go then, but turned back to his touch on her elbow. "Yes, my lord?"

"I think it best that you and Abigail lie down in your clothes," he said soberly.

Lady Mary swallowed, and then she nodded. "Of course. That is eminently practical, my lord. We shall do so."

24

THE MORNING of the eighteenth of June was an anxious one, and the scene in the Place Royale surpassed all imagination. There were thousands of wounded French, Belgians, Prussians, and English. Carts, wagons, and all types of other attainable vehicles were continually arriving heaped with sufferers. The wounded were laid, friends and foes indiscriminately, on straw, with narrow avenues between them, in every part of the city.

The humane and indefatigable exertions of the fair ladies of Brussels greatly made up for the deficiency of adequate numbers of surgeons. Some women strapped and bandaged wounds; others served out tea, coffee, soups, and other soothing nourishments; while many occupied themselves stripping the sufferers of their gory and saturated garments and dressing them in clean shirts and other habiliments.

Despite their unceasing ministrations, however, the ladies could not banish from their thoughts their fear for the ultimate outcome of the battle still raging.

That Sunday morning the general terror and confusion in Brussels reached its highest point. One common interest bound together all ranks and conditions of men. All other subjects, all other considerations, were forgotten. All distinctions were leveled, all common forms of courtesy were thrown aside and neglected. Ladies accosted men they had never seen before with eager questions. No preface, no apology, no ceremony was thought of. Strangers conversed together like friends. All ranks of people addressed each other without hesitation—everyone seeking, everyone giving information. English reserve seemed no longer to exist.

News arrived of the French having gained a complete victory, and it was universally believed. A dreadful panic seized the men left in charge of the baggage in the rear of the army, and they ran away.

It was impossible for Lady Mary and the others to disguise their strong overpowering dread that the news might be true. At one point Lady Mary burst out, ''I can scarcely bear it another moment. We are so near and yet unable to learn what is really passing! It is horrid to know that within a few miles such an awful contest is waged, to hear even the distant voice of war, and to think that in the roar of every cannon our brave countrymen are falling, bleeding, dying . . .'' She broke off, smothering a choked sob behind the back of one hand.

She had been to the Place Royale earlier that morning and had only just returned. She thought she would never forget the sight of that sea of suffering, broken humanity. Everywhere she had looked, each face that she had peered into, she had dreaded that she might find her son's dying gaze. But now she wished that she had. It would have been so much easier, knowing for certain where he was. If the news of French victory were true, she would be forced to depart from Brussels without ever learning his fate.

Abigail stared at her mother with wide eyes. She could not recall ever hearing her mother speak with such agitation. She was shaken and dismayed. Her mother was the rock that she and the others had leaned upon for days.

But Abigail's instinctive fright at witnessing her mother's sudden frailty was chased away by the abrupt realization that Lady Mary Spence, like any of them, could not be expected to remain unaffected by the long and protracted suspense of the past three days. The constant agitation, the varying reports and incessant alarms, the wild fluctuating of their hopes and doubts, could not be wholly endured even by one as strong as her mother.

Abigail looked at her mother with suddenly sharpened eyes, taking note at last that her mother had lost weight and that there

were darkened circles like bruises under her eyes. It shamed
Abigail that she had not noticed before how much toll the ordeal
and the ever-present responsibilities for the wounded had taken
of her mother.

Abigail slipped an arm about her mother's trim waist. "It
will be all right, Mama. It must be all right," she said unsteadily.

Lady Mary turned her misted gaze on her daughter's earnest
face. What she saw brought a smile wavering to her lips. She
straightened her shoulders and pulled from under her cuff a
handkerchief of fine muslin to briskly blow her nose. She felt
better immediately. "Of course it shall be all right. We have
only to trust God and continue to believe in our troops. Our
army has never before been defeated by Bonaparte, after all."

She had intended to speak with conviction, but even to her
own ears her voice sounded falsely bright. Abigail gazed at her
mother. There was a wealth of such an age-old understanding
in her eyes that Lady Mary was nearly overcome. She wondered
when her little girl had so grown up that a word of reassurance
for her was no longer wholly sufficient. She felt a sudden aching
loss for Abigail's discarded naiveté. She made a determined
effort to smile. "Why do we not go up to see Lady Cecily?
She will be too much alone with her thoughts just now." They
went upstairs to Lady Cecily's sitting room, where they
discovered the earl already before them.

Lord Kenmare did his best to show a calm exterior to reassure
the ladies, but inside he was eaten with anxiety. He was restless, unable to stay immured at the town house without news,
and he had come and gone from the house several times already
in search of accurate information.

It was just before noon. The rain had finally stopped and the
sun appeared. Lady Cecily, who had insisted upon sitting at
the window so that she could glance out of it, called sharply
to her brother. "Robert, something is happening!"

Lord Kenmare went quickly to the window, where he was
swiftly joined by Lady Mary and Abigail. He instantly perceived
what his sister was referring to when he looked down into the
street and saw the flurry of activity. The horses, men, carts,
and carriages of all descriptions, laden with baggage, which

had filled every street all night, had apparently received orders to march.

"What does it mean, my lord?" Abigail asked anxiously.

"We shall know soon enough, depending upon the direction they take," Lord Kenmare said grimly.

The ladies exchanged quick glances. Abigail's frown was worried and uncomprehending, while Lady Cecily looked sick with apprehension. Lady Mary knew that her expression must mirror the same feelings. "If they take the Antwerp or Ostend Road . . ." She broke off, appalled at the obvious conclusion that must be drawn.

"Exactly. If they do so, we will not be holding our ground this day," Lord Kenmare said, never removing his eyes from the frenetic scene below.

Lady Mary found in her anxiety that she was digging her nails into her palms. But she was scarcely aware of the stinging discomfort as she, too, watched the commotion below. She felt her daughter's hand steal into her own and she relaxed her fingers to reassuringly clasp Abigail's hand.

"I cannot bear to watch any more," Lady Cecily said, shading her eyes with one hand. But the next instant she had dropped her hand and leaned forward again to the window.

The baggage wagons and various carts and carriages sorted themselves out and started moving up the Rue de Namur.

"They are moving toward the army," Lady Mary exclaimed. When Lord Kenmare glanced at her and smiled, she felt her heart turn over in her breast. A giddy feeling came over her and she clutched Abigail's hand harder for the support that the warm contact gave her.

Unaware of the devastating effect of his own charm on a certain lady's vulnerable heart, Lord Kenmare said, "Yes. Our fellows must still be in the fight, no matter what we have heard this morning to the contrary." He turned then to his sister and lifted her cold hand to clasp it warmly between his own palms. "We shall not be haring home just yet, Cecily."

Lady Cecily's lips trembled. A sheen of tears glistened in her eyes. "Thank God. All is not quite lost, then."

"Quite. We shall have luncheon as usual, and then I shall

saunter out again to discover what intelligence I can,'' Lord Kenmare said.

Luncheon was a subdued meal. Each of those about the table was preoccupied with his or her own thoughts, and none seemed to have much appetite, especially Lady Cecily, who only picked at her plate before pushing it aside. Before the meal was finished, she quietly excused herself from the table.

As she rose, Lord Kenmare looked at her with a worried frown. ''Cecily, are you quite all right? You look unusually pale to me.''

Lady Cecily managed a small wan smile. ''Of course I am, Robert. It is just this beastly, awful suspense we are all in. I shall be so glad when it is all over,'' she said. She asked the attending footman to ring for her maid. ''I shall go upstairs for a bit and rest, I think.''

''Perhaps that would be best,'' Lord Kenmare said. He watched his sister walk slowly and awkwardly from the room, and when the door was closed behind her, he said, ''I do not like how strained Cecily appears.''

''I shall myself look in on her presently, my lord. But I am certain it is only the natural tiredness that comes with the approach of one's confinement that affects Lady Cecily,'' Lady Mary said reassuringly.

''Thank you, my lady. You greatly ease my mind where Cecily is concerned. I feel compelled to go often in hopes of hearing what is happening with our army. I would have been fearful of being absent when my sister most needed support, except that I know that she will not lack for care while you are with us.''

The expression in his eyes was incredibly warm. Lady Mary felt herself glowing with his confidence in her. ''You may rest assured that I shall look after her, my lord,'' she said quietly.

The rest of luncheon was accomplished in passing conversation between the earl and Lady Mary. Usually so voluble in company, Abigail seemed unnaturally content merely to listen. When the covers were removed, Abigail said, ''Mama, should you mind it if I call on Michele? I have been thinking about her all morning.''

''Of course you may, Abigail. I only ask that you take a

footman with you, for I confess to some anxiousness about the safety of walking about the streets alone today,'' Lady Mary said. Abigail kissed her mother's cheek, assuring her that she would take a manservant for an escort, and dashed upstairs to change into her walking dress. She left soon afterward in the protective custody of a sturdy footman.

Lord Kenmare escorted Lady Mary to the drawing room and then stayed to talk with her for some time. She was surprised that he should wish to spend the time in her company when he had expressed the intention of going out after luncheon. They did not speak of anything of moment that she could see, but yet when he at last rose to say that he meant to reassure himself about a couple of household matters before he left, she felt that in some way they had helped each other to momentarily forget their mutual apprehension over the battle raging at that moment.

Abigail came into the drawing room just as the earl was leaving it, and they exchanged greetings in passing. Lady Mary was surprised that Abigail had returned so quickly. ''How was your visit with Michele?'' she asked casually.

Abigail answered her mother with a subdued air. ''It was not as entertaining as I had anticipated.'' She was playing absently with the curtains at the window, turned away from her mother.

''Do you wish to tell me about it?'' Lady Mary asked softly. She did not falter in her steady employment of rolling bandages, even though the undercurrent in her daughter's voice struck a protective chord within her.

Abigail abandoned the window and placed her hands on the back of a chair. She said quickly, ''Sir Lionel brought a rumor to Michele about Viscount Callander. He told her that Lord Randol was dead. And then in the next breath he proposed marriage to Michele! Wasn't that rather horridly unfeeling of him, Mama?''

Lady Mary's fingers had frozen at Abigail's revelation. She resumed rolling the bandage. ''Indeed it was, Abigail. I am surprised that Sir Lionel showed so little consideration for one whom I was always persuaded he had a strong partiality for.''

Abigail moved her hands restlessly across the back of the chair. ''Yes, everyone knew it. He made no secret of his admiration for Michele. In any event, Michele says that she spurned him furiously and he went away all cold and proud and hurt. She allowed me to read the letter that she is sending to him in apology for wounding his feelings." Abigail reflected a moment, finally saying, "In the same circumstances, I do not think I would have pitied Sir Lionel, for he never gave a thought for the hurt that he inflicted. You will say that Michele is more mature than I am. Isn't that so, Mama?"

"Not at all, Abigail. I think that each of us acts according to her own nature. You might not have been so cruel in your rejection to Sir Lionel's suit and therefore would not have felt the need of apologizing to him," Lady Mary said. She hardly knew what it was she was saying. Her head was spinning with the distressing rumor of yet another young gentleman gone.

Abigail shook her head swiftly. "Oh, Mama! You don't understand at all. I am so ashamed of myself, don't you see?" A sob seemed to tear its way out of her chest, and she collapsed across the chair's back, crying wildly.

Lady Mary was startled by her daughter's unprecedented upset. "Abby!" She threw aside the lint and went quickly to gather her daughter into her arms. "My dear sweet child, whatever is the matter?"

Abigail clutched at her, still weeping. Her reply came in a series of hiccuping breaths. "Michele is so noble and you are so strong and Lady Cecily is so brave to have a baby. I am the only one who goes about shaking inside, and I am luckier than anybody! I have Bruce safe. I know he is alive and will be well. If what Sir Lionel said is true, Michele has already lost her beloved. We don't even know whether William is coming back! Oh, how I detest this horrid war!"

Lady Mary's throat burned with the effort not to burst into long-denied tears of her own. She said unsteadily, "We are all of us sick of the fighting, darling, and we are all afraid. You are not alone in those sentiments, believe me. I am not the tower of strength you think me. Sometimes I am so terribly afraid— for William, for you, for all of us. As for Lady Cecily, she hasn't any choice in having the baby. Its arrival will not be denied."

Abigail gave a watery giggle. She mopped her eyes. "No, I suppose one cannot simply send it back," she agreed.

Lady Mary hugged her. "That's my girl. Why do you not go upstairs now to read to Captain McInnes? He must be growing mad at being alone with his own thoughts."

Abigail regarded her mother in utmost surprise. "Go up to a gentleman's bedroom, Mama? But surely . . . Whatever would Grandmama say?"

"I suspect that the viscountess would swoon at the least hint of such scandal." Lady Mary smiled slightly. "I have every confidence in you, my dear. And I promise upon my honor that I shall not breathe a word about it to your grandmama."

Abigail kissed her mother quickly. "Thank you, Mama." She exited the drawing room on her happy errand.

Lady Mary remained standing where she was for some minutes, staring into space. Then, as though her thoughts were too unpleasant to bear, she went over to the pianoforte and ran her fingers over the keys, picking out a playful air that had always served to brighten her spirits. But it was not quite the antidote that she had hoped it would be, and for some unaccountable reason she felt tears in her eyes.

That was how Lord Kenmare found her when he entered. At his quick step, Lady Mary whirled with a gasp. He was startled by the expression of fright on her face, but it was gone so quickly he was uncertain that he had actually seen it. "I am sorry, my lady. I did not mean to startle you."

She came forward with a light laugh, hoping that he was not observant enough to note how she blinked against the betraying dampness in her eyes. "It was of no consequence. I was so caught up in my thoughts that I did not hear you immediately, my lord." She studied him a moment, as though debating within herself, then appeared to come to a decision. "My lord, how long was it that you knew of Abigail's attachment to Captain McInnes?"

Lord Kenmare regarded her, surprised by her question. But he could see that it was important to her. "Your daughter confided in me two days ago, my lady. She requested that I ask word of him whenever I had occasion to go out for news."

Lady Mary turned away. "I see. She never confided in me."

The earl heard the peculiar forlorn note in her voice and he came up behind her. He laid his hands on her shoulders. "When

Abigail came to me, she was thinking only of the fact that I was often out searching for news. The impropriety of her request never crossed her mind, and assuredly I do not hold it against her in such times. I am certain that she never meant to slight you, my lady," he said quietly.

Lady Mary held herself still under the comforting warmth of his hands. She had the oddest wish to turn, to bury her face in his shoulder and burst into tears. But that could not be. She must remain strong. Everyone depended on her. She could not lean even for a moment on someone else, no matter how compassionate his voice or how solid and comforting his nearness, for fear of completely crumbling away. So instead she pinned a smile to her lips. She turned and his hands fell away from her. She felt curiously bereft without their strength. Again, for the third time that day, she felt the hot prick of tears in her eyes. "Silly of me to mind so much, is it not?"

"Not at all." Lord Kenmare was breathing with deliberate slow control, fighting the urge to catch her up in his arms and kiss away the rare, bruised look of vulnerability in her eyes. He imagined what her reaction would be if he gave in to his shocking impulse to gather her up in his arms and give full rein to his ardor.

Once, he had allowed her to glimpse the extent of his passion for her, and she had turned from him in revulsion. The memory was not a pleasant one and therefore his voice was cooler than he perhaps intended. "I came to inform you that I am going out now to discover what news I can. If you will be so kind to let Cecily know when she wakens, I will be grateful."

"Of course, my lord," Lady Mary said, forcing the words past the seeming obstruction in her tight throat. She offered her hand to him, and when he took it, she said earnestly, "Take care."

Lord Kenmare permitted himself the liberty of kissing her fingers with a banked passion. "Be assured that I will, my lady," he said, the timbre of his voice curiously deepened. He turned then and left her, before he could say anything that he might regret.

Lady Mary stood staring after him, shaken by his graceful intimate salute. For an instant there had been something unmistakably naked in his eyes that she thought she understood. But surely it could not be.

Her fingers still tingled from the touch of his lips and her hand crept up to her cheek, there to be cradled against her face. "Robert," she whispered.

25

LORD KENMARE left the house just before three o'clock and walked about two miles out of town in the direction of the army. He observed with some surprise the most curious scene he had yet witnessed. Every kind of carriage was on the road, carrying the Sunday population of Brussels out to the suburbs out of the Porte Namur. They were sitting about tables drinking beer and smoking and making merry, as if races or other sports were going on instead of a great pitched battle. But there was a feverishness in the darting eyes, an edge of tension in the laughter, that could not be completely disguised.

Lord Kenmare neither heard nor saw anything of moment among the crowd, and he turned to retrace his steps. Suddenly a considerable shouting and the pounding of hooves rose behind him, coming rapidly closer. The earl swung around. A regiment of cavalry galloped full speed down the Rue de Namur, heedless of carriages and pedestrians alike.

As others were doing, the earl leapt to one side, narrowly escaping being trampled. In the brief second of their passing, he recognized the cavalry to be the Cumberland Hussars. The cavalry thundered on down the road into the Place Royale, crying out at the top of their lungs that the French were on their heels. The havoc and panic raised by their passage were incredible, and as carriages were untangled and pedestrians dusted themselves off, shouted queries and curses flew through the air. But after several minutes, when no French could be espied in the distance, the Sunday loiterers again settled to their beer and their nervous gossip.

Lord Kenmare strode quickly in the wake of the fleeing cavalry. He entered the great square of the Place Royale, only to pause, gazing upon some hundreds of wounded men who were stretched out on piles of straw. Men and women of upper and working classes alike moved among the wounded, offering soup, coffee and tea, fresh blankets and shirts. "Good God," he said blankly. He had listened to Lady Mary speak of the wounded, but nothing could have prepared him for this.

"Aye, it is a rare sight indeed. And there will soon enough be more of the same."

Lord Kenmare turned to see who addressed him. A Life Guardsman stood next to him. The soldier was obviously worn out and he sported a bloodied rag about his head. "Here, you need that looked to," Lord Kenmare said, instinctively looking about for help for the man.

The Life Guardsman shrugged off the earl's concern. He touched the bandage lightly with a dirty finger and grinned crookedly. "This trifle? Believe me, I am damned fortunate compared to some of the other fellows. I'm off to my bivouac for a long and deserved sleep."

Lord Kenmare detained the man for a moment longer. "You've just returned from the field, then. When you left, how was the battle going?"

The Life Guardsman turned around, glancing about to see if anyone was within hearing, and lowered his voice. "Why, my lord, I don't like the appearance of things at all. The French are getting on in such a manner that I don't see what's to stop them." He saw that his grave words had proved disquieting, and he apologized. "I am sorry, my lord. But that is my honest impression."

Lord Kenmare smiled fleetingly, dispelling his heavy frown. "Quite all right. Look here, you still need to have that wound taken care of. Why do you not return with me to my residence, and I shall have a physician to—"

Suddenly an alarm was raised, drying the words in his mouth. Shouts that the French were entering the city swiftly led to panic. In a moment all was in an uproar. Those who had been attending the wounded ran in all directions. Beside Lord Kenmare, the Life Guardsman bit out a curse and ran toward a party of the Eighty-first Regiment that had remained on duty in the city during the action. Without being totally aware of his actions, the earl followed after him. Lord Kenmare found himself amidst the soldiers, a sword steady in his hand and his heart pumping.

The panic was as quickly over as the one previous, when about seventeen hundred French prisoners appeared under the escort of some British dragoons. Held high above the Horse Guards could be seen two eagles, the distinctive standards of Bonaparte's forces, which had obviously been taken as prizes of the battle. A ragged cheer broke from the throats of those in the square, citizens and wounded alike.

Lord Kenmare looked blankly at the sword in his hand. He had no notion from where he had snatched it up or what he thought to accomplish with it. If the alarm had been authentic, he would have been in the middle of a desperate battle in the Place Royale, while those with a claim on his protection were left to their own devices. His beloved sister and her unborn child, Lady Mary and Abigail, and all the others of his household would have been left to the mercies of the enemy while he indulged in vainglorious heroics.

All at once Lord Kenmare realized that he had been chafing for days at his passive spectator's role, when so many he knew were in the thick of the fight. But his duty had bound him, as it still did, first and foremost to the welfare of his household.

Lord Kenmare gently laid aside the sword beside a wounded officer lying on a pallet of straw. It was time to finish the errand that he had come on so that he could return to the town house. He recalled that he had offered hospitality to the Life Guardsman to whom he had been speaking; but when he looked about for the soldier to give him directions, he did not find him.

The afternoon crept by with almost palpable slowness until Lady Mary received an urgent summons by Lady Cecily's maid. She rushed upstairs to Lady Cecily's bedroom and saw instantly that the maidservant had not been mistaken. Lady Cecily lay in bed, her face white and beaded with perspiration. Her eyes were closed. She was breathing abnormally quickly, obviously fighting off pain. Lady Mary felt a sinking sensation. In a lowered voice she told the maid, "Quickly, order someone to go for the physician. And tell them in the kitchen to put water on to boil."

"Yes, my lady," the maid gasped. With a last rolling glance toward her mistress, she rushed from the bedroom.

Lady Mary went up to the bed. She touched her friend's shoulder and said gently, "Cecily, why ever did you not tell me?"

Lady Cecily's eyes flew open. Reflected in the brown depths was relief, shaded by rueful amusement. "I did not want to set about another wild rumor," she said.

Lady Mary spluttered on a genuine laugh. She was amazed by the uplift of her spirits from an exercise that had become a rarity for them all in the last thirty-six hours. "You silly peagoose," she said affectionately. She turned to the washstand and wet a towel in the cool water. Gently she touched it to the prostrate woman's hot face, and Lady Cecily sighed with the relief it brought.

The minutes ticked by on the bedroom clock. The maid returned to whisper that a physician could not be got. Lady Mary's eyes flashed. Thinking swiftly, she ordered a message that a physician or a midwife was needed immediately to be carried to the house she had leased for the Season. If anyone could find the medical help that Lady Cecily required, it would be the housekeeper Berthe, she thought hopefully. Thereafter she set herself to the task of making Lady Cecily as comfortable as it was in her power to do.

The clock ticked on inexorably, marking the shortening intervals. Still there was no word, even as Lady Cecily was rapidly approaching the point where the midwife would be required.

Lady Mary thought that she had never spent a worse vigil than this one. The passing hours were made even less bearable by the continued absence of the earl. For some reason she felt certain that if he had been at the town house and had known of his sister's sudden confinement, there would now be a physician in attendance.

With another quick glance at the clock, Lady Mary hoped that the earl had not fallen afoul of difficulty.

Lady Cecily's thoughts were an echo of her own, for she said with a hint of fretfulness, "I do hope that Robert is safe. He has been gone now for hours."

"I trust that he is," Lady Mary said, outwardly calm. But her eyes did not see the towel that she was once again wringing out, rather she was looking inwardly at all that her imagination was conjuring up to account for the earl's extended absence.

"Mary."

She looked around, startled by the imperative demand inherent in Lady Cecily's normally soft voice.

"Mary, I wish you to tell me the truth," Lady Cecily said. "I have seen—at least, I have thought I have seen—a certain light in your eyes whenever you gaze on my brother. Are you in love with him?"

Lady Mary felt herself flush. Denial was on the point of her tongue. But there was such poignant appeal in Lady Cecily's steady gaze that she could not withstand it. It seemed that this ragged time had torn aside all protective layers and would leave them with only naked honesty. She said in a low voice, "Yes, I am."

Lady Cecily let go a long sigh. "How perfectly wonderful. I am so glad."

"Is it wonderful?" Lady Mary asked, with a sad little smile. She would not say so to Lady Cecily, for her heart could not bear for her to do so, but she still harbored doubts that Lord Kenmare thought of or saw her as anything more than Abigail's mother. He had desired her, true, but she had made herself so very available, and there was no doubt of his virility. Even now she inwardly shivered, feeling the echo of all that he had called up in her.

"Of course it is. Robert has needed someone sincere and sweet and marvelous for a very long time," Lady Cecily said. She saw that her words had not made the impression that she had intended and she realized the reason. "Mary, he cares deeply for you. I know that he does."

"Perhaps." Lady Mary bent her attention once more to her

task of wiping the perspiration from Lady Cecily's brow, making it obvious that she preferred to leave the topic behind. But she could not so easily turn aside her own thoughts.

The pulse beat dully in her throat at the thought that Lord Kenmare might care something for her, but she shook her head. She thought that she knew better than Lady Cecily the truth of the matter. She had seen warmth and friendliness in Lord Kenmare's eyes and he had always shown her the greatest consideration. He had made quite plain that he wanted her physically. But not once had he ever given any sign that his emotions ran deeper. Oh, perhaps, when he had kissed her fingers earlier that day, she had been positive of seeing more. But her certainty had faded, until now she questioned that she had really seen anything at all in the earl's eyes.

Tears threatened to close her throat, and she swallowed, dismayed by her own lack of stoicism. She was more worn down than even she had suspected.

Lady Cecily bit off a sharp exclamation and doubled with the pain of birth. Lady Mary forgot herself then, because events were suddenly escalating. After a swift assessment, she called to the hovering maid and issued a series of rapid orders even as she began rolling up her sleeves.

When Lord Kenmare entered the house he was immediately accosted by Lady Mary. She greeted him with outstretched hands, and when he took hold of them, she pressed his fingers. "Thank God! We heard that the French were in the town. I . . . we feared that you might have come into some jeopardy," she stammered.

Lord Kenmare smiled warmly at her. "I am grateful for your concern, my lady. As it turns out, some of the French are indeed in town, but as prisoners under the escort of our fine dragoons."

"But this is marvelous news!" Lady Mary exclaimed, color flying to her cheeks with her excitement. "Surely that must mean that it is almost over and we have carried the day."

"I wish that were so, but I fear that the end of the tale is still to be worked out," Lord Kenmare said. He realized that he was still holding her hands in his and he felt all sorts of fool.

She must think him the most graceless idiot alive, he thought, and awkwardly stepped back from her.

Lady Mary felt the stiltedness of his movement and she flushed. Obviously she had discomfited him by clinging to him in such an ungenteel fashion. With trembling fingers she smoothed her skirt to cover her discomposure. "I . . . I have news for you, my lord. You have become the uncle of a fine lusty boy," she said.

"What?" The earl stared hard at her in mingled disbelief and gladness. He took a hasty step and caught her elbows. "My lady, is it true? My God! And Cecily—is she . . . ?"

Lady Mary laughed at his agitation. "Yes, it is indeed true. Lady Cecily is quite well and she is asleep now. If you like, you may look in on them both."

The earl let her go and he loosened his cravat slightly. He had a somewhat dazed expression on his face. "No, no, I shall not disturb them. But when? I was gone only a few hours."

Lady Mary went to the decanter to pour a glass of wine, which she offered to him. "Lady Cecily was apparently feeling some discomfort for a little time before your departure, but she did not wish to spread what could possibly be another false alarm. She said that there had been too many of those in recent days."

Lord Kenmare accepted the glass of wine and laughed. "That is just like her. What an idiot Cecily is," he said in a tone of deep affection.

"Precisely so," Lady Mary said, smiling at him. "I sent immediately for a midwife, of course, and the rest of it I shall leave to your imagination."

Lord Kenmare eyed her appreciatively. "I am deeply grateful to be spared the details, ma'am. My stomach is not of the stoutest order, as you have so shrewdly guessed."

Lady Mary's eyes laughed at him. "I was certain of it, my lord."

After a few more words the earl went upstairs to visit his sister. He found her reclining tiredly in bed on her side, protectively curled about a small bundle. He quietly congratulated her, half-fearing that his presence would waken his tiny nephew.

Lady Cecily was glad of his company and asked that he stay for a few moments. As they talked, Lord Kenmare learned that Lady Mary had delivered the baby herself just as the midwife had arrived. "My God, but she is an amazing woman," he said, awed.

"Yes, she is. You would be a fool to allow her to get away, Robert," Lady Cecily said. She smiled at her brother's sudden glowering frown. "I have hinted to her that you are not precisely indifferent toward her."

The earl gaped at her. "Are you mad, Cecily? Whatever possessed you to do such a thing?"

"Blame it upon the extremity of the moment," Lady Cecily said flippantly. She sobered immediately when she saw how much she had distressed him. "Pray do not look so anxious, Robert. Mary is very much in love with you, you know. There, I have given away her secret, which is very bad of me, but I am out of all patience with both of you for not knowing what is for the best."

Lord Kenmare laughed grimly. "Another of your harebrained attempts to decide the fates, Cecy? I pity myself far less than that gallant unsuspecting lady. She is not so used to your little exaggerations as I."

"No such thing. It is as I have told you, Robert. She could not lie to me at such a moment," Lady Cecily said, complacently, glancing down at her small son. "I refuse to skirmish with you, Robert, so you might as well go sulk somewhere else."

Lord Kenmare gave a reluctant laugh. "Very well, you shall have it your way. But I warn you, I shall be extremely ill-tempered if I learn that your thoughtlessness has led to hurt for Lady Mary." Lady Cecily only smiled at him. He grunted and left her then to proud contemplation of her new son.

26

SUNDAY NIGHT was bitterly cold. Too exhausted to care, the Earl of Kenmare lay down on top of his bed without undressing and slept soundly until four o'clock A.M. Upon waking, he went immediately to the front windows to see what was passing in the park. He had the satisfaction of seeing baggage and soldiers still moving toward the field of battle, which he considered very favorable.

With renewed energy he called his valet to him and set about the task of peeling off his rumpled clothing, bathing, and getting dressed again in riding coat and breeches. Afterward he went downstairs and breakfasted in solitary, none of the rest of the household being yet up. He loitered about the house until nearly six o'clock before he decided to ride toward the field of battle and gather what news he could. He left a message for the butler to relay to the ladies so that they would not be made unduly anxious by his absence, and he asked that preparations for leaving Brussels wait against his return.

Astride his gelding, Lord Kenmare had not proceeded far when he chanced to see Mr. Creevey, and he stopped to speak to the gentleman. He reached down to catch the other gentleman's hand. "Good morning, sir. Have you any news?"

Mr. Creevey's expression was somewhat strange and there was an odd light in his eyes. He wrung the earl's hand. "Aye, my lord! I have just come from the Marquis Juarenais's. He has told me that the French are defeated and have fled in great confusion." He pulled out a handkerchief to wipe his brow. "Pray excuse me, my lord. My feelings so overwhelm me that I hardly know if I am standing on my head or my heels."

"It is certain?" Lord Kenmare asked sharply, his heart pounding.

"Indeed, that is just what I asked of the marquis. He was

asleep when Madame Juarenais took me to him to hear the news from his own lips. When he awoke and saw me by his bedside in doubt of the truth of the good news, he almost began to doubt himself. But then he recollected and it was all quite right,'' Mr. Creevey said. ''General Sir Charles Alten, who had commanded the Hanoverians, was brought in late at night, very badly wounded. One of his officers, who was on the field about eight o'clock last night when the French gave way and who had gone on with the Duke of Wellington in the pursuit as far as Nivelles, brought in this intelligence to Alten about three o'clock this morning, knowing that his general would wish to hear it.''

''It is wonderful news,'' Lord Kenmare said hoarsely, hardly aware that he spoke aloud. He felt suffused with the most astonishing emotions and he literally shook with the force of it all. ''My God, what incredible glorious news!'' Moistness gathered in his eyes and he blinked it back. Such was his euphoria that he never thought to be ashamed of his public display of emotion.

Mr. Creevey beamed and tears glinted in his own eyes. ''Indeed it is, my lord! I am sorry, my lord. But I was just on my way to convey the glad tidings to Mrs. Creevey and the Misses Ord, and—''

The earl waved the gentleman on his way. ''I shall not keep you then, Mr. Creevey.'' He sat in deep thought, unaware when Mr. Creevey actually left him. He turned abruptly in the saddle, calling, ''Creevey, if you would be good enough . . .'' But he saw that the portly gentleman was already lost to sight.

Lord Kenmare sat atop his gelding in unusual indecision, torn by his conflicting duties. He should return at once to the town house to impart the glad news to the ladies and the rest of the household. But that would mean the loss of precious time in answering their astonished queries, when the very fiber of his being demanded the action of riding to the battlefield to see for himself and to attempt to locate those closest to them whose fates were still unknown.

A gentleman was hurrying by and the earl suddenly made up his mind. ''You, sir!'' The gentleman stopped, looking around in surprise at the commanding voice. Lord Kenmare stepped his gelding closer to the man. He held up a gold piece. ''I have a message that I need taken to my household, sir. Will you take it for me?"

The gentleman bowed. "Certainly, my lord. But tell me what you wish them to know."

The earl gave him the address of the town house. "Say that the battle is won and that I have gone to find Spence and Wilson-Jones. Have you got it?"

The gentleman assured him that he had, and accepted the gold piece. He stood watching as the earl cantered away in the direction of the field of battle. The gentleman glanced down at the gold piece in his palm. His fingers folded tightly over it. He gave a short, harsh laugh. "The battle is won? Not likely, my lord, not likely at all. I'll not waste time carrying another false rumor when I am leaving this cursed place as quickly as I can." He started away out of the park, in quite a different direction from the Earl of Kenmare's town house.

There was shouting and running in the streets. In the bedroom, Lady Mary and Abigail started up, the color driven from their faces, and they ran to the window. A multitude of persons milled aimlessly about, clutching whoever was around and shouting with excitement, some with tears streaming down their faces as they laughed and cried together.

"I distinctly heard someone shout 'Boney's beat!' " Abigail exclaimed wonderingly.

"Oh, can it be?" Lady Cecily breathed. She cast a glance down at the tiny body nestled close to her breast. She would have gotten up from her bed and gone to the window herself but for her sleeping infant.

Below the window, a party of wounded Highlanders who had obviously made their way on foot from the field of battle were shouting with the most vociferous demonstrations of joy. Those who had use of their arms threw their Highland bonnets into the air, calling out in broad Scotch accents, "Boney's beat! Boney's beat! Huzza! Huzza! Boney's beat!"

Lady Mary felt her pulse fluttering in her throat. She turned away from the window and practically ran toward the door of the sitting room. "I am going down."

"And I!" Abigail said. Not waiting for her mother's permission, she ran ahead.

Lady Mary paused only fractionally, her eyes on Lady Cecily's anxious expression. "I shall return at once," she promised.

"Thank you, Mary," Lady Cecily said fervently.

Lady Mary left the bedroom. Swiftly, without pausing for shawl or bonnet, she went downstairs. Every door stood open, every room was deserted of servants, and she experienced a curious sense of *déjà vu*. But now the roar outside the open street door was not edged with fear, but instead sounded with hysterical joy.

Lady Mary's heart pounded as she stepped out onto the steps. The rejoicings and acclamations deafened her. To her dazed eyes it seemed that the voluble Belgians had gone mad, pumping one another's hands and hugging all the while as they cried out joyfully. They literally danced in the street. The British, though not as loud in expressing their extreme feelings of triumph and heartfelt gratitude, had nevertheless put aside their native reserve so that each greeted his or her neighbor with fervent exclamations.

The Highlanders continued to throw up their bonnets and shout. Their tumultuous joy attracted round them a number of old Flemish women who were extremely curious to know the cause of this uproar and kept gabbling to the soldiers of their own tongue. One of them seized a Highlander by the coat, pulling at it and making the most ludicrous gestures imaginable to induce him to attend to her. The Highlander, forgetting in his transport that the old woman did not understand English, kept shouting that "Boney was beat and running away ta his ain country as fast he could go."

At any other time, Lady Mary would have laughed to see the old Flemish woman holding fast to the soldier, shrugging up her shoulders, and making absurd grimaces while the Highlander roared at her, "Dinna ye ken that Boney's beat—what, are ye deaf? I say Boney's beat, woman!"

Abigail appeared beside Lady Mary, seized her hands. Tears streamed down her radiant face. "Mama! It is true! It is true! We have beaten Bonaparte!"

Lady Mary was too dazed to absorb it. "Is it quite, quite true?"

A complete stranger overheard her and laughed uproariously even as tears streamed down his heavily jowled cheeks. "Indeed, madam! It is a glorious day. The allies have gained a complete victory. The French are defeated, routed, dispersed!" He waved his arms for emphasis. "They have fled from the battle, pursued by our conquering troops."

Lady Mary could not speak for the closing of her throat. She felt bombarded by the welter of emotions—triumph, sorrow, anxiety, and gratitude. The war was over at last, at a great horrible cost that must still be reckoned.

She still did not know the fate of her son.

"But the war is over," she repeated.

"Yes, Mama, yes!" Abigail exclaimed, laughing.

"I must go up at once to Lady Cecily," Lady Mary exclaimed. Her pale cheeks were rose with excitement and her gray eyes blazed with the full light of joy.

"We shall go up together," Abigail said, catching her mother's hand in hers. "I cannot wait to see her face, or Bruce's, or the rest, at such great wonderful news!"

"Nor I!" Lady Mary said. But curiously enough, it was not Lady Cecily, whom had grown to be so dear a friend, that she desired most in the world to share this moment with, but rather Robert, the Earl of Kenmare.

27

THE ROAD between Brussels and Waterloo ran through the Forest of Soignies and was completely confined on either side by trees. The earl quickly found his gelding's progress slowed to a crawl as he maneuvered the road's choked condition.

The road was covered with broken and overturned wagons, heaps of abandoned baggage, dead horses, and terrified people.

In some places horses, wagons, and all were driven over high banks by the roadside in order to clear a passage. Those behind attempted to get past those before. Officers' servants struggled to secure their master's baggage; panic-stricken people forced their way over every obstacle with the desperation of fear.

The confusion combined with the quantity of rain during the past three days had made the road nearly impassable. Lord Kenmare realized that it was impossible for the newly wounded to be brought in from the field. Grim-faced, he set himself to the monumental task of getting himself and his horse threaded through the melee in one piece. He had to get to the battlefield, for he knew as certainly as he breathed that that must be where he would find the two men for whom he was searching.

It was hours later when at last he emerged from beyond the forest onto the plain. He yanked up his reins, thunderstruck and shaken to the bone by the horror of what he saw. Only days before there had been tall cornfields waving in the warm wind as far as the eye could see. Now the corn was broken and trampled into the mud. The dead lying there among the ruins of nature could not be numbered. The mangled and lifeless bodies were stripped of everything of the smallest value.

Near a hedge that had been completely trodden down, where the fighting had been particularly severe and the carnage dreadful, huge pits were filled with hundreds of dead, British and French alike. Lord Kenmare averted his eyes and kicked his horse forward once more, but the images of the massive grave remained with him and he knew with sickened certainty that he would never forget.

Besides the tremendous pits, the dead were being burnt in different places, and their ashes, mingled with the dust, were being scattered over the field. A wayward breeze brought the tainted smoke to Lord Kenmare, and he gagged. Clenching his jaw, he rode on slowly, looking for the particular regimental uniforms that he had come to find.

Slowly, slowly, Lord Kenmare became aware that here and there life still breathed among the dead. He had been so stricken with horror that he had seen the entire field of battle as one vast charnel pile of death, not realizing that the wounded lay there as well. But the occasional groans or the harsh breathing that he heard as he traveled past at last penetrated to his consciousness.

That was perhaps the most affecting thing of all, to see those wounded lying wherever they had fallen or had been able to crawl. Half-crazed with pain, they had endured the driving rain and now a day of blazing heat was upon them. They lay without succor, without food or drink, and with little hope of regaining such common necessities.

It was when Lord Kenmare had almost despaired of finding what he sought that he came across a wounded man in a torn and filthy uniform barely recognizable as that of the Fifth Division. The soldier did not look up when the gelding's shadow fell across him, but instead continued to sit on the ground and hold his comrade's lifeless hand in his own.

"He just now sighed and went away," he said.

The unexpected sound of the soldier's roughened voice startled Lord Kenmare. He looked sharply from the soldier's lowered head to the face of the dead man and he realized what the soldier had meant. "I am so very sorry," he said inadequately.

The soldier raised his head and tears were coursing down his face. "We both knew that it was hopeless for him. But I couldn't very well leave him alone, could I?"

Lord Kenmare fought the tightening of his own throat. "No, you couldn't do that. You've been a damn fine friend."

The soldier nodded gravely, returning his attention to his dead comrade. "Yes. That is what he said."

A silence fell. The gelding eventually began to become restless and pawed the ground. Lord Kenmare corrected his mount with a slight pressure of the reins. He detested himself for breaking into the wounded soldier's private vigil of grief, but nevertheless he said quietly, "I am seeking two others of the Fifth—Captain Wilson-Jones and an ensign by the name of William Spence."

The soldier did not look up, nor did he give any other indication that he had heard. Lord Kenmare, reflecting with pity that the man had gone demented, was on the point of giving up and going on when he was surprised once more by the soldier's voice. "Wilson-Jones, yes. I saw him. Wounded in the thigh, he was, but still on his feet when the French broke and ran. Likely joined the pursuit."

"And Spence?" Lord Kenmare asked quickly. But his luck had played out. The soldier never said another word to him.

Again Lord Kenmare was faced with an unpleasant choice.

He surveyed the battlefield. Other figures moved about among the dead and wounded, seeking those they knew or attempting to offer aid to those still living. He had been astoundingly naive to take on the task of finding two men among so many, but now through an incredible piece of luck he at least knew that Wilson-Jones had probably survived. He had the choice of remaining to search for Lady Mary's son or going on to trace the path of the scattered armies in hopes of finding his brother-in-law, who could very possibly tell him what he wanted to know about William Spence.

The reluctant decision made, Lord Kenmare stepped down from his horse. He was careful to keep the reins firmly in hand, as the gelding had exhibited a reluctance to remain amid the smell of death. The earl began the slow progress of searching the area around the soldier he had spoken with in an ever-widening ragged circle. This was where the Fifth Division had made its fight and this was where he would find Ensign William Spence if the boy had not survived. His mind quickly became numbed to the necessary task of turning over sprawled bodies so that he could see the dead faces.

The sun was high in the sky and brutally hot when he finally gave up. Lord Kenmare gathered the reins in his hand, mounted, and turned his gelding in the direction of the Forest of Soignies.

He squared his shoulders, attempting to free himself of the queer feeling of failure that had dropped over him. But he could not rid himself of it. Though he was relieved not to have found William Spence's body, he was also all too aware that in the carnage he might have overlooked the boy, who could have been too gravely wounded to call out, or that the boy might have been one of those already tossed into the pits.

The memory of Lady Mary's anxious and yet hopeful eyes continued to haunt him. He had to continue looking, for he felt the greatest reluctance to return to the town house without something definite to relate to Lady Mary. The earl decided that his only course now was to make a pilgrimage to every hospital tent and every other gathering place of the wounded, in hopes of discovering the fate of one lone soldier among so many.

Once free of the carnage of mingled living and dead, he set himself to the difficult task of making his way safely through to Brussels.

28

THE Earl of Kenmare went into the drawing-room, where he had been told he would find Lady Mary. She looked up and an unmistakable light leapt to her eyes. She rose from the settee to meet him. "My lord! You are back," she said with a warm smile. As she looked into his face, her own expression abruptly altered. "My lord, what has occurred?"

Lord Kenmare clasped her hands gently between his. "I have come to tell you of William, my dear lady."

The color drained from Lady Mary's face, leaving her chalk white. In a hoarsened voice she said, "Tell me quickly! Is William dead?"

The earl felt compassion as he looked into her eyes. "I am sorry, my lady," he said gently. "I have not been able to find him, nor any word of him. I very much fear that he must be."

Lady Mary swayed, blindly throwing out her free hand in denial. Even as Lord Kenmare exclaimed and moved to catch her, she fainted dead away. She lay limply in his arms, her face icy when he touched her skin, and she did not rouse when he sharply called her name.

The earl called for assistance. The butler immediately entered the drawing room, alarmed by the sharp summons. He was appalled at sight of the senseless lady in his master's embrace. "My lord! What can I do?"

Lord Kenmare shot swift orders for Lady Mary's maid to be alerted. He gathered Lady Mary up in his arms and carried her upstairs to her bedroom. He laid her gently on the bed and straightened, pausing to look down at her.

She appeared so white, so frail, to have born the burdens that had assailed her over the last tumultuous days. But he knew the steel that lay beneath that exterior. At least, he thought he had known it. He had counted upon Lady Mary's ongoing strength to carry her past the news of William's probable death. Instead his thoughtlessness had completely devastated her. His fists clenched in impotent helplessness.

The maid entered then. "My lord! I am told that my mistress has fainted. Why, she has never done so before!" the woman exclaimed, staring in alarm at her still, pale mistress.

"Lady Mary has sustained a grievous shock," Lord Kenmare said.

The maid's eyes widened in horrified comprehension. She put one hand to her mouth. "Never tell me that young Master William is dead!"

The earl nodded. "I very much fear so. Pray see to your mistress's comfort. I shall send for a physician."

He swung around on his heel and left the bedroom. He was shaking in reaction. Intolerable to be so much in love with a woman and yet be unable to tell her so for fear of her rejection. All he had been able to do was to give her unbearable news, he thought, despairing that Lady Mary would ever forgive him.

Lady Mary did not regain consciousness.

The thoroughly frightened maid relayed the fact to the earl. Lord Kenmare was almost beside himself with alarm. He had sent for a physician to come from one of the hospitals set up in the town, but his messenger was told over and over again that unfortunately there were none available to spare for any but the direst emergencies. "By God, I shall make it known that this is an emergency of the highest order!" he vowed, setting off himself to dragoon the first physician that he could find.

He returned much later with a physician. The physician was hollow-eyed from lack of sleep and his mouth seemed permanently drawn tight because of the horrible things that he had seen and had to do among the wounded. He was brusque to the point of rudeness to be hauled away from his innumerable patients only to see to a foolish lady's fainting spell. But once he learned that Lady Mary had not wakened from her swoon, he became as attentive as the earl could wish.

While Lord Kenmare paced the hall outside the bedroom, the physician examined Lady Mary. She stirred faintly and murmured something incoherent at his touch and the sound of his voice, but she did not waken from her stupor.

The physician came out of the bedroom with a frown carved deep in his face. He gently closed the door, ignoring the earl's impatient query until he had done so. Lord Kenmare ushered him into his own apartment so that they could speak privately. The physician glanced at the earl. "The lady has obviously suffered a most severe shock. What happened?"

Lord Kenmare ran a shaking hand through his hair. "I informed Lady Mary that I believed her son to be dead. I had no notion what the news would do to her. She has been such a constant steadying influence upon us all throughout everything, and I thought her strength sufficient to bear . . . My God, what have I done?" He dropped into a chair and covered his face with his hands.

The physician said in a hard voice, "It will hardly mend matters for you to fall to pieces, my lord."

The earl straightened as though suddenly cut by a whip. His eyes blazed. "I assure you that you need not concern yourself on my behalf, sir!" he said coldly.

"Good." The physician smiled slightly. "I apologize for my roughness, my lord. I felt it was required by the moment. I have seen so much true suffering that I have little sympathy left for unavailing guilt. As for the lady, she will take no real hurt from this long sleep of hers. If she is like so many others who have been out tending the wounded, I suspect that her ladyship wore herself to the bone caring for others while criminally neglecting herself. Her nerves must already have been stretched taut when she was given the sad news of her son. I am not at all surprised by her collapse."

"Then she will recover?" Lord Kenmare's voice had quickened, his expression showing the fear that he felt he hoped for too much.

"I should rather think so. Give orders that she is to be kept warm, and have someone ply her as well as they are able with drink and broth. Her ladyship will almost certainly waken with a sense of wonderment at all the fuss."

The earl seized the man's hand and pumped it, all his anger dissolved. "Thank you, sir."

"Yes . . . well, I must be going. I have been away from hospital too long as it is." The physician turned toward the door, the earl beside him, but he suddenly swayed. He caught himself with a hand on the back of a chair.

Lord Kenmare took hold of the physician's arm, immediately perceiving that the man was done in. "You are in no shape for it. Why, you are dead on your feet. I will have supper brought to you and you will rest here before you return to that charnal work of yours."

The physician attempted to shake himself free, protesting, "But I must go. There are lives depending upon me."

"Yes, and how much good do you think you will be, unable even to walk across the room without rolling like a drunken sailor?" Lord Kenmare asked, deliberately brutal. He ignored the blaze of anger in the physician's eyes as he maneuvered the man to a settee, at the same time calling for a servant. When a footman appeared, he gave rapid orders for sandwiches and cider to be brought in.

"This is unnecessary, my lord," the physician said stiffly. Despite himself, he accepted the small amount of brandy that the earl poured for him. It burned his throat and he coughed, but the warming of his insides from the liquor was very pleasant.

"Indeed, but then, we aristocrats are known to be a whimsical and stubborn lot, and it is far better to humor us, you know," Lord Kenmare said. The supper was brought in and placed before the physician, who reluctantly picked up one of the beef sandwiches. Even as he bit into it, he eyed his arbitrary host with hostility and resentment.

Lord Kenmare remained in the sitting room to see that the physician did not leave before he had eaten, and when the physician was finished, he told the footman who came to remove the tray that he wished extra sandwiches made up and wrapped for the physician to take away with him. "I shall not be present to be certain that you consume your share, but at least I shall have the gratification of knowing that your colleagues will not starve," he said.

The physician had leaned back against the settee. He chuckled tiredly at the earl's quip. "Indeed, my lord, I will be certain that your gracious hospitality will be spread as far as it will stretch." He was overtaken by a wide yawn, and he apologized. "I have been working on the wounded since the first were brought in, and the trickle that became a stream is now a flood. At six o'clock each morning I have taken the knife in my hand and continued incessantly at work till seven in the evening. Of course, this evening you appeared to drag me off before I was quite done." The last was said with the faintest note of disgruntlement, but apparently was not enough to rouse the earl's ire. The physician gave the veriest flicker of a smile. "I suppose that I must thank you for that small inconvenience, my lord," he said, raising his glass slightly in acknowledgment.

Lord Kenmare inclined his head. He observed that the physician still sat in a leaning posture against the settee back, and he thought that it would not take much before the man was asleep. "I shall go see about those sandwiches so that you may be on your way. Pray excuse me for a moment, sir," he said, and exited the sitting room.

The physician closed his eyes for a moment. It was such a luxury to relax, even for a moment. Just for a moment, he thought drowsily. Just until his lordship returned. The hand that still clasped the glass of cider dregs wavered and sank to rest upon his stomach. Seconds later a snore issued from his half-open mouth.

Lord Kenmare reentered the sitting room, the package of wrapped sandwiches in his hands. He took in the situation at a glance. Setting aside the sandwiches, he took the glass away and eased the physician into a reclining position on the settee. He threw a cover over the sleeping man and left the room.

The earl gave orders that the physician was not to be disturbed and that he himself would waken the gentleman. He glanced down at the package of sandwiches that he had retrieved on his way out of the sitting room. He gave them over to a footman. "I shall give these into your care, I think. Take them to the fellows in the garden house. They'll not mind the additional meal."

Three hours later Lord Kenmare returned to the sitting room. It had grown dark and the room was lighted only by the fire in the grate. He quietly ordered the candles be lit, and, seeing that the physician still lay as one dead, he seated himself nearby and unfolded a newspaper to read.

Nearly another hour passed before the physician at last opened his eyes. He blinked, disoriented by his unfamiliar surroundings. Recollection came quickly. Abruptly he sat up. His angry gaze fell on the earl, who was calmly regarding him over the edge of the newspaper. "*You*, my lord!"

The earl's mouth twisted at the loathing in the man's voice. "Yes, it is I," he agreed. He set aside the newspaper. "How do you feel?"

"How do I feel? How do I *feel*? I have been kidnapped, sir! How should I feel?" the physician spluttered.

"Perhaps you might tell me," Lord Kenmare said, interested.

The physican opened his mouth, preparing to deliver a blistering retort, but a strange look suddenly passed over his face. He said slowly, wonderingly, "I feel alive." He gl anced at his host again and frowned. "I should take you thoroughly to task, my lord. But I find instead that I am grateful to you for your perception of my condition."

Lord Kenmare bowed from the waist. "I accept your apology, sir."

The physician threw him a reluctant grin as he swung his feet to the carpet. "How long have I slept, sir?"

The earl glanced unconcernedly at the clock on the mantel. "It was just under four hours," he said, rising from his chair. He ignored the physician's dismayed exclamation and indicated the gentleman's black bag. "I hope that you are sufficiently alert, doctor, for I have patients for you to see before you return to hospital."

The physician stood up and bowed. "I am naturally at your service, my lord," he said with the quirk of a smile. He took up his bag and followed the earl out of the sitting room.

Lord Kenmare showed the physician into Lady Cecily's bedroom and introduced him. "My sister, Lady Cecily Wilson-Jones, and her three-day-old son, James Arnold Robert Wilson-Jones."

"How do you do, sir?" Lady Cecily asked, holding out her hand in correct fashion even as she threw a mischievous glance toward her brother. "My brother tells me that you saw Lady Mary earlier. How was she?"

"Lady Mary is apparently suffering from nervous shock, my lady, but it is my opinion that she will completely recover," the physician said.

"I am so glad," Lady Cecily said, smiling.

The physician examined both mother and child, his hard mouth softening in the presence of new vigorous life amidst the horrific consequences of war. He pronounced them both healthy and thriving and complimented the attending physician for a job well done.

"I shall relay your gracious opinion to Lady Mary and the two maids who assisted her," Lady Cecily said gravely.

The physician shot a surprised look at her. He grunted, and after a few additional words of encouragement and advice, took his leave of Lady Cecily.

Lord Kenmare took him next to see Captain McInnes. Abigail was discovered to be sitting at the young soldier's bedside, reading aloud to him. At the gentlemen's entrance, she leapt up, flushing. She well knew that it was not proper for her to be alone with the young Scot. But the earl's manner so reassured her that she quickly regained her countenance, even deciding to remain during the physician's examination of the wound.

The physician surveyed the cleanliness of the area and the beginning of neat healing before he redressed the wound. "A most skillful job," he remarked. "So many I see go instantly to gangrene for lack of proper care."

"If it had not been for Mama, the gangrene would have killed Captain McInnes," Abigail said proudly.

"Aye, I owe my very life to the kind lady," Captain McInnes said, nodding.

The physician looked to the earl for explanation, suspecting that he was being made game of. Lord Kenmare smiled slightly at the man's questioning expression. "Lady Mary took it upon herself to clean the wound, while I had the unpleasant task of holding down your young friend during the whole of it," he said. He thoughtfully rubbed his chin. "The ungateful wretch had the audacity to plant me a regular flush hit."

Captain McInnes laughingly protested, "Now, sir, I have apologized most profoundly for my lack of proper respect."

"So you did," Lord Kenmare agreed, grinning at him.

When the earl and the physician had left Abigail and her swain to their book, Lord Kenmare ushered the physician in to visit the officers ensconced in the two spare rooms, before leading him back downstairs and outside to take a peek in the garden house at the wounded soldiers that were bivouacked there. After the tour was done, the physician said, "Lady Mary is a most remarkable woman."

"Yes, she is," Lord Kenmare said quietly. The gentlemen returned to the house and he saw the man to the front door.

When a footman handed the physician a covered basket, he glanced inquiringly at the earl. "What is this, my lord?"

"Some cheeses and bread and a couple of bottles of good wine. You must keep up the habit of eating, doctor," Lord Kenmare said.

The physician laughed, and for once his expression was totally devoid of its underlying tired bitterness. "I thank you most sincerely, my lord. I shall share these with my poor colleagues, who must be cursing my very existence for my shameful desertion of them these last hours."

"Doctor, whenever you should wish it, there are a meal and a bed for you or any other physicians," the earl said. He grinned suddenly. "My household would naturally benefit greatly from regular medical expertise, and I prefer that those doctors be alert."

The physician smiled. "Thank you, my lord. I shall relay your handsome offer of hospitality, and its attendant pleasant conditions. I am certain that it will prove too great a temptation for most of us to resist."

Lord Kenmare offered his hand, and the physician, recovering from his surprise to be treated thus as a social equal, shook hands with him. Then he left and the earl turned back into the house.

After a moment of reflection Lord Kenmare went upstairs to Lady Mary's bedroom. He gave a quiet command to the maid, scandalizing the woman by his unorthodox suggestion. But she was too exhausted to object overstrenuously, having sat beside her motionless mistress for too many hours.

The maid left to go to bed, leaving the earl to sit with Lady Mary. She assuaged her conscience with the reflection that what no one knew would not hurt her mistress's reputation. It was such queer times that it most likely would not matter in any event, she thought.

Lord Kenmare saw to the fire. Then he seated himself in the chair that the maid had vacated. Thus it was that his was the first face that Lady Mary saw when she at last slowly opened her eyes.

"My lord." Her voice was faint but firm.

He took her hand and folded it gently in his own. He said softly, "Yes, I am here."

Greater awareness entered her gray eyes. "My lord, was it true? About William, I mean?" she asked lowly.

The earl's expression altered. There was almost a flicker of fear in his eyes. "I cannot lie to you, my lady. It was true."

"Yes, of course it was." She closed her eyes. Before he could panic, she sighed and raised her lids so that she could look at him. "I had so hoped it was all a nightmare. But it is not, is it? The war, the awful cannonade sounding on forever, the wounded and dying in the streets. Abigail's Scot and Michele's fiancé and all the others. And . . . and my William."

She started to cry in great heaving gasps. Lord Kenmare raised her from her pillows and crushed her against him.

The pain inside him was nearly impossible to bear as he listened to her pitiful sobs. He could feel her slight body racked by deep shudders, and he tightened his arms about her, rocking her slightly as one would a child that had cried out in the night. He spoke to her, not really realizing what it was he was saying. "Oh, my dear. My dear love. If only I could change it all. If only I could love you and protect you from all the unhappiness. Oh, Mary, don't cry."

But she was heedless of anything other than her sharp loss.

When at last her wild grief abated, he eased her back down onto her pillows. Lord Kenmare reached over to the bedside table to pour water from a pitcher into the waiting bowl and to wet one of the neatly folded cloths that had been placed there. With the damp cloth he gently wiped her face clean. He gave his own handkerchief to her to blow her nose, and once these simple ablutions were done, he smiled at her and said, "I suppose I must let you rest now." He made to rise, meaning to call back her maid.

"Robert!" She caught his hand.

He looked down at her, startled alike by her use of his Christian name and the desperate appeal in her hold of his fingers. "Why, whatever is it, my lady?"

"Pray do not leave me. Not just yet," she begged. Her eyes darted about the quiet room and returned to his face. "You will think me nonsensical. I . . . I am a bit fearful of the shadows tonight, you see."

"Of course I shall stay," Lord Kenmare said quietly. He settled himself again in the chair and held her hand while she fell asleep. Though she slept, he never once thought of letting go her hand.

He watched the firelight play across her drowsing face and he must have dozed a little himself, because he was roused by the maid's touch at his shoulder. He blinked up at the woman, then looked quickly down at Lady Mary. Her face was serene in repose, and beneath the coverlet her breast rose and fell rhythmically.

"I shall sit with her ladyship now, my lord," the maid whispered.

He nodded. He rose stiffly from the chair and went away to his own bedroom.

29

ABIGAIL was naturally alarmed and upset by her mother's collapse. She was only partially soothed by hearing from her mother's maid that Lady Mary seemed to be resting. She looked to the Earl of Kenmare for an explanation, but until the following morning he completely forgot her request to speak with him. When he recalled it, he asked that Abigail join him in the study downstairs.

Abigail came in and seated herself, looking up at him rather anxiously. "Pray, what did the physician say about my mother?"

Lord Kenmare sat down on the edge of the desk. "He said that Lady Mary is suffering a nervous collapse, but with proper rest and care he expected her to recover completely."

Abigail's expression reflected her relief. "I thought it must be something of the sort. Mama always appears so strong and capable. Others grow used to relying upon her to an extraordinary measure, but she never complains. But I know that this hideous war, and especially William's continued absence, have placed a dire strain upon her spirit."

Lord Kenmare sighed. "Abigail, possibly I should speak to you about your brother."

"Yes, my lord?" She looked up with a clear, steady gaze.

Lord Kenmare went to sit with her on the settee. He took her hand, saying gravely, "What I must say is difficult." He felt her stiffen beside him. "Abigail, I have been unable to locate William or, indeed, any word of him. It is as though he has dropped off the edge of the world."

"You mean that you believe he is dead." Abigail made a flat statement of it, her voice tight.

"I very much fear that may be the truth of it," Lord Kenmare said very gently.

"You told Mama this, didn't you?" Abigail's eyes glittered with anger and something else. She pulled her hand free of his. "I shall not believe it, do you hear? I shall not believe it until I have myself seen my brother's lifeless body and laid it in the ground," she said furiously.

"Abby . . . " For the first time he used the diminutive of her name as he reached out to capture her hand once more.

Abigail leapt up, rounding on him. Her hands were doubled into fists held rigid to her sides. "I shall never believe it!"

She whisked herself off to the study and ran blindly up the stairs, not stopping until she had thrown open the door of Captain McInnes's bedroom. She stood just inside, standing stiffly, her breast heaving.

Captain McInnes regarded her in astonishment and alarm, at once perceiving her distress. "Abigail! Why, whatever has occurred, lass?"

Abigail told him in a clipped, staccato fashion what the earl had said. "But I refuse to believe for even one moment that William is dead." Her voice faltered on the last word.

Suddenly her cornflower-blue eyes were awash with tears. "Oh, Bruce!" She rushed across the carpet and threw herself to the floor beside the bed, her arms and head across the coverlet.

"Hush, lass," he murmured comfortingly. With his good arm he drew her up so that she half-reclined against him. "We will keep the faith for your brother for a wee bit longer."

After luncheon, Lord Kenmare sent up an inquiry asking if he might visit with Lady Mary in her sitting room later that day. He was told to his surprise that her ladyship had requested that she have no visitors. "Her ladyship is not wanting to see anyone, my lord. My lady told me all quiet-like that she wished to be alone for a time," the maid said. Beatrice's expression was troubled. "She has refused already to see Miss Abigail, and now she has locked the door even against me."

"What the devil!" Lord Kenmare exclaimed, astonished and disturbed. This behavior was not characteristic of the brave, practical lady that he had learned to love. He was on the point of going upstairs to knock at her door himself when he realized how odd that would look to the household. Lady Mary Spence was a guest in the house, and not even a relative. He could not demand entrance to her rooms. ''I suppose that we must bow to her ladyship's wishes and grant her the privacy that she has requested,'' he said.

When he was relating the incident later to Lady Cecily, she shook her head. ''It is only to be expected, of course.''

Lord Kenmare looked at his sister in frowning surprise. ''What do you mean, Cecily?''

''Why, don't you see, Robert? Mary has been such a rock through the whole horrid affair. She carried us all, and not once did she allow herself to burden others with her own fears. Pray, do you actually expect her to reverse herself now and burden us with her grief?''

Lord Kenmare sighed. He drew a hand through his thick hair. ''Yes, I see. It would not be like her to do so, would it? But to deny admittance to her daughter—that is what has so disturbed me. She has always been available to Abigail. My lord, did you see the girl's face at luncheon? She has been crying her eyes out.''

''Perhaps Lady Mary is aware that Abigail has someone else whom she may turn to now beside herself,'' Lady Cecily suggested.

Lord Kenmare lifted a dark brow, his blue eyes quizzical. ''Indeed! I suppose you are referring to Captain McInnes.''

''Exactly so.'' Lady Cecily nodded. She smiled at her brother's continued frown. ''Come, Robert. Allow Mary to know what she is doing. She will come around, believe me.''

It was a day and a half later that Lady Mary finally made an appearance in the dining room. The earl was the first to see her paused in the doorway. He got hastily to his feet. ''Lady Mary!''

She entered, pale and composed, and took her usual seat at the table. She did not at first appear to notice the fixed stares of the earl, her daughter, and Captain McInnes, who had also jumped to his feet, and Lady Cecily, or of the butler and footman who stood ready to serve. She placed her napkin on her lap, and only then did she glance around her. She smiled faintly. "I perceive that I have caused some consternation. I do apologize for doing so."

The gentlemen seated themselves again. Abigail reached out and tentatively touched her mother's arm. "Mama? Are you quite all right?"

Lady Mary regarded her daughter. There were shadows in the depths of her gray eyes. "I shall be. But I do not think we shall talk of me this evening. I understand that you and Captain McInnes may have come to an agreement."

Lord Kenmare's brows shot up and he exchanged glances with Lady Cecily. Lady Mary had broached a subject not usually discussed in the presence of persons outside the family, and in the process she had instantly and effectively banished all sympathetic inquiries regarding herself.

Abigail blushed and her eyes flew to the face of the gentleman sitting beside her. "How did you know, Mama?"

"I am not quite so caught up in myself that I do not listen to what Beatrice tells me," Lady Mary said humorously.

"But we only decided this afternoon and never breathed a word to anyone," Abigail said, marveling at how certain and accurate was the servants' grapevine.

Captain McInnes cleared his throat. There was an anxious look in his eyes. "I hope that our decision meets with your approval, my lady."

"I approve most heartily, Captain. I shall at once write the happy news to the viscount and viscountess. Perhaps it will make up a little for what else I must relate to them."

There was a little silence as everyone remembered the earl's somber opinion that William Spence had perished. Abigail broke it, saying brightly, "I should like to be married in London, I think. Grandmama would like it excessively if she could do the thing, of course, and Bruce—Captain McInnes—does not mind a great society wedding."

"Och, no. It is likely the only grand London affair to which I shall ever be invited," Captain McInnes said. There was laughter all around, doing much to lighten the mood of the company again.

"Very well, I shall throw that particular carrot to your grandmother, Abigail. She shall be delighted, naturally," Lady Mary said. She suspected that her daughter and future son-in-law had decided upon this course to save her from having to deal with all the details, and she treasured their generosity toward her.

The evening meal was much livelier than it had been the previous two nights. Lady Mary made an effort to appear her usual self, but she could not quite conceal the distance that she felt from everyone. There was almost a clear wall of glass erected between herself and the others that was strikingly noticeable to those who knew her well and which to others would have seemed like a cloak of hauteur. Nevertheless, the company stayed up late playing cards, and when at last good-nights were said, it was nearly midnight.

Lord Kenmare was not particularly sleepy, and so remained downstairs for a time after the others had all gone up. He stared into the fire, sipping from time to time from a glass of wine.

When he at last made his way up the stairs, it was the small hours of the morning. He dismissed his sleepy valet after the man helped him off with his boots, saying that he would undress himself. The grateful manservant stumbled off to his bed while Lord Kenmare started to divest himself of his coat. He had tossed it and his cravat aside and half-unbuttoned his shirt when he heard a thundering rap on the door downstairs.

Lord Kenmare threw open the window and looked down at the stranger standing on the front steps. When the man moved his head, the moonlight caught his face. Lord Kenmare exclaimed, "Wilson-Jones!"

Major Wilson-Jones tilted back his head at the earl's voice above him. He gave a wide grin. "Open your doors and your cellar, my lord! I am home!"

The earl dropped the window sash and yanked his dressing gown on over his half-buttoned shirt and breeches. He flew downstairs in his stocking feet to the front door, unbolted it, and threw it open. He and Major Wilson-Jones threw their arms about each other, slapping each other's backs, laughing. When they parted, Lord Kenmare grabbed his brother-in-law's hand and gripped it. "My word, it is good to see you, Wilson-Jones. Come in, come in!" He drew his brother-in-law inside and shut the front door.

A sleepy footman had appeared, attired in his nightshirt, its tails hastily thrust into the top of his breeches. "Bring a bottle of the best Bordeaux and food at once for the major," Lord Kenmare instructed him. As the footman hurried away, he urged his brother-in-law into the darkened drawing room. Lord Kenmare lit a match and touched the small flame to a branch of candles.

Major Wilson-Jones had gone to the occasional table to pour himself a brandy. As the earl finished with the candles, he limped toward a wing chair.

Lord Kenmare said in quick concern, "You're wounded. I'll send for a doctor at once."

Wilson-Jones waved aside his lordship's concern as he dropped into the chair. "It is a thigh wound only. It plagues me from lack of attention and overexercise, but it is not a grave wound. Ah, it is deuced wonderful to sink into a chair with cushions! Robert, at this moment the last thing I wish is some impatient physician poking and prodding at my leg." He toasted the earl with his glass and downed the brandy in a single swallow.

The footman entered with a heavily laden tray in his hands and a dusty bottle held securely under his arm. The major's eyes lit up and he straightened from his slouching position. "*That* is what I need. I am famished with hunger and thirst. I've had nothing but a bit of broth and biscuits since leaving the city six days ago."

Lord Kenmare took the bottle from the footman and immediately broke open the seal. He splashed a liberal amount of the Bordeaux into his brother-in-law's held-out glass. He watched as the major threw back his wine. He held up the bottle and said regretfully, "Pity to waste such a fine vintage on a man who would be just as happy with a tankard of bitter."

Major Wilson-Jones grinned as he attacked the rump of beef on the tray. "A sacrifice indeed," he said, and then for some time he was too busy devouring the beef to speak.

Lord Kenmare sat on the arm of a wing chair, swinging his foot. "You've a fine son," he observed in an offhand manner. He was rewarded by his brother-in-law's amazed expression and cessation of chewing.

Major Wilson-Jones swallowed swiftly, nearly choking. "A son, you say? A son!" His eyes took on a bemused expression, then suddenly sharpened again. "And Cecily?"

"She came through her confinement with flying colors," Lord Kenmare said, smiling.

Major Wilson-Jones glanced at the ceiling. "I suppose Cecily and the boy are asleep," he said regretfully.

"Yes, at least for now. The brat invariably tries out his lungs in the early hours, when he so eloquently demands his feedings. You may meet him then," Lord Kenmare said. He regarded the inroads that his brother-in-law had made in the beef and said dryly, "I see that he comes by his appetite honestly."

Major Wilson-Jones laughed. He held out his empty wine-glass. "I shall trouble you for another glass, my lord. I've not yet done, and my throat begs for lubrication!"

"I am entirely at your service, sir," Lord Kenmare said, tilting the bottle over his brother-in-law's glass. He poured some wine for himself. Lifting the glass, he said with a nod, "Your health, Reginald. I am damned glad to see you alive, you know."

"Never more than I am to find myself still living," Major Wilson-Jones said. In between more leisurely mouthfuls of beef and frequent attacks on the bottle of Bordeaux, he described his experiences since marching out of Brussels on the previous Thursday. He had been eighteen hours on horseback, he said, and in that time he had had two horses shot out from under him. When he could not procure another mount, he had taken up a fallen man's sword and fought as a common foot soldier.

"It was a near-run thing, I can tell you; the worst action that I have ever seen," Major Wilson-Jones said somberly. He cracked a huge unintentional yawn.

"I saw the field afterward," Lord Kenmare said grimly, nodding.

There was a short silence while Major Wilson-Jones gazed into the fire. Just when Lord Kenmare began to think that his brother-in-law had become mesmerized by the flames and fallen asleep, Major Wilson-Jones turned his head. Shadows that had nothing to do with the flickering firelight darkened his eyes. "I do not think that I shall ever be able to form an adequate description of that slaughter, or what I felt to see some thousands of wounded wretches, British and French, dying side by side.''

"There are still some alive. Wounded are being brought in even now, days afterward," Lord Kenmare said. He thought how inane he sounded, but there were no adequate words that he could offer to his brother-in-law that could possibly erase that haunted look.

Major Wilson-Jones drained his wineglass again, then stared at it as though seeing it for the first time. "I have no doubt that hundreds who were not discovered when the dead were buried and who were unable to crawl to any habitation must have perished from famine," he said.

Lord Kenmare was wholly sensitive to the aura of pain about his brother-in-law. He wondered as he studied his brooding companion if the kind gentleman of ready laughter that he had once known had perished. Wilson-Jones could not be allowed to submerge himself in such bleak reflections, he thought. Without quite making a conscious decision regarding the matter, he said, "I've a puzzle for you to mull, if you like. An intimate acquaintance of mine has fallen in love with a lady of sterling quality, but he hasn't declared himself to her for fear of having his suit rejected.''

Completely diverted from his black reverie, Major Wilson-Jones stared at his lordship. "You, Robert? Why, who is this paragon who has so tied you in knots? Is she known to me?''

Lord Kenmare frowned at him. "My good man, I did say that it was the dilemma of an intimate acquaintance. But yes, you have met the lady in question.''

Major Wilson-Jones grinned. "Aye, an intimate acquaintance indeed! I never thought to hear of your invincible heart falling again to Cupid's arrow. I suppose you do not intend to tell me the lady's name?''

"Not at all," Lord Kenmare said cheerfully.

"I shall discover it from Cecily, then. You cannot possibly have hidden anything from her eagle eyes." Major Wilson-Jones looked thoughtfully at his lordship. "I suppose that you do not actually wish my advice. But I shall give it to you anyway. My lord, make a clean breast of it all to your lady. Life is too precious to waste it in nonsensical fears." He suddenly cracked another yawn. "Lord, but I am tired." He dropped his head back and in an instant he was asleep.

Lord Kenmare rose to his feet. Quietly he took the wineglass from his brother-in-law's slack fingers. For a long moment he regarded Major Wilson-Jones's haggard face and comatose form. Setting aside the wineglasses, he picked up his brother-in-law's ankles and placed a footstool under his boots. Then he left the drawing room, gently closing the door behind him.

30

THE FOLLOWING morning Major Wilson-Jones limped stiffly out of the drawing room, bleary-eyed and demanding breakfast. Lord Kenmare had persuaded Lady Cecily to come down to the breakfast room for the first time since the birth of the baby. When she heard the major's irascible voice, she paled. Her startled eyes met her brother's laughing gaze for a single second. "Why didn't you tell me?" Then she flew out of the breakfast room, her napkin fluttering to the carpet.

She met Major Wilson-Jones in the entry hall. She threw her arms about his neck, laughing and crying. "Reginald!"

Major Wilson-Jones swung her about in his arms, also laughing.

Lord Kenmare had followed his sister into the hall, flanked by Lady Mary, Abigail, and Captain McInnes. "A fine spectacle indeed!" he said.

From the depth of her husband's arms Lady Cecily looked accusingly at her brother. "You knew! And you never breathed a word to me, when you know how anxious I have been."

"The poor man was dead on his feet. I wished him to have at least one night's peace before he made the acquaintance of his infant son," Lord Kenmare said.

"My son!" Major Wilson-Jones had an appalled expression on his face. "I had actually forgotten." He shot a swift glance down his wife's newly trim figure.

Lady Cecily laughed up at him, a tender light in her eyes. "Shall we go up to see him, my love?"

"I should like that, I think," Major Wilson-Jones said, clearing his throat. Hand in hand, they went up the stairs.

"Wasn't that simply wonderful?" Abigail breathed, glad tears in her eyes for Lady Cecily's happiness.

"Yes. Yes, it was," Lady Mary said quietly. There was a darkened expression in her eyes. She took a deep breath and seemed to throw off her thoughts. She glanced at the earl; then her eyes fell away from his. She turned back into the breakfast room, and Captain McInnes hurried to offer his escort to her.

Lord Kenmare stared after her. He was certain he had seen reproach in Lady Mary's gray eyes. "Damn it," he breathed. He started back into the breakfast room, but Abigail nipped his sleeve.

"My lord! I meant to ask a favor of you, if I might," she said quietly.

He glanced down at her. "Of course, Miss Spence. Whatever it is in my power to do."

"I hope that it is," Abigail said. At his puzzled look, she sighed. "I have tried and tried to talk to Mama about William. But she will not. She has put up that . . . that *barrier* she resorts to whenever she wishes to put one off. My lord, you have become close to my mother, have you not? I will be so grateful if you could offer her the sympathy that she will not accept from me."

Lord Kenmare kept his face carefully expressionless. "I shall hold myself ready to do so, Miss Spence."

Abigail smiled gratefully at him. "Thank you! I knew that I could rely upon you."

Lord Kenmare offered his arm to her and they returned to the breakfast table. He wondered whether he would be able to justify Abigail's faith in him. He was weighed down still with that oppression of spirits that had first assailed him when he had been unable to find William Spence. He had failed to bring the same sort of joy that he had just seen in his sister's face to Lady Mary. Even if she might someday forgive him, he did not know that he could ever forgive himself.

* * *

Before breakfast was quite finished, the doors flew open and a familiar figure strode into the room. He stood grinning at the expressions of astonishment and frozen shock on the faces of those at the breakfast table. "Never tell me that you thought me dead," he said.

"William!" Abigail shrieked.

As one, she and her mother jumped up and raced to him. They cast themselves against him, laughing and crying at once. William staggered under the weight of their enthusiasm, but he made no complaint. Instead he laughed and gathered both ladies close.

Tears streamed down Lady Mary's face even though her eyes blazed with a glad light. She cupped her son's face between her hands and with her eyes devoured its dear lines. "Oh, William, William! How I feared for you. But you have come back!"

"Did I not tell you that he would, Mama? Did I not?" Abigail asked, laughing deliriously.

"Yes, yes!" Lady Mary laughed. She was suddenly struck by the brightness of the room, and she glanced about in surprise. How strange that she had not before noticed that outside the windows the summer sun was blazing. Her oppression of spirits had blinded her to it. But William, her dear son, had returned safe and unharmed. On that thought she stepped back to run newly anxious eyes over him. "William, are you quite all right?"

"I've never been better in my life," William said cheerfully. "I haven't a scratch to boast of, incredible as that is, what with fellows dropping about me right and left. Why, there wasn't an officer left among us after the blistering French fire." He suddenly became aware of the other two occupants of the room. Unable to bow owing to the ladies clinging about him, he nodded to the gentlemen. "My lord, good morning. And to you, Captain."

Lord Kenmare had hung back during the joyful reunion, but now he came forward to offer his hand to William. With complete sincerity he said, "I am glad to see you in one piece, Spence."

Abigail was recalled to something more than her brother's

incredible appearance. She pulled Captain McInnes into the group. "William, I am engaged to be married," she announced proudly.

William looked at her with astonishment and then at Captain McInnes, whose craggy face had slightly reddened. William grasped the officer's hand and pumped it energetically. "My dear fellow! Dash it, this is news indeed! She will lead you a fine dance, I warn you."

"Och, I am thinking it will be a grand dance," Captain McInnes said, slanting a warm look at his betrothed. Abigail blushed with pleasure at the pretty compliment.

"But come, William! Come sit down and tell us where you have been—what you have been doing," Lady Mary urged, drawing him toward the table.

William looked approvingly on the dishes of eggs, kippers, ham and biscuits, strawberries and grapes on the sideboard. "I shan't mind sitting down in the least," he said half-jokingly.

Lord Kenmare read rightly the appreciative and hungry expression in the young soldier's eyes. He gestured quietly for a footman to serve up a well-filled plate for the apparently famished young gentleman. "You'll join us, of course," he said.

William agreed that he would. He set to with relish, and as he polished off a huge breakfast he told a tale of a last-minute desperate charge, the confusion of the enemy, giving chase, and at the end, of being pointed out to the Duke of Wellington as the fellow who took command over his section after all the officers had fallen. The duke had ordered him to remain until he had cleared a few details; then his grace had heard William's story and immediately entered in his dispatches a recommendation for William's promotion. He had then ordered William to deliver the dispatches to the packet sailing from Ostend for England, a side trip that had necessarily delayed his return to Brussels.

"And then, upon my arrival, I am told to my complete surprise that my family have removed to another address. By the by, his grace the Duke of Wellington sends his regards to you, Mama." William sent a teasing look at his mother. "He apparently recalled with some pleasure a waltz that he once enjoyed with you."

Lady Mary was much astonished that the great man should remember such a trifle. She felt Lord Kenmare's eyes upon her and she met his amused glance, at once recalling the circumstances that had arisen from the first waltz. She smiled at his lordship, shaking her head.

"A promotion! How wonderful for you, William," Abigail said, her eyes shining.

"Yes, indeed. I am very happy for you, William," Lady Mary said. "Your grandfather will be most pleased when I tell him."

"I should like to tell the old tartar myself, actually. He has always the most devilishly mocking expression in his eyes. I'd like to see the moment of surprise come over him," William said.

"But you will not be able to, William. Grandpapa is not here. He and Grandmama left Brussels days ago," Abigail said.

"Did they indeed?" William said with a lurking grin. "I would not have thought the old gentleman would turn tail so easily. Won't I roast him for it, though!"

"You shall have your chance at my wedding, which will be in London as soon as we return home to England," Abigail said. "You shall have leave, won't you, William?"

Lord Kenmare had been startled by the talk of a London wedding. It had not occurred to him before that the Spences would be leaving Brussels. He was left prey to disturbing feelings, and he judged it time to leave the scene of the happy reunion. He rose, saying, "I am somewhat *de trop,* I think, and as I do have a few small matters to attend to, I shall make my excuses. Spence, I am glad to see you again."

"Thank you, my lord," William said, gratified by the earl's kind attention.

Lord Kenmare raised Lady Mary's hand to his lips. He saw that she was looking at him in a quizzical fashion. He smiled, his mouth quirking attractively at one corner. "Lady Mary, your servant." He bowed to Abigail and left the breakfast room.

Captain McInnes decided that he, too, was unneeded, and he also made his adieus. Abigail instantly protested, saying that she would go with him, but he silenced her with a shake of his head. "You shall want to hear every word," he said, understanding her consuming interest in her brother.

Lady Mary saw that the footmen were hovering about, obviously ready to clear away the remains of breakfast. "Come into the parlor. There is so much we have to relate to each other. William, I am just so happy that you have come back to us." She and Abigail took hold of William's arms and bore him off with them.

The morning was spent and luncheon had come and gone when William announced that he must go to his quarters to freshen up and change if he were to be presentable for the evening. Lady Mary and Abigail were reluctant to let him out of their sight, and so they requested one of the earl's carriages to drive them. The ladies dropped William off at his quarters, letting him go only after extracting his promise that he would return to the Kenmare town house for dinner.

When the ladies had returned to the house, Abigail declared her immediate intention to make up to Captain McInnes for her desertion of him and she sped upstairs. Lady Mary had put her hand on the banister to follow her daughter up the stairs, though at a more leisurely pace, only to be directed by a footman to the drawing room, where the Earl of Kenmare awaited her.

31

LADY MARY entered the drawing room. "My lord, I was told you wished to see me."

Lord Kenmare turned away from his contemplation of the fire. He went to her and took one of her hands. "Lady Mary, pray be so kind as to give me a few moments." He drew her over to a settee.

Lady Mary sank down. "Of course, my lord." She watched as he returned to the drawing-room door, and she heard him quietly request the footman without that they not be disturbed.

Then he shut the door. When he returned, she said, "It is something of some moment that you wish to discuss, I assume."

He seated himself opposite her. "Yes. Would you care for a glass of wine, Lady Mary?"

Lady Mary nodded. "Please. It has been a very long afternoon with William. I hope that you do not mind, but I mean to remove my bonnet and be comfortable," she said, untying the ribbons under her chin.

"Not at all, my lady." Lord Kenmare got up to go to the occasional table. He picked up the decanter, unstopped it, and poured out two glasses of wine. "I apologize for waylaying you like this, before you even had a chance to change out of your walking dress," he said, returning with the wine.

Lady Mary had discarded her bonnet and gloves. She accepted the glass of wine with a murmur of thanks. "That is quite all right, my lord. I know well that you would not have done so unless it was of the first importance."

"I believe it to be, indeed," Lord Kenmare said. He did not sit down again, but instead went to stand at the mantel. He regarded Lady Mary's expression of mild curiosity. He had her complete attention. She was waiting to hear what he had to say, but he found it more difficult to speak to her than he had anticipated. What right did he have to speak to her, after all? She was a friend and a guest in his house. It would only be natural were she to take affront at his presumption in violating the precepts of conduct of a host.

"My lord?" She was looking at him in growing inquiry.

Lord Kenmare shrugged in resignation. He loved her, but he had never had a chance in fixing his interest with her. The terrible war had effectively seen to that, as well as his attempt to make love to her. The occasion had resulted in a show of revulsion on her part and must forever place him outside her affections. So he had very little to lose by arousing her anger.

He set aside the glass of wine, untasted. Thrusting his hands into his pockets, he faced her. "The thing of it is, Lady Mary, I am curious what you have decided for your future. As your friend and the one who has been most nearly responsible for your safety these past weeks, I have taken it upon myself to discuss the matter with you," he said.

"I see." Lady Mary's voice was totally without inflection and he could not read her expression. She raised her glass and sipped at the wine.

Lord Kenmare left his place at the mantel and seated himself beside her. He took her free hand, to hold it gently between both of his. "My lady, I am concerned for you. Otherwise I would not presume to speak so bluntly," he said. "Pray consider what I am saying to you. The hideous war is over, at great loss to you and to me and to everyone else. We have all faced the deaths of family and dear friends. Now it is time to think of getting on with our lives. Have you given any thought to what you shall do, now that Abigail plans to wed?"

Lady Mary looked into his eyes. "I have decided to return to England with Abigail in a fortnight."

He was taken aback. He had thought to have some time to make himself agreeable to her, but her cool announcement had taken him totally by surprise. "A fortnight? But I had assumed . . . My lady, why?"

She glanced away from him. She was in tears, but it would not do to let him become aware of it. "There is very little to keep me in Brussels now. As you have said, the war is done with. Though William must remain on until he receives leave, Abigail and Captain McInnes will be journeying to London. I expect that it will be most pleasant to travel in their company."

Lord Kenmare was not unobservant where his chosen lady was concerned. He took the wineglass out of her trembling hand and set it aside on a half-table. He drew his handkerchief out of his coat pocket and gently dried her tears. She did not protest his ministrations and when she met his eyes, he saw a vulnerability in hers that he had glimpsed only twice before. He slowly bent his head, giving her time to draw away. But she did not, and her lips parted soft beneath his.

The warmth of her, the scent and feel of her, were like a shock to him. Unable to stop himself, he gathered her up tight in his arms and kissed her with bruising force. She did not resist, but neither did she respond to him with the passion that he knew lay within her.

Lord Kenmare tore his mouth from hers. Setting her free with such abruptness that she fell back against the settee cushions, he got up and strode over to the mantel. He discovered that he was shaking, and he placed his hands on the mantel for a measure of support. With his face turned away, he said thinly, "Forgive me, my lady. It was not my intention to take advantage of you."

There was a short silence.

"Since coming to Brussels, I have been peculiarly unlike myself. All those years I was content in the raising of my children, and never once was I tempted by any of the gentlemen who were brought to my notice by my kind friends. I had such memories from my marriage. Those few short years with my husband seemed likely to sustain me for my lifetime. But here in Brussels . . . It was so like a dream, actually. The gaiety, the frenzy to forget all that might happen—it all contributed to the strange metamorphosis in me."

Despite himself, Lord Kenmare had turned to regard her with fascinated curiosity. Lady Mary's voice had been distant and she was regarding her hands, which were clasped loosely in her lap. He dared to ask, "What metamorphosis is that, Lady Mary?"

She looked up. Her wide gray eyes reflected the firelight and he could not be certain of her expression. "It was the waltz that began it all, I think," she said. "Otherwise the Comte l'Buc would most likely have never taken such particular notice of me." She rose from the settee and went to stand beside him. She contemplated the strained expression on his face. "I do not think that I shall ever be quite as content as I once was. Perhaps I am wrong. Perhaps after I have returned home, after Abigail's wedding, I shall be able to take up my former life without regret. I do not know. But I shall have to try, shan't I?"

Lord Kenmare wasn't certain of where she was leading. The only thing that he was sure about was that she meant to return to England too soon. His sister's admonition to him not to lose Lady Mary rang in his memory with alarming relevancy, as did his brother-in-law's advice that life was too short to allow uncertainty and fears to dissuade one from some action.

With a feeling of urgency, Lord Kenmare threw caution to the winds. He took Lady Mary's hands in his own. "My lady, I must speak what I feel, even though you turn from me. I am aware that you must despise me for my past conduct toward you, but pray listen to what I have to say—''

"Despise you?" Lady Mary regarded him in the greatest astonishment. "I do not understand. Why, you have been all that is most kind and considerate."

"Thank God for that! I had thought that you could never forgive me for the role I played in your collapse," Lord Kenmare said.

"I am not so silly, my lord. Quite the contrary, your forbearance has been most exceptional and I have been quite cognizant of it." Lady Mary colored slightly at the vivid memory of how she had begged him to remain beside her bed while she slept.

"That makes what I have to say easier." Lord Kenmare raised her fingers to his lips in salute, and when he had done, he did not release her hand. His voice vibrated. "My lady, it is my hope that you will do me the signal honor of accepting my suit for your hand."

Lady Mary stared at him. She saw the burning intensity in his blue eyes and she could sense how still he held himself. He felt something for her, she had no doubt of that. But in declaring himself, Lord Kenmare had said nothing of loving her. He had held her in his arms and called her his "dear love." But since that night, he had never given any sign that he even recalled his soft words. Lady Mary felt as though her heart was breaking. Controlling her voice with difficulty, she said, "Marry you? I could not possibly." She started to turn away.

"Damn you, Mary," he breathed. She had erected that glass barrier between them once more. Fury lent him the courage that he needed. He swung her about. She gasped, her eyes wide in startlement, and then he savagely took her mouth.

His fingers tangled in her hair, holding her captive while he ravished her mouth. His arms pinioned her body, crushing her to him. She was pliant in his arms. Her lips parted under his, inviting him to invade her.

His heart beat wildly in his breast. He knew absolute fear. She had not responded to him, not truly. Not like before. For a second he wrenched his mouth free of hers and stared down into her face. Her eyes opened and she regarded him from the shimmering distance that she hid behind.

"Oh, God, Mary!" His mouth descended once more to find hers. With desperation born of fear, he set himself to arouse her with all the skill at his command. He must break through to her. He must, he thought. Or lose her forever.

Lady Mary felt her senses assaulted. His mouth moved sensuously on hers, teasing and demanding at once. When her lips parted again for him, his tongue explored her mouth with a maddening leisure that brought fire to her veins.

His lips left her mouth to trace down her throat, to the sensitive juncture of her neck and shoulder. She uttered a moan, beginning to arch into him. His hands slid over her hips to fit her against him, but this time she did not resist the intimacy. Her arms slipped up over his shoulders and she drew down his head so that she could take his mouth with a hunger that equaled his own.

At last, at last, he thought, and swung her up into his arms to carry her to the settee.

When he at last raised his head, he said raggedly, "You see, my lady? There is passion, at least. If you will not marry me, then become my mistress. Give me that much of yourself and I . . . I shall be satisfied, I promise you."

She should have been outraged; but his desperation came through his words, taking the insult from his proposition. "My lord, are you trying to say that you love me?"

He stared at her. "Isn't that what I have been telling you?"

"No, my lord. You have not said it," said Lady Mary quietly. Her fingers pulled gently through the short hairs at the back of his head.

Lord Kenmare's shoulders sagged, but he held her eyes with his. "Yes, Lady Mary. I do love you, most desperately and irrevocably."

"And I you, my lord," she said softly. She pulled his head down and kissed him deeply.

After a moment, he broke free. He had an expression of dawning hope in his eyes. "Then you must marry me," he said unsteadily.

"Of course I must," Lady Mary agreed.

He sat up abruptly, pulling her up with him. "Mary, I ought to thrash you. You have put me through the devil of a time these past several minutes."

"Yes, but we have ironed out all of our differences. Except one," Lady Mary said. There was a hint of rueful amusement in her eyes.

"You will make me a countess, my lord. I do not know whether I can bear to fall in with my mother's—Viscountess Catlin's—ambitions for me after so many years. Perhaps I should consent only to becoming your mistress. Then . . . Robert! *Robert!*"

Lady Mary's outraged laughter was distinctly heard through the drawing-room door. In the entry hall, the butler and the footman exchanged a glance. Neither would deign to allow himself comment, but there was a faint smile on each of their faces.